ALIENS VS. PREDATORS

RIFT WAR

THE COMPLETE ALIEN™ LIBRARY FROM TITAN BOOKS

RIFT WAR

WESTON OCHSE
& YVONNE NAVARRO

TITAN BOOKS

**ALIENS VS. PREDATORS:
RIFT WAR**

Print edition ISBN: 9781789098440
E-book edition ISBN: 9781803361192

Published by Titan Books
A division of Titan Publishing Group Ltd
144 Southwark St, London, SE1 0UP.

First edition: August 2022
10 9 8 7 6 5 4 3 2 1

A CIP catalogue record for this title is available from the British Library.

Printed and bound CPI Group (UK) Ltd, Croydon, CR0 4YY.

Did you enjoy this book?
We love to hear from our readers. Please email us at readerfeedback@
titanemail.com or write to us at Reader Feedback at the above address.
www.titanbooks.com

To Zachary Ochse, because there is no better son.

PROLOGUE

The Ovomorph pulsed with life. Writing within the amniotic fluid was a creature perfected by an unknown hand eons ago. Then the Yautja encountered them, harnessed them, and found a use for them.

Now the creatures were bound to the Yautja system of honor and the hunt, so thoroughly that the two species would never be separated. This egg, in all its hideous beauty, was the beginning of a cycle that would help transform a young Yautja into a strong and valued member of their society, as he or she began to fulfill their destiny.

Seeding a planet for the unblooded was the first step in the developmental process. The source of the Ovomorphs remained hidden behind various impenetrable levels of bureaucracy and wasn't deemed necessary for those who were to become future hunters. During the down times, however, traveling between the stars, Ar'Wen couldn't help but wonder where the creatures had originated.

Xenomorphs had been their primary antagonists as far back as any record he had found. If there was a time when they hadn't been the Yautjas' mortal enemies, their greatest prey, it lay beyond memory and was of no consequence. What mattered to Ar'Wen was that he was here, a shepherd of sorts whose mission was to provide for others that which they could not provide for themselves.

This planet was the fifth one Ar'Wen had seeded on behalf of the elders. Oomans called it LV-363. The Yautja identified it as a rift world because the surface was split by deep gashes, as if a giant, zealous juvenile had taken an oversized wristblade and tried to carve something into its surface. The elders had designated it as perfect for seeding, with a wide variety of fauna that included two- and four-legged mammals, including primates of sufficient size to host the embryos. It also would provide an excellent battleground for groups of juveniles who were ready to become blooded.

The rifts would add to the difficulty and create several unpredictable problem sets that the juveniles would need to overcome. Neither the juveniles nor those who were training them would know of Ar'Wen's presence. It had taken time and effort for him to rise in the hierarchy, to the point that he was entrusted with the seeding process. Those beneath him in the training strata weren't privy to his activities.

As well, there was another reason for choosing the rift. Senior xenobiologists on their homeworld of Yautja Prime believed that if a Xenomorph implanted a species of the local fauna—in this case the winged insectoids—a mutation might emerge. There were those who rejected the theory, but to Ar'Wen it seemed entirely plausible. The winged creatures were at the top of the planet's food chain, and had no viable predators. The only exception was a type of microphage that strained the host's endocrinological system, slowing its hunger and keeping it from ranging too far or killing too many of the other species.

It was as if the land itself had installed a governor on the insects' ability to flex their superiority over every other life-form on the planet.

Setting aside his musings, Ar'Wen returned to the task at hand. His mission was always the same. Having prepared the Ovomorphs, he had located the best area for placement, seeded the testing ground, set the beacon, then returned his ship to a hidden location. Once he had accomplished the first three tasks, he opened the manifest that identified those who would participate in the hunt.

In that moment, everything changed.

Instead of leaving before the blooding began, he chose to stay.

The time had finally arrived to settle an old score.

Ar'Wen had been waiting for this chance for fifteen years, since the day that had ruined his life—the day when the one he'd most trusted had let him down, leaving him for dead, broken on a planet to which he refused to give a name.

Because of his many years living a solitary existence, Ar'Wen had become a scholar of all things relating to vengeance. Ironically, there was a phrase from ooman history that identified it as "a dish best served cold"— meaning, he believed, as a deadly surprise. The Yautja believed in the here and now, and chose to reap the whirlwind whenever the opportunity arose.

Other species he'd encountered believed that the best method to achieve vengeance was to act as if their nemeses didn't exist, starving them of any satisfaction that might be gained from their deed. To Ar'Wen, that was a coward's way.

No, he would have his vengeance.

He would reap the whirlwind.

Of more immediate concern, however, there were oomans present on this ugly rock. Several groups, scattered across the surface, each one appearing to be entirely cut off from the others. From what he could ascertain they were drug collectors, gathering for resale as much as they could of the pollen that grew along the upper edges of the rift, like fuchsia-colored beards. Those in charge were oomans who used their people like tools, wasting them, breaking them, and then leaving their remains like so much garbage.

That was humanity by definition. The waste of a species.

Ar'Wen hadn't had much interaction with them, but in the course of his preparations he'd studied the records. They possessed distinct potential, and yet so many of their kind utterly lacked the willpower that would enable them to reach for anything resembling greatness. That a species would prey upon its own in such a self-serving, self-destructive fashion lay beyond anything Ar'Wen had ever been taught or believed.

Ever a contradiction, oomans had the ability to be nearly as honorable as Yautja, and some rose to the challenge. He'd seen the recordings. He'd heard the stories—yet they also had the capacity to define what it meant to be horrendous. They had yet to learn that the worst of their species would always drag down their best.

Societies were by their very definition hierarchical, with the members of each culture grouped into castes—and there they should remain. Yet instead of seeking to become perfect within their own appropriate niches, oomans tried to claw their way to the next level.

A waste of time and destined to fail.

Here was a host of oomans preying upon the suffering of others. They were what their culture deemed a "criminal organization," and their motivation was profit. They had identified a population with a built-in need and determined the best way to exploit it—oomans called them "addicts"—a weaker caste who allowed themselves to be controlled in order to procure what they needed. This placed the drug collectors at the top of their own food chain.

Another ooman trait—one which inevitably would lead to their downfall—was *pity*. An utterly useless concept, concerning oneself with another's inability to achieve. All this meant was to suffer in their stead. If anything could be said for the ooman criminals, it was that they exhibited no such wasteful behavior.

In the end, he supposed, the oomans might provide additional hosts for the Xenomorphs. That, at least, would provide them with purpose.

Putting aside thoughts of a clearly inferior species, Ar'Wen, returned to the task at hand. His mission was to enable the young and inexperienced Yautja to graduate from unblooded and become young bloods.

All they needed to do was survive.

All *he* needed to do was bide his time.

1

LV-363 had few redeeming qualities. Breathable oxygen. Normal gravity. Almost no human occupation. Enough flora in the rifts to create humidity, and a never-ending supply of Khatura, which could only grow on the desolate planet.

Murray ran the operation, and the addicts harvested the flower pollen, but it was Shrapnel who did most of the work. Even the other merc, Margo, didn't do as much as he did, but wasn't it always like that? He never got his rightful due. To Murray and the bosses, he was only good for lugging crates and slugging riftwings. It was pure ageism. What he counted as experience, the rest of them considered "over the hill."

Shifting the M41A pulse rifle to his right shoulder, he moved closer to the rift, a deep gash in the landscape. He wore heavily personalized and modified body armor that he'd bought on the black market from a Colonial Marine. He'd adjusted the knees and elbows to allow for more freedom of movement, and was able to carry three weapons and a drop pouch with extra ammo. Then he'd added a clear polymer paint that could be programmed to match the colors and textures of whatever was around him, making him blend in with almost perfect camouflage.

Shrapnel slid his helmet goggles into place and ran through the various visual fields. Peering over the edge, he inhaled, appreciating the funky aroma of the mass of flora that grew there. Ship life was nothing but recycled air, and no matter what filter upgrades were installed, after months in the can the air on board smelled like vomit and flop sweat. Even the sweat was strictly regulated, though. It was dry in space, and water was at a premium.

The treacherous drop to the bottom was studded with bushes thrusting their roots between rocks in an effort to get closer to the sun. This north-south crack in the planet's surface was one of hundreds like it, gifted with full sun for only two hours a day. Far below he could just make out movement on the rift floor—six-legged rodents they called jivenings and what looked like an albino raccoon with a gray striped tail. In the trees he thought he spotted a couple of the native monkeys that for the most part stayed hidden in the daytime. Tiny birds moved from flower to flower on the various plants along with flybees, insectoid creatures that looked like a fly but acted like a bee.

Nothing on this godforsaken planet played by the rules.

The rift was silent during the long hours of darkness,

but as light began penetrating the gloom, birds began calling to each other or marking their territory. Clouds of flybees swarmed here and there. Beetles rubbed their wings before they took to the air, searching for smaller prey to eat. Among the native flora and fauna, a pair of human figures dangled from cable harnesses.

For the most part, all of these were harmless. Shrapnel noted and dismissed them, knowing that his two harvesters were safe. He was watching for something much bigger and more dangerous. The largest and most dominant apex predator on the planet: the riftwing.

Human-sized and omnivorous, these aggressive winged insectoids boasted proboscises and needle claws. Impervious to the narcotic pollen of the Khatura plant, riftwings scanned for their prey on multiple visual spectrums. Their wings moved like those of a dragonfly, almost too fast to see, but the thrumming sound they made in the air offered a clear indication when one was near. Another was the call it gave when it was on the hunt, a *jai-reeee* that filled the rift with sound and sent all other creatures scuttling for safety.

Shrapnel keyed his mic.

"Enid, status."

"Harvest back one ready to lift." The tired and muffled voice of a woman came back.

"You're working too slow," he said.

"I—I'm wo-wo-working as fast as I can," she said.

"Khaleed, your status."

Silence.

"Khaleed."

Still nothing.

Shrapnel strode over and tugged at the cable. He should have received a tug back, but got nothing in return. He tugged again.

Still, nothing.

"Margo, get your ass over here," he said.

The other merc trotted over from where she'd been sitting. She wore no armor, just a ship's jumpsuit and rubber boots to keep from getting static electrical shocks. Margo had a pistol on her hip and an M37A2 shotgun angled across her back.

"Khaleed?" she asked.

Shrapnel nodded.

Margo had probably been pretty a decade before, but now, with a broken nose and a flattened cheekbone from being hit by space debris during an out-of-station chase, any beauty had been shorn away. One eye hung droopy where the cheek was flattened, and an ear on the same side had a missing lower lobe. She wore her black hair short with a buzz of fuzz going down the center. Her neck was tattooed from when she'd been in the marines.

"Do you think he did it again?" she asked.

"He better not have, or old Murray will have our asses."

"Weren't you watching?"

He glared at her, then heard the sound of wings.

JAI-REEE!

He brought his rifle around and aimed, moving in quick efficient steps until he was above where Enid hung.

The sound came again.

From the depths of the rift it rose, like an immense dragonfly with the face of a monkey and a meter-long proboscis designed to suck the fluids out of its victims. The thrum of its wings caused every other creature in sight to dash into hiding. As Margo pulled at the cable in an effort to haul Khaleed back to the surface, Enid began crying, the sound rattling in his ear.

"Take it easy, girl," Shrapnel said. "I got the thing covered."

A second *JAI-REEE!* split the air.

This one was larger and bore the markings of a fighter. It had scars along one side and a weeping wound on one of its spindly legs, which were very much like those of arthropods. Its trochanter was fat with muscle, descending into a thick femur with two tibias and ending with a tarsus that had the claws of a raptor.

"Please… oh… please… oh… please." Enid's feverish cries came through the comms.

"Fucking hell," Shrapnel ground out. He took aim at the monster closest to his harvester—the smaller of the two—and let loose with six rounds that zipped across the space and punched through its carapace. Green blood exploded out the back and the riftwing faltered, then fell, crashing against the side of the rift until the sound receded into silence.

The larger one spun toward him with a predatory appreciation.

He shifted his aim and was about to open fire when it dove out of sight, dropping to the bottom where it would probably feed on its dying kin.

Margo heaved the last bit of cable and dragged Khaleed over the edge. Sure enough, he was mask-free and stoned out of his mind. The masks let the harvesters breathe, but filtered out the narcotic Khatura pollen. The asshole addict had found a way to remove the mask, despite all of the safeguards that kept it locked and harnessed. The mask's metal mechanics were supposed to make it unremovable.

Other than that, Khaleed was fine—just on cloud four hundred and nineteen, with his face covered in the red powder. His heart rate was probably through the roof. The pollen was unprocessed and uncut, thus at full strength. They'd need to give him a shot to slow things down, and then shove him in his bunk. He'd be useless for the next rotation, which meant the other harvesters would have to double their work.

Shrapnel stalked over to the sitting figure, whose eyes rolled up to the whites to stare at the fireworks oscillating through his frontal cortex. Drool laced down his chin just below an idiot's grin. The merc pressed the barrel of his rifle against the side of the man's neck and heard a satisfying sizzle. The barrel still hot from the passage of rounds.

It didn't even phase the stupefied man.

"Really, Shrap?" Margo scowled. "Can't you be human for once?"

He prodded the drugged addict with the barrel of his rifle, shoving hard enough to make him turn halfway, then roll back.

"You call this human? He's a fucking addict."

Margo stepped closer and got into his face, and he hated her for it. She thought she was a badass, but she wasn't. He was just biding his time. Still, he listened to her.

"He's not your toy," she said. "He's property. He belongs to the cartel. You want to explain to them why you ruined their property?"

He backed away, wishing for something to shoot.

"Mr. Shrapnel, can I come up?" Enid asked in a voice so tiny he had to strain to hear it. He spun back toward the rift and bared his teeth.

"Nice try. Keep harvesting."

"But the riftwings…"

"What about them?"

"They might—"

"You should be more frightened of me than them," he growled into his mic. "Do you understand me?"

The sound of her weeping was replaced with a strangled, *"I understand."*

While Margo dragged Khaleed back to basecamp, Shrapnel took up his position again. He was down to ninety-two rounds. That should be enough for a while, and he had to admit, he did love shooting the riftwings.

He only wished there might be something else to shoot at and kill.

Something. Anything.

Anyone.

Anything to relieve his boredom.

2

Ny'ytap and T'U'Sa sat at the controls of the hunt ship. Their faces were lit only by the orange and red lights of the console as the two male Yautja concentrated on entry into the planet's atmosphere.

They'd been dropped by the mothership at the edge of the system and had worked their way to the rift planet, scanning for any stray ionic activity. Nothing registered, except for the trace of a vessel that might have passed several weeks earlier. This could have been the seeder ship.

Ny'ytap was the larger of the two and bore an acid scar on the side of his face, a remnant from his own blooding. Once a renowned battlemaster, he'd been reduced in rank to elite captain. While elite captain was something most Yautja could only wish to attain, he'd let it slip on more than one occasion that he'd never get a chance at clan leader, much less elder.

T'U'Sa was faster than Ny'ytap, faster than Ca'toll, always first to the prey and often laughing at others who were too slow. He was the youngest of the hunting captains, and the most eager to show his abilities.

Ca'toll sat in the back with their nine juveniles.

She was the smallest of the adult Yautja, but she'd beaten both T'U'Sa and Ny'ytap in many a hunt. As one of the few female hunting captains, she might not be the fastest or the strongest, but what she lacked in those traits she more than made up for in guile. She watched closely as they descended to the planet's surface.

The previous ship would have seeded the planet with Ovomorphs to prepare for the blooding of the nine. Each of their wards came from honorable families belonging to the Rhyhalotep Clan, and it had been the desire of the clan leaders to have their offspring learn the old ways. Some of the young ones wouldn't survive. If things really went wrong, it might be that *none* would survive.

Ca'toll, T'U'Sa, and Ny'ytap had worked together as hunting captains on three previous occasions, so it had been an honor when the clan elders selected them to lead this particular initiation. Other captains might try to keep their wards safe, but what good would that do? No, the three of them were known not to coddle their wards. Those who survived would hold a special place in the records, able to proudly state who their hunt captains had been, and why they were held in such high esteem. Through their actions, the way they conducted themselves, they would emblazon their names into the lore of the clans.

As long as they survive, Ca'toll reminded herself.

Some of the Ovomorphs would have already hatched, spurred to action by the diverse selection of the planet's indigenous species. Others might still be waiting, however, and if an unblooded were to come across one that was hatching, they would be required to use minimal weapons and defeat the spiderlike facehugger as a test of their inherent speed and skill.

While some hunting captains might arrange for controlled kills, Ca'toll and her two companions eschewed such shortcuts. They believed in the chaos and the glorious randomness of the hunt.

Previous scouting reports had indicated there were several mammalian species of moderate size, easily sufficient to host a Xenomorph. Of particular interest, however, were the reports of the large avian predators that lived in the rifts. These creatures were as tall as a small Yautja, but possessed wings like an insect. They were also omnivorous, eating anything and everything by grabbing hold and drawing life fluids through a proboscis.

The hunting captains had decided not to tell the juveniles about these creatures, in order to see how they would react. Their armor would protect them from serious harm, at least in theory, but it was the fear stimulus the captains would be tracking.

Fear was a killer, and Ca'toll had revealed what she had been told when she was blooded—that fear was nothing more than then anticipation of the unknown. To be afraid of the unknown, she had told them, was absurd.

Fear—*h'dlak*—was to be quashed.

Death was inevitable.

Death was honorable.

Fear was ignorance. It was not honorable.

Thrusters slammed the ship down, making Ca'toll squint. She saw through the console screen that they'd landed in a clearing surrounded by a thicket of trees and scrub. Remote sensors around the ship indicated that in the immediate vicinity, there were no lifeforms larger than a bilge rat.

Ny'ytap stood and began giving orders. Within moments the ship was secured and cloaked. They hauled their supplies and ammunition down the ramp and half a kilometer away toward the nearest rift, where they would set up their forward operating base. Standard operation procedure dictated that they mustn't operate anywhere near the ship. It was their sole lifeline back to the mothership and the clans. If it was destroyed, they would all be dishonored. If that happened, they might as well as be dead—even if they were rescued later, they'd be termed bad bloods and outlaws, hunted by the likes of Ny'ytap in his prime.

As they prepared to break into groups, Ny'ytap pulled the other two adults aside.

"We followed the ion trace and found an ooman ship nearby," he said, voice like glass rattling against stone. "That means in addition to the seeding ship, there are oomans infesting the area. We must avoid them, and not engage."

T'U'Sa grinned. "Then what are we to do with them?" His voice was like gravel in the wind.

"Nothing," Ny'ytap snapped. "We leave them alone. We are here to blood the young ones and return them to their clan as warriors."

"Not all Yautja still continue the old ways," Ca'toll said. Her voice was sharp and low, sweet grass with razors.

"Those who do rise higher in power," Ny'ytap countered. "We are here to determine if these nine are destined for greatness."

"Why don't we move the ship, if we're so close to the oomans?" T'U'Sa asked. "Contact is inevitable."

"Nothing is inevitable except for honor earned and a swift death," Ny'ytap responded. "The oomans are near where the Ovomorphs were seeded. We will stay where we are."

"Didn't the seeder realize that?" Ca'toll said. "It makes you wonder what he or she was thinking."

"Perhaps the oomans arrived after the seeding." T'U'Sa shrugged. "It doesn't matter."

She peered at him. "And if a Xenomorph attacks them?"

"Then it attacks them," Ny'ytap said. "We will not interfere." He made an irritated sound with his mandibles. "We have our mission, they have theirs, whatever it may be. They should never know we are here. Explain it to your unblooded so that they understand—to be seen is to be dishonored."

She nodded assent. So did T'U'Sa.

WESTON OCHSE & YVONNE NAVARRO

They separated and Ca'toll took her three aside. Hetah was the only other female Yautja in the group. Small for her size, she was cunning and quick. Ptah'Ra was big shouldered and would grow into them, making him one of the largest Yautja she'd yet to see. Sta'kta was sized between the other two and thick around the waist. He barely fit into his armor and refused to have it adjusted.

Her blooding crew wore her colors: red, gray, and white in an oscillating camouflage pattern. The hunting captains could cloak their armor with a push of a button, but only in extreme circumstances. By order of the Clan, the unblooded were expected to survive while being seen. It was part of the challenge that would prove their mettle.

Ny'ytap and his crew wore jet black, while T'U'Sa's colors were black and green. Everyone wore the clan symbol of the Judone Tree. The unblooded's armor would shift visual spectrum frequencies as the wearer passed into new locations, but it wasn't as effective as those worn by the adults. This limitation would increase the need for them to count on stealth, and decrease their desire to cling to technology.

They'd spent a lot of time in the ship, entering the system from the Lagrange point, and it showed. Ca'toll needed her unblooded to unwind, to develop a sense of themselves and of the planet. For them, this was the first time off their homeworld, and they still had the tendency to be wide-eyed and wondering. The young ones needed to become focused.

26

So she took Hetah, Ptah'Ra, and Sta'kta aside, gave them instructions, and soon they were moving through the upper limbs of the trees. Hers was an old hunting game simplistically called "follow the leader." She picked places among the limbs that were just right for an individual's weight, but the slightest misstep could send them crashing to the earth below. Taking intentionally longer strides, she forced her followers to observe her carefully and stretch the limits of their agility. If they didn't follow correctly, they'd pay the price.

The trees grew tallest nearer the rift, as if the organic substance at its edge and the outflowing damp air promoted growth. The taller the growth, the more lush the foliage and the more frequent the fauna. Birds of all colors and sizes exploded from the branches as they approached. Tree rodents found bolt holes, and branch snakes hissed at their passing, but the Yautja, young and old, were as silent as a stealthy breeze, pushing through the forest until they came out just above the rift.

Ca'toll stopped suddenly, crouching on a long, thick branch, and Hetah and Ptah'Ra halted behind her. But Sta'kta slipped, and had it not been for the other two, he would have fallen several hundred meters into the dark maw of the rift below. He hung for a moment before the other two pulled him to safety.

Far to one side, Ca'toll spied movement. Using the targeting oculator in her bio-helmet, she zoomed in.

Ooman, male.

Armored, weapon.

Over the edge of the rift in front of him hung another figure on a cable. Female, unarmored, no weapons. Her face was covered by a curious mask. Below them in the semi-darkness, she spied one of the flying creatures she had researched. Riftwings—dangerous only if you let them sneak up on you.

An alarm went off inside Ca'toll's visor. Biometrics picked up the movement and shape of a Xenomorph. She zoomed to the maximum, and there it was, far down on the floor of the rift.

Hunting.

Soon to be the hunted.

The game is on.

3

Ny'ytap watched his two hunting captains take their unblooded in different directions—one to the right and the other to the left. Part of their mission was to scout, but another part was to familiarize themselves and the young ones with the flora, fauna, and terrain. Knowing one's environment was essential for any battle. This was standard whenever they arrived on a new planet; learning the process was part of the blooding program.

He stretched his shoulders inside his armor. He was older by half than his two captains. He should have been clan leader by now, but he'd forsaken that to become a battlemaster, in order to obtain greater *yin'tekai*—honor—by defeating a rival clan who was trading Yautja technology for monetary gains. To become such a warrior was a magnificent achievement, but like becoming a temple guard, it also disqualified one from ever becoming a clan leader.

This rankled him still. In truth, he'd never thought they would block him from becoming what he'd been destined to become. His father had been a clan leader, as was his grandfather. He'd certainly earned it, but because of his scarring, the clan elders seemed to have decided that he'd seen enough combat and had elected him to run their blooding program.

For many, this was the highest rank they could attain, so he should be proud of the accomplishment. But for Ny'ytap it felt like a demotion or, worse, retirement. He was an elite. A veteran. He was a weapon of war being wasted in the monitoring of pups.

Nevertheless, he had a mission. His was the responsibility of ensuring the safety of the unblooded—in this case, the offspring of an influential clan. As always, there was danger inherent in blooding the young Yautja and preparing them for adulthood. They would be put in situations where they might get killed, but death was still something to be avoided. The unblooded were destined for greater roles in Yautja society. So, while the blooding wasn't fixed, it could be... moderately controlled.

Before they'd left the home world, Ny'ytap had been pulled aside by many former clan leaders and fellow battlemasters. They treated him as if this would be his last blooding assignment. He'd snapped at them for even the implication, but deep down he felt as if it might be true. Ny'ytap, however, did not want to go gently into the darkness. He wanted to die fighting. He desired to bathe himself in the blood of his enemies and take them down with him.

When he'd been younger, his desire for battle had caused many to label him as a tyrant or a bully. The reality couldn't be farther from the truth. He was neither of those things, and cared deeply for his wards, as if they were of his own clan. Yet his blood sang with the need for battle. Any battle.

It had taken many years and tremendous effort to control it.

As a youngling, Ny'ytap had fought any and every Yautja who came into his path. He didn't care. He just needed to fight. His essence begged for it, and yielded him little control over his own behavior. As he matured and became more experienced, he learned better ways to harness that energy so that he could unleash it when it mattered. After all, his fellow Yautja weren't his enemy.

Everything else was.

It had been far too long since he'd been challenged. Ca'toll couldn't challenge him. T'U'Sa couldn't either, regardless of what the warrior thought of himself. Ny'ytap doubted there was anything on this dull planet capable of even coming close, and pride fought with pity at the idea.

"*Ooman, armor, weapon sighted.*" It was Ca'toll, and she passed the coordinates.

"Leave him," he responded. "Stealth. Don't let him know we are here."

Stealth had always been a major part of the training. Too many young blood Yautja, given their new armor, felt impervious to harm and longed to wade into battle. Indeed, that was how Ny'ytap had earned his scar. Although the armor rendered Yautja mostly impervious to the blood of the Xenomorphs, too much of that acidic liquid, concentrated in one area, could do serious damage. He'd become blooded that day, but had worn a scar ever since.

The whole left side of his face had been burned, even scarring his left mandibles so that his speech was slurred in everything he said. He often thought that the scarring had kept him from his greatest desires. Self-scarring was one thing, but accidental scarring was a mark of shame he would have to wear for as long as he lived.

Ny'ytap motioned for the young ones to follow. Like him, they were dressed in jet black armor. He instructed them proceed with minimal camouflage, because it would require them to rely on their inherent skills. There was a switch on his wrist that could either activate or deactivate the camouflaging—and even invisibility—of his wards' battle suits. If all went well, he would not need to use it.

Vai'ke was the largest of the unblooded and almost as large as Ca'toll. He was a brute whose father was a clan leader, and he expected to become one as well, one day. Ny'ytap knew the feeling. Vai'ke acted as if the universe should give him whatever he wanted. Ny'ytap's challenge would be to put the young one in situations that would break him of that sense of entitlement.

Cau'dki was a smaller version of Vai'ke. His family was less connected, but what he lacked in connections he made up for by being a bully. He'd been stopped on several occasions after pushing Ba'sta into a corner. Ny'ytap had overheard Cau'dki ordering the others to hang back and let him get the first kill.

Ba'sta was the runt of the nine unblooded, the progeny of an older clan that had shrunk over the years as warriors died or married into other clans. Still, his family held prestige. The problem was, Ba'sta couldn't manage that prestige—didn't know how to wield it to his advantage. Instead of walking with his head high, he slumped as though the weight of the world was on his shoulders, all because he was one of the last of his lineage.

Ny'ytap's three unblooded followed in order as he loped ahead, his eyes measuring each movement for potential danger. They ran perpendicular to the rift, out several kilometers to verify the safety of their perimeter. The further they moved away from the rift, the shorter the flora and the more disperse the fauna. Out here, nothing larger than a ship rat moved along the ground.

Ny'ytap listened closely, assessing the noise made by the young ones behind him. He realized that Ba'sta's small size made him the most fleet of foot. His passage could barely be detected, while the other two seemed to run through bushes instead of running around them. The clamor was maddening.

Ny'ytap flicked on his camouflaging and poured on the speed. He juked left, then right, then left, then left again. Irritated, he watched as all three of his wards passed without noticing his presence. When he had all-but vanished from sight, they should have stopped to take stock. Instead they kept plowing ahead.

Another thirty meters and they finally stopped, finally acknowledging that he was missing. Vai'ke took charge. He grabbed Ba'sta and pointed back the way they came. Then he directed Cau'dki to continue forward another thirty meters. Once the other two reached the designated goals they began to move in a circle, keeping equidistant from where Vai'ke stood.

Good.

Ny'ytap found himself grinning. At least they were using a proper search pattern, proving that in basic training they'd learned more than how to change their own diapers and sharpen their wristblades. This put him in a quandary, though. He was inside the circle of their attention. If they continued, they would find him.

No, he wasn't ready to give them a win—it was too early in the program. He waited until Cau'dki was near, then grabbed the unblooded by one arm and threw him back to where Vai'ke stood.

The self-proclaimed leader backed away to keep from falling and let his wristblades flash, ready for a possible attack. Cau'dki growled in in anger. He scrambled to his feet, and the two of them went back-to-back.

Leaving Ba'sta by himself.

Ny'ytap moved like a breath through the scrub, at one with the wind, the sun, and the aroma of the world. The two who were back-to-back continued to turn, blades out, any fear that might be on their faces concealed by their bio-helmets.

Ba'sta squatted and cocked his head. When Ny'ytap was within three meters, the unblooded whispered.

"I hear you, Battlemaster."

"What is it you hear?" Ny'ytap asked, voice soft.

"The space between things. I hear the difference. You are the space between things, where there shouldn't be anything." While the two larger and more dominant youths readied themselves for a possible opponent, Ba'sta had already found his. He didn't know exactly where Ny'ytap was, but he faced in the right direction, ready to roll left and right.

The others had left him alone.

The former battlemaster toggled off his camouflage and became present once again. The unblooded straightened when they saw him. Ba'sta remained crouched at the ready.

It pleased Ny'ytap.

He had so much opportunity to teach, and they had so much to learn. This might actually be fun, after all.

Then he snarled as he grabbed Ba'sta and approached the others.

INTERLUDE

Ar'Wen remembered when he'd been young, a time which seemed like eons ago. In fact, even though he knew they were his memories, they felt as if they belonged to someone else. He'd been shorter then and had yet to grow into the body of the hunter he eventually became.

Before his blooding, the elders had arranged them in pairs so that they could learn to fight together. Once blooded, unless they were led by a battle captain, they would never work together again. Being a hunter was supposed to be a solitary existence.

But they trained together, and he was partnered with a female known as Mei-Jadhi Kaail—Sister Rage. Not only was she a sister of blood, but a sister of battle as well. She was by far the most formidable of their brood. In the combat pits she'd bested more unblooded than anyone else. It should have been a victory to have someone like her as his partner, but Ar'Wen was intimidated in spite of himself.

He'd never fought a female before, and when he had lost to her, he hadn't been sure how to interpret what he'd had experienced. Some of the others were ill-advised enough to make fun of her, but they only did that once. Once Mei-Jadhi Kaail unleashed her anger on them and proved her martial superiority, they quickly came around and respected her as they should have in the first place.

When they'd been partnered, Ar'Wen had been conflicted. Was she trying to act too much like a male? And what might that mean? Males and females in Yautja society were treated virtually the same, so why would he wonder about such a thing? As he assessed his thoughts, it became clear that she was merely being herself. His thoughts and doubts were born of a lack of experience—he had not known any unblooded female other than Mei-Jadhi Kaail.

If she was the definition of a female, then none of the others should have questioned her actions or her value. To do so was a waste of time, and could prove dangerous.

One of their training programs called for the unblooded to break off into their battle pairs. For the target team, their task was simple. They had to get from one point to another on a map without dying. It would be a simulated death, and to create the illusion they wore attenuation vests that had special light receptors that, when triggered, sent a shock violent enough to render the wearer incapacitated.

They would be the target team, and were given an hour to prepare and plan. Once the program began, the other teams would be after them. All of the other trainees were equipped with electrically charged combisticks. He and Mei-Jadhi Kaail would remain empty-handed. None of them wore armor.

They loaded the map into their helmet displays. A red line showed the path they were supposed to follow. Mei-Jadhi Kaail said that they should concentrate on speed, rather than concern for safety. Her idea was to run the gauntlet as quickly as possible, weaponizing the flora along their route of travel, and he had no argument to the contrary.

When the starting chime sounded, they were off at full speed. She immediately ripped away a willowy branch and held it in her right hand as she sprinted forward. One end of the branch was jagged. Ar'Wen had to struggle to keep up. He'd always been fleet of foot, but he was careful. Mei-Jadhi Kaail threw caution to the wind and raced ahead so fast that at one point she was almost out of sight.

Along the way, he paused to grab a pair of broken bamboo reeds so he would have one for each hand. Pushing himself to the limit, he caught up with her.

They came upon the first pair of adversaries, one on either side of their chosen path. The nearest one struck out with a combistick, but Mei-Jadhi parried with the willow branch and slashed at the unblooded's face. The other tried to attack Ar'Wen the same way, and received a *thwack* to the head and groin. He went down in a heap.

Their path wasn't supposed to have been broadcast to their opponents, but after their fifth attack in so many meters, Ar'Wen couldn't help wonder if the overseers had shared the information. Even if that was the case, they gave as good as they got... right up until the ninth assault.

Out of nowhere a rope came down and snagged him, lifting him bodily from the ground. The shock came fast and furious, and Ar'Wen felt himself jerking at the end of the rope, unable to so much as think. He was lucky he didn't empty his bowels.

He was fighting against blacking out from the pain when Mei-Jadhi doubled back, grabbed his legs, and used them to climb up his body until she was standing on his shoulders. He thought she might try to release him, but she made no move to do so. Instead, she stood on his shoulders and launched herself upward, shoving her willow stick in between the feet of the opponent and twisting, sending him cartwheeling to the ground.

The pressure released on the rope, and Ar'Wen dropped as well, landing hard on his shoulder when he hit the ground.

Mei-Jadhi Kaail grabbed the combistick his opponent had dropped and took off running down the trail. Shaking his head—both to clear it and in disbelief— Ar'Wen climbed shakily to his feet. The rope was still around him, so he gathered it in his hands to prevent it from catching on anything, and trotted in her wake.

There were no more attempts to ambush them, so they arrived relatively unscathed. Mei-Jadhi danced in place, spinning her newly acquired combistick like a baton. The unblooded hunters they had bested along the trail arrived two by two at the finish line, none of them looking happy at the result. Each had felt the wrath of Mei-Jadhi Kaail, and Ar'Wen had gotten the worst of it.

The one from whom she'd taken the combistick, a young Yautja named Tre'Ner, marched up and tried to grab it. Instead, she slapped him on the side of the head and then activated the stick's electric nodes, sending him to the ground. Adding insult to injury, she kicked at him like he was a dying animal.

A pair of training captains emerged from the monitoring hut, where every encounter was observed, recorded, and graded. The captain stood chest and shoulders taller than the rest of them. All had already been blooded, and were approaching the ends of their careers.

"We were successful." Mei-Jadhi held her head high, staring unflinchingly at each training captain.

But one of the captains shook his head.

"You cheated," another said. "You used a weapon." He gestured to the combistick in her hand.

"The rules were clear." Her eyes flashed. "I could grab anything I wanted along the path. I grabbed this."

"You took it from me," Tre'Ner said.

She ignored him and clicked her mandibles.

"You told us we could take whatever we found along the path, from any plant that stood there," she said defiantly. "I took this weapon from that plant." She pointed at Tre'Ner.

His eyes widened in fury and he rushed her. Mei-Jadhi

didn't move until the last moment, then twisted her torso and let the other unblooded student slip off her hip and fall to the ground.

"I see no warriors here," Mei-Jadhi said. "If I did, things would be different." She stared hard into the training captain's eyes. "Does that answer your question?

The training captain stared hard at her for several seconds.

"Carry on." Both captains turned and left.

Ar'Wen stooped and helped the fallen unblooded to his feet. When he was upright, Tre'Ner held out his hand. Mei-Jadhi tossed him his weapon.

"Next time, hang onto it."

Tre'Ner didn't respond. Instead, he snatched the combistick out of the air and followed the captains in the direction they had gone.

Ar'Wen grinned. Mei-Jadhi had lived up to her name, and making her an enemy could prove dangerous. He appreciated being paired with her and hoped that it would continue.

Little had he known where the wish would lead.

4

Khaleed felt as if his eyes were bleeding and his lungs were on the outside of his chest—and he loved every second of it. He was a god and nothing could stop him. The universe was his and he could shape and destroy galaxies at a whim.

He raised a finger to a speck floating in the air and touched it.

Wham!

A billion lives gone from the god Khaleed.

Another speck came near.

Kaboom.

Another billion lives.

He was the god of all things and the universe should take notice.

"Okay, dirt bag. Back on the cable," Shrapnel the Asshole said.

Khaleed pointed a finger at him.

"Kaboom," he whispered, but nothing happened.

Shrapnel smacked his hand away. *"Enough of that,"* he

growled over the comm. *"You're just a lowlife addict harvesting the same shit that made you who you are—and this time we've double-locked your mask so there's no getting out of it."*

Mask.

Harvest.

Khaleed remembered.

Heavenly pollen.

Inhaling.

And tears burst fireworks in his eyes.

Before he could move, he was manhandled and locked into the harvesting cradle. Khaleed wanted to scream and shout, but the metal composite mask wouldn't let him do much more than breathe and mumble to himself. He reached up, but his hands were slammed with the butt of the Asshole's weapon.

May he die a thousand deaths at the hands of intergalactic monsters.

Then he realized it was all okay—he was going back to be near the flowers, the nectar, the source—that place where universes were born and dreams died.

The flower.

Through the mask's comms, he heard Shrapnel disengage the lock and order him to descend.

Khaleed didn't care that his legs were dangling hundreds of meters from the rift floor. What was below didn't matter. It was what was in front of him that did. He pressed the descent button and dropped into the darkness—the same darkness that was a life without the pollen, without Khatura. If Shrapnel the Asshole only knew what it was about... but then Khaleed might have to share, so he couldn't tell him.

No.

No.

Never.

There was a sound, something moving beneath him. He jerked around, head twitching like a chicken trying to understand algebra. Where was it? *What* was it? Could it be one of those flying things... what did the Asshole call them?

Riftwings.

He shuddered, then waved his arms to try and scare away anything that might be sneaking up on him. The contraption he was in was ridiculous. Khaleed had the ability to move side to side along the net, but to go up or down he had to ask the Asshole to retract or lower the cable. He felt like a worm at the end of a fishing line, instead of a human who had an actual job.

Then he went still in the darkness.

There were a dozen flower bulbs in front of him, each unopened and just about ready to spit pollen. He wondered what an entire bulb might taste like. What if he was able to chew one, or swallow one whole and feel it open inside him? So much of the plant was inconsequential, but the red pollen that came from the stamen was the golden thread.

The sun crested the rise, lit the rift, and warmed his

back. Almost instantly the bulbs opened into flowers, each large and glowing and the genesis of all things wonderful. Then came the pollen: a shower of red specks flowing from the middle of each, drifting along the air currents in graceful, glittering dust spirals.

Amazing.

Extraordinary.

Wondrous.

Khaleed had the harvesting vacuum attached to his side, designed to collect the pollen and nothing else. He gripped it, depressed the power button, and felt the whir of the engine at is came to life. The first red fragments entered the equipment, followed by more and more and more. He so wanted to rip off his mask and inhale the entirety of what he was harvesting, but they'd tightened it until it was painful.

Then he heard it again, over the sound of the vacuum.

A sound like no other.

Khaleed paused his harvesting and looked down into the lit portion of the canyon. Asshole must have been watching him, and he jerked on the cable.

"*Don't stop. Get to work. We have quota.*"

"Bu—but I hear something," Khaleed said.

"*You don't hear nothing but a chicken wing,*" Shrapnel said.

"What's a chicken wing?"

Shrapnel laughed harshly. "*You outworlders never had real food. Everything you've ever eaten was pressed or facsimiled—protein compounds with taste bundles.*"

"That still doesn't tell me what a chicken wing is," Khaleed replied. His voice stuttered as he stared hard into the twilight beneath. Was that a four-legged creature near the rift floor looking up at him? Did Shrapnel think *it* was a chicken wing?

Holy hell in a harvest basket.

The flowers took on a life of their own. Each one seemed to want him to harvest. He couldn't help speaking with them in his head, opening two-sided conversations where they thanked him and he thanked them and everyone was thanking one another.

He paused as an asteroid of a thought hit him.

Weyland-Yutani.

He'd worked for them, once upon a time. Khaleed had been a corporate officer, actually. Men and women deferred to him as he walked through the halls. Doors opened for him that wouldn't open for others. He'd been someone to reckon with. Then came the vacation. Then the party. Then the Khatura.

Oh, the lovely Khatura.

He'd been hip deep in credits back then, and could afford anything he wanted. A few women here. A few men there. Food for gods and a few snorts of Khatura. Then some more. They promised him it wasn't addictive. They said it was just something to make life more interesting.

The sound of flapping wings.

Khaleed felt the riftwing grab at him and he waved his arms as hard as he could. The creature dislodged, but it still hovered behind him. Unable to turn, he could feel the wind from its wings and the chilling touch of the protuberance from its face as it sought a soft spot on his neck, thankfully covered by the metal composite mask.

He tried to cry out, and it emerged as a gurgling sound. Then he began to weep. He wanted to go home. He knew he'd been married and he and his partner had adopted two young girls. He'd had a wonderful life. He'd been respected. He'd been loved. He'd been on top of the world.

"Let me back up," he yelled as best he could into the comms.

"Keep working."

"But there's something down here!"

"There's always something down there, addict."

"But it's trying to eat me," he pleaded.

"Then let it. It'll only spit you out once it discovers how rotten your body is."

Asshole Shrapnel. If there was anyone that Khaleed wanted to kill, it was that man. He had the empathy of a snail and the appreciation of a rock. His brain was rusted metal waiting to be polished.

The thought made him laugh.

"What's so funny?" Asshole asked.

"Rusted metal," he replied. "Snails. You suck."

"Fucking addicts," he received in response.

Khaleed might be an addict, but at least he was human.

5

Ptah'Ra's mouth was dry and his skin was clammy. He hated being nervous. If his father were here, he would have been slammed across the room.

But wasn't fear just another emotion to be embraced? That's what he had been told. Like the excitement of the hunt or the joy of defeating one's enemies. Nervousness was nothing but a physical reaction to fear of the unknown, and something that wasn't known shouldn't be the source of fear.

He glanced at the other two unblooded—oh, how he hated that term. It was the equivalent of being called a child and no matter what he did, until he was able to take down a Xenomorph, he would remain a child.

But the time was finally here. The elders had seeded the planet with Xenomorphs, and given them the appropriate amount of time for them to attach to the local fauna. Ptah'Ra hoped to see something extraordinary—he'd heard tales of giant lizards and double-headed snakes from other planets. Even flora wasn't safe. An elder had told the story of his own blooding, and how several unblooded had gone into a thicket, never to emerge alive. When the hunting leader had finally hacked through, they'd found the bodies drained of blood and the roots of a tree pulsating nearby. They'd never figured out how the tree had done it, and had opted to bypass the thicket and blood themselves in another place.

Stories like that were supposed to remind them that *nothing* was safe, and that they needed to always stay aware of their surroundings. Ptah'Ra agreed without question. Not the fleetest of foot, normally he was the first one to spy the quarry in a hunt. Where he lacked speed he more than made up for it in marksmanship. In training, they weren't allowed the use of aiming devices, and that was fine with him. He didn't need them, and promised himself that once he had been blooded, becoming his own hunting party leader, he still wouldn't use them.

No, the one fear he possessed and kept hidden from the others was his fear of heights. When they'd been briefed on the rifts, he'd been told they were going to have to transit to the bottom. His was the fear of a pup. No blooded hunting or war leader would ever be afraid of a simple drop to the ground. So why had his mind chosen to warp his thoughts?

Every time he was near a place that had the most modest drop his mouth would go dry, his hands would sweat, and his knees would shiver. The only thing his body wanted was to turn the other way and flee.

It was unreasonable,

It wasn't fair, either.

He glanced over to where Hetah stood, unmoving, staring into the depths of the rift. A few meters further stood Sta'kta. His head was cocked as he scrutinized the winged birds and insects. If they ever found out, Ptah'Ra would never live it down. As soon as they learned the truth, they would share it with the rest of the clan.

He closed his eyes to control his breathing. Then came the command for them to descend. Each of them had a cable with a locking claw at one end. Ptah'Ra fixed it tightly into a rock crevice, gave it a few worried tugs, then gripped it with both hands.

Hetah dove from the branch on which she was perched. When the cable snapped taut it bounced her to the side of the rift, where she began to walk as though she was on the ground. Then Sta'kta took three great leaps and rappelled halfway down. Meanwhile Ptah'Ra, hating every moment of it, skidded backward, glancing down every few meters to see how sickeningly far away the ground remained.

Too far.

Ca'toll descended without a cable. Hunting leaders didn't need one. They were able to leap from rock to outcropping to brush to clumps of tree root, all with ease.

To one side hung one of the oomans, suspended in a netted cradle. Appearing to be a male, he was unaware of their presence and seemed to be mumbling to himself.

Ca'toll had reported that the oomans were after some sort of native drug. What drug would be worth risking one's life this way?

A silent alarm flashed on his arm.

He acknowledged and searched below until he saw it. A juvenile Xenomorph, prowling the rift floor, tail whipping. Here and there it would spy a rodent or a bird and lunge for it, but the fauna of this planet were still too fast, frustrating it.

Ptah'Ra thought he saw something else. Was this part of some specific lesson? Were they being graded for something that hadn't been revealed?

He blinked. First it was there and then it was gone, like the after-image from a flash of light. Closing his eyes, he opened them again, and all he saw from his gut-wrenching vantage point was the Xeno drone on the rift floor. It peered upward and spotted one of the cables. Leaped and missed. It leaped again.

Missed.

In a fit of anger it ran in a circle, tail whipping madly, then it leaped and made the bottom of the cable—the cable that held Sta'kta.

Ptah'Ra felt his breath catch, and squeezed the cable harder. How lucky was it for Sta'kta that a Xeno had come up right in front of him? He'd be the first blooded, and win their bet.

The Xeno gripped the cable with its front and rear appendages and began to pull itself up. Above it, Sta'kta held onto the cable with his left hand and drew a blade with the other.

Ptah'Ra felt the excitement of the hunter. All eyes would be on Sta'kta and his prey as he waited for it to come to him. A true hunter would kill with a single stroke of the blade. Would Sta'kta be able to do so? Or would he panic and hack and slash? The moment between being unblooded and blooded was a special one that could not be replicated. Only once would it occur, and the method used could set a Yautja on a good arc through life.

He had never seen a Xeno this close. The vids weren't half as realistic. It looked as if it could easily leap from cable to cable. Its head twitched left and right like that of a predatory bird.

It was twenty meters below Sta'kta when it stopped.

The unblooded hadn't made a move, so why had it stopped?

Then Ptah'Ra saw the reason.

Oblivious to the danger, the ooman had begun lowering himself toward another of the opened flowers. Far above, a different ooman—this one with a weapon— also remained oblivious. How these creatures survived their own stupidity, Ptah'Ra would never know.

What was becoming obvious, however, was the ooman in the net was not long for life.

The Xeno moved several more meters up the cable then leaped sideways, catching the netting hard enough to make it swing from side to side. The sound of the ooman's terror was muffled by the odd mask that covered his entire face. Above, the armed ooman started, then leaned over the edge and fired several times in the direction of the Xeno.

All of his rounds missed.

Then another ooman, a female previously unnoticed but in a net some distance to one side, began to scream. Both oomans tried to claw their way upward, fighting the safety of the net and attempting to ascend the sheer rock surface as though they had the expertise of a Yautja. But they'd never be fast enough.

The Xeno reached the nearest one and grabbed him with its rear feet. Panic had caused the ooman to become entangled in his netting, and all he could do was thrash helplessly. The Xeno thrust its face close to the ooman's, trying to understand the metal composite mask. Its jaw elongated, then elongated more, jaw within jaw, teeth within teeth. It snapped against the metal.

Once.

Twice.

Saliva dripped from its mouth onto the ooman's shoulder and his dying screams filled the silence as the Xeno's teeth found a spot below where the man's neck was covered. It savaged the ooman's chest, filling the air with the smell of blood and sizzling skin and bone.

Ptah'Ra's nostrils flared and he inhaled. Forgotten was the floor beneath him. Forgotten was his fear of heights. Forgotten was the possibility of falling.

Now all he wanted to do was hunt.

INTERLUDE

Ar'Wen watched as the ship landed in the pre-coordinated clearing, setting down without issue, and knew that inside, young Yautja were preparing and suiting up. The three hunt leaders exited, each followed by their unblooded. He felt a reverie, observing the solemnity of the hunt leaders and the barely contained excitement of the unblooded. Remembered when he had been on a similar ship on a similar hunt, before he'd become the warrior he was now.

He hadn't been afraid. He'd looked forward to the hunt like it was something predestined, and each day alive was but one more day he hadn't yet reached his true potential. He'd felt as if his skin had been vibrating with anticipation.

Unbeknownst to them were the oomans—not really an issue—and the new Xenomorphs which Ar'Wen had ensured were successfully bred for their hunting pleasure. He couldn't help but laugh. The hunt leaders likely thought this was going to be a standard and relatively uneventful blooding, but it would be very far from ordinary. Soon they would discover that this expedition was more than they bargained for. Those who survived would be the stronger for it.

Those who didn't, well…

He recognized two of the hunt leaders—Ca'toll and Ny'ytap. The third was unknown to him. Ny'ytap had been a bully back when he was an unblooded. He was large even for a Yautja and had learned to wield his mass from an early age. While he was convinced his skills at hunting were better than anyone else's, he couldn't conceive of the idea that he might lose.

Ar'Wen was delighted in the choice of hunt leaders. It had been too long. His old nemesis would have to slowly become accustomed to the idea that there might be an opponent that was smarter and craftier. Ar'Wen might never show himself to the others, but his longtime enemy would know, eventually, and be forced to appreciate the results of his work.

He counted the unblooded as they disembarked. The elder clan colors were familiar, and he knew them as the usual assortment of young Yautja ready to become more than they believed they could be. For the blooding, the youth were brought to a place in teams, but for those who survived, they'd spend the rest of their lives largely alone, unless they became part of a war party or a procession. Such was the life of a hunter. It had never been a group life, but a solitary existence where each

Yautja placed his or her mark, and then found ways to take down a designated target.

For now, they were on *his* planet.

And Ar'Wen had prepared it for them.

As surely as Sister Rage had left him behind in pursuit of her own goals, he would ensure that few of the arriving Yautja left this world to realize their futures. The elders had use for all of them, in one shape or form. To the hunt leaders he was a *ghost*, but to the elders he was known as *the one who prepared the way*.

For the moment, Ar'Wen enjoyed watching the three young ones rappel down the side of the rift as if they had nothing to fear in the entire universe. He'd once felt the same way. He'd once been on top of the world, where nothing could destroy him. So he sat and watched and appreciated who he once had been... in the before time.

6

Enid screamed as she watched Khaleed die, but she didn't hear her own voice, nor did she hear the sound of Shrapnel's weapon as he fired downward. The image was burned into her brain, of the insectoid creature chewing on the stump where Khaleed's head had been.

Terror sent adrenaline slamming through her blood-stream and her world, her entire *existence*, narrowed down to one thing: the net onto which she was holding and the cable that tethered her to the top of the rift.

"Take me up!" she screeched as loud as she could. "It killed Khaleed—he's dead! *Help*!"

There was a soft *thump*, more a vibration down the cable than a sound, and the lock disengaged. The steel line tightened and Enid felt herself rising, but so slowly! She scrabbled at the line, trying futilely to climb it. When that didn't help, she hooked her fingers into claws and grabbed at the netting.

Nothing she did worked. How stupid—like Khaleed, she was an addict, too, for crying out loud. A hundred and five pounds if she was lucky, no lung power, and certainly no muscle. She'd count her blessings later, that she was even coordinated enough to know which was way was up.

Black spots danced across her vision and she craned upward. There was sky up there, but it was so far away. She was panting in fear, on the brink of hyperventilating. Her head turned unwillingly back to where she could see Khaleed—or what was left of him. The creature had a vaguely insect-like form, a lot like a riftwing, but that's where the resemblance ended. It clung to him, its shining, oversized black head dipping forward and back as it feasted. Khaleed's body hung beneath it, shuddering and dripping strands of mucous from the beast's mouth.

Enid jerked her head hard enough to feel a crack in her neck as she tried to pull her gaze away. Her head swung around and she focused on something, *anything* else—

"There's something else down here!" she howled into the comms. She didn't know what Shrapnel could hear, but inside the helmet her voice sounded like little more than a piteous squeak. "Please get me up get me up get me up—"

"I'm working on it! For fuck's sake, stop screaming in my ear!"

Enid couldn't tell if the cable was moving or not, nor could she stop herself from wailing as she stared at a *second* creature almost as horrifying as the first. Like her, it hung from a cable, and also like her, it was human-shaped... more or less. The whole thing was dark and armored, with what seemed to be some kind of helmet over its head so that she couldn't see its features. Spikes jutted from the bottom of the helmet, falling like tendrils of hair that were as thick as her fingers.

It was on the far side of Khaleed and his attacker, but she could still make out heavy coverings on its shoulders, arms, and chest. It was hanging from a cable, and long appendages that resembled thin knives wrapped around the line. Unlike the insect-thing, it had no shine to it, as if it could fade into the shadows at will.

"I don't wanna die!" she shrieked as she pawed blindly above. "You gotta—"

There was a *bump* and she let out an airless gasp. Shrapnel seized her by the back of the neck and dragged her out of the rift. He flung her behind him and she slid across the ground, rocks and dirt dragging the sleeves of her suit up and gouging into her bare skin. Stunned, Enid rolled onto her back. Her chest heaved as someone bent over her and shoved a keycard into the slot on the back of her facemask. It snapped open and then she was screeching all over again.

"Monsters! Killers! Never seen them before! They'll kill us all if you don't—"

A big, dirty hand clamped over her mouth and nose, cutting off her air.

"Shut up, you stupid addict," Shrapnel snarled. "We heard you already. The whole *planet* heard you."

Another voice slid behind Shrapnel's, sharp and dangerous.

"What the hell's going on?"

Shrapnel pulled his hand away and Enid pulled air into her lungs.

"Don't speak," he warned her. "Or I'll break your fucking head." He shoved her to the side and turned.

Murray, the cartel boss, stood a few feet away. Tats spiraled across the skin of his crossed arms, old and muddled ink split by too many scars to count. Shrapnel opened his mouth but Murray cut him off.

"Not you." Murray's eyes were pale and disturbing, the color bleached away by the vicious suns of more than a few harvester planets. They found and focused on Enid. "Her."

Whatever spit she had in her mouth instantly dried up and she had to fight to get her throat to push out the words.

"There are creatures down there," she managed to rasp. "One of them killed Khaleed. It pulled his head off and was eating the rest of him."

"A riftwing," Shrapnel said with a dismissive wave.

"No!" Enid cried. "I know what those look like—we all do. This thing was different, some kind of giant creepy crawly. It climbed up the cable to get to him!"

Murray frowned. "Are you sure you ain't just high?" He glanced at Shrapnel. "Did you check her before you sent her down?" Before the guard could answer, Enid reached an arm toward him.

"Please, Murray, you have to believe me. And there was another one, too, but it was different. Upright like a human, but covered in some kind of armor. It came down on its own line, on the far side. Just hung there, watching everything that went down."

The boss man's frown deepened into a scowl before he turned and strode away.

7

As she watched the Xeno decapitate the terrified, masked ooman, it wasn't in Ca'toll's genetic makeup to feel empathy, and certainly not for a member of a lower species.

On the other hand, she did grimace at the inequity of the situation—the man could neither fight nor flee. Without weapons, tied in place, he'd been nothing more than an arranged meal. On the far side was another ooman, a female, also masked and trapped in place, and Ca'toll noted with interest that the cables upon which the oomans were tethered were strategically placed so that even at full stretch, they could never reach each other.

There had been several shots into the rift from above, but the shooter's aim had been poor and useless. As she measured the distance between the cables, the thrashing, bawling female was pulled up and out of sight.

Leaving the juvenile Xeno to its grisly meal, Ca'toll motioned to her unblooded to follow her down to the rift floor. All three looked longingly at the dangling

Xeno, especially Ptah'Ra, but they obediently dropped silently to the ground behind her. They mimicked her movements, crouching and carefully taking in everything that lay in front of them.

The bottom of the rift was anything but flat. Although the walls were smooth and too slick to climb or anchor anything, rocks of every size were scattered across the ground, with no way to tell if they'd fallen from above or had been birthed as part of the planet's long-ago creation. There would be no unimpeded movement, no easy path ahead or in retreat, but the bigger boulders would provide excellent cover for tactical maneuvers.

Provided a hunter could go from one to another without disturbing the unhatched Ovomorphs.

Xenomorph eggs were notoriously sensitive. The breeze of the slightest passage, running across an egg's surface, was enough stimulation to make its top "bloom," split into four sections and release the facehugger within. Once that occurred, it took only a short time for the facehugger to erupt.

Plenty of time for a single, precise shot to destroy it.

Which would then cause any nearby Ovomorphs to bloom… in an ever-widening circle.

The eggs had been placed toward the center of the rock-studded rift. Some were wedged between boulders. Ca'toll led her group along the wall, easing past the closer ones without breathing until they reached an Ovomorph that was more solitary. None of them had been there long enough to develop the tendrils along the ground that might enable it to communicate with other Ovomorphs. If such a thing was possible.

The three young Yautja positioned themselves around it, keeping a safe distance and waiting for Ca'toll's instructions.

The monitors in her helmet made it easy to see how her charges were handling the situation, and she was pleased to see that none of the unblooded seemed afraid. They all showed normal blood chemistry levels, and the stats represented elevated predatory instinct—she would have been disappointed to note anything otherwise.

Ca'toll lowered the sound in her helmet so that her words would be barely audible.

"Enable your nitrogen sprayers," she told her unblooded. She glanced around, and each nodded their readiness. "Deploy on three. One... two... three." The cryo hit was perfectly timed, the Ovomorph frozen solid almost instantaneously. "Secure it in a non-acid net and take it up," she ordered. Ca'toll moved to assist, but Hetah's sharp transmission stopped her.

"Xeno twenty meters behind you, coming up fast."

"Who gets to kill it?" Sta'kta voice practically thrummed with eagerness. Ca'toll shot a glance over one shoulder, then spun to face the creature skittering toward them.

"Your kills will come later," she barked. "Right now, get that egg up before it can be damaged. I'll follow. *Move!*"

They obeyed immediately, ascending via their cables in unison and drawing the netted Ovomorph up with them—so fast they were over the rim and peering down by the time the Xeno made its leap.

All the Xenos down here were adolescents, and this one seemed to be solidly in the middle range of what had hatched from the seeded Ovomorphs. She could have killed it with barely a breath. Instead she dodged low and to her left so that the inexperienced Xeno simply swept past her, swiping at the empty air where she been. She wanted her unblooded to watch her kill this Hard Meat, their first full viewing of a battle between a Yautja and a Xeno.

She'd use her acid-resistant telescoping spear, her combistick.

The juvenile spun and launched itself at her again, moving on pure instinct. On a different playing field, this would serve it just fine—it would likely be able to kill its target and go on to bigger and better, learning as it grew. Here, however, it faced a seasoned Yautja hunt captain.

There was no need to draw it out. Indeed, doing so would set a bad example for her wards, who might have a sense that it was okay to make a game of the killing. That was far from the truth, and could cost them their lives.

The apex of its jump put her fully extended combistick squarely into the center of Xeno's chest area, deep into its acid reservoir. Reflex made the creature extend its neck to snap at her before it squealed, and its acid blood sprayed around the combistick. Ca'toll lifted the Xeno off the ground with hardly any effort, making certain it could find traction enough to drag itself off the weapon on which it was impaled. It screeched as it did so.

There was enough damage to make it a mortal wound, but that didn't mean the Xeno was finished—it could still inflict a lot of damage before it died. She braced the angled combistick against her left arm and—wristblades extended—her right hand shot forward in a blur, first one way then the other. With the completion of the second sweep the Xeno's racket stopped abruptly. Its long, smooth skull lolled to one side as its body went still.

It was only a matter of moments before more Xenos would show up, drawn by the now-dead one's caterwauling. Ca'toll didn't wait. She withdrew the combistick and the Xeno dropped, flopping onto one side. A final, fast twist of her wristblades and she had the Xeno's dripping head in one hand.

Bounding to her cable she rode it up, her trophy dripping acid as she went.

8

T'U'Sa heard the commotion through the comms. The hunt was on. Ca'toll's team of unblooded had already recovered an Ovomorph, and she'd killed a juvenile Xenomorph. He'd wanted to be the first. He *deserved* to be the first. After all, he was faster than any of them— but he was also the youngest, and that was something that was always held against him.

Still, he was a hunting captain, and T'U'Sa would lead his team to their own education and discovery, despite Ny'ytap's warnings.

His three wards were also fast, chosen by him for that specific reason. Stea'Pua, U'Brea'Sua, and T'See'Ka could have been brothers. They were all about the same size and they all moved with similar speed. He wanted them to fight against each other first, ply their training in a friendly environment before things got decidedly *unfriendly*.

As tradition had it, they each wore light armor and wristblades. He was going to give one of them a chance to carry a combistick, but he was going to make them earn it.

They'd found a clearing. He set the weapon in the middle of it, then without a word signaled them to pace around it, jogging slowly, their eyes on the object in the center. If any of them weren't paying attention to what was in front of them, as they passed he'd slap them across the face. It didn't take many revolutions for them to realize that they needed to maintain awareness of *everything* in their surroundings, every potential threat, no matter what the goal.

What they didn't yet understand was that none of them should have been paying attention to the combistick at all. The weapon wasn't going to move.

Who would make the first move? They were waiting on a signal from him. They could wait forever. He wasn't about to signal. He'd let them decide.

Four more revolutions.

Stea'Pua dodged forward.

The instant he changed course, T'See'Ka and U'Brea'Sua moved in, as well. But Stea'Pua grabbed the weapon and held it tightly. He looked to the hunting captain for a signal.

The test continued.

Having missed the opportunity, the other two slid back and returned jogging in a wide circle. Each time one got close to him, T'U'Sa slapped the unblooded on the back of the head.

Finally, T'See'Ka lunged for the stick and grabbed it. U'Brea'Sua followed suit and latched onto the other end. All three found a solid grip, and they played tug-of-war for a moment, until Stea'Pua leg-swept T'See'Ka, sent him to the ground, and grappled his hands up the length of the combistick.

U'Brea'Sua wasn't a pushover, though. He kicked out with his leg to catch Stea'Pua just above the left knee. Stea'Pua staggered and went down, one leg all but useless, but still he held on.

T'See'Ka got to his feet, grabbed the weapon again, and elbowed U'Brea'Sua in the head. U'Brea'Sua spun and double punched T'See'Ka in the face, and this forced him to relinquish his grip on the combistick. The jolt dislodged Stea'Pua, as well. T'See'Ka rolled with the blow, a backward somersault taking him to the far edge of the circle.

The combistick was his.

Stea'Pua came to his feet, as well, panting slightly, staring at T'See'Ka—who had claimed the best of the weapons.

"What do you see?" T'U'Sa asked.

"I see that I won," T'See'Ka said. "I have the weapon."

"What are you going to do with it that you couldn't have done with your wristblades?"

T'See'Ka's eyes narrowed. "I don't understand the question."

"You were so eager to gain the combistick that you fought against your fellow unblooded. What did you achieve?"

T'See'Ka shifted from one foot to the other.

"You told us to get the weapon."

"I didn't say a word."

"But that's what you implied."

"Was it?" T'U'Sa strode to the smaller unblooded and stood over him. "Are you not Yautja?" he demanded. "Do you now feel like a worthy hunter? Is that what you want? A better weapon? Do you not trust your wristblades?" He knocked sharply on the top of T'See'Ka's head. "Do you not trust your skill?"

The weapon dropped to the ground.

T'U'Sa whirled. "And you two," he growled.

They both came to attention. T'U'Sa fixed his gaze on U'Brea'Sua.

"Why did you relinquish the stick?"

"It was taken from me."

"No one can take anything from you that you don't want to give."

U'Brea'Sua only looked at him.

"Were you afraid of the pain? Do you think the Xenomorphs care about your pain? What happens when you slice one up the middle and get bathed in their acid? Are you going to run home to your mother?" He strode with purpose to U'Brea'Sua and grabbed the unblooded by the chest armor, lifting him with one hand until his feet dangled in the air. "You want to be Yautja? Then show no fear."

He turned to Stea'Pua next. "And where were you? Watching? Did you think this was a tournament?"

"I-I—"

"You *what*?"

"They were faster than me."

"How can that be? I chose all of you for your speed. You are equal. You are all fast." The hunting captain ran at Stea'Pua and feinted an attack. The unblooded flinched and received a glare in return. "Unless, of course, you are hesitant. That will get you killed. Stopping to think will end you. Do you think the Xeno will give you a moment to get your bearings?"

"N-N-No."

"Of course not." T'U'Sa shook his head. "Fine. Now we go into the rift."

They started to follow, then T'U'Sa stopped.

"T'See'Ka, where's the weapon?"

"You said we don't need it."

"I said you *shouldn't* need it, but it's stupid to leave a perfectly good weapon behind," T'U'Sa snarled. T'See'Ka hurried back for the combistick, but held it as though it might snap at him. They neared the edge of the rift, and a sound spiraled up from below.

"*JAI-REEE!*"

T'U'Sa commanded all three of his wards to lower themselves to the rift floor. The idea for today was not to hunt, but to familiarize them with the way a hunt was organized. They'd hunt later, after they'd experienced the nuances of interactions with the Xenos. It was important for them to digest the information, make it a part of themselves.

They hit the rift floor without misadventure, but on the way down he spied several riftwings, testing the updrafts and calling out with their signature *JAI-REEE* screeches. As one, the four Yautja began to move north. It had all been pre-arranged—Ca'toll would move south. Ny'ytap would hold the center.

Right away T'U'Sa saw evidence of the Xenos. A number of Ovomorphs had hatched and several medium-sized local creatures lay in smoldering pools of acid, steam rising from their bodies. Then, however, he saw a riftwing that had been caught by a facehugger.

That was unexpected, but the potential dynamics were intriguing. Sometimes Xenos would take on some of the physical aspects of those in which they had gestated. The idea of a flying Xeno made him grin. He'd thought this mission might be the same as so many others—routine. Suddenly it was anything but.

T'U'Sa had his unblooded spread out behind him, with T'See'Ka in the center and holding the combistick. They didn't carry the same technology he did, though. As a hunting captain, he was able to track movements as if he were a solo elite. Like Ny'ytap had once been, T'U'Sa wanted to be elite. He wanted to make a name for himself.

The clan elders had assured him that if he could excel at being a hunting captain, he would be promoted. He certainly didn't want to end up like Ca'toll. Because of what she was, she had already reached the ceiling of anything she could hope to accomplish. He wanted to move past that. He wanted to see honor and grab it by the throat.

His attention was caught by movement from above.

JAI-REEE!

A live riftwing was spiraling above them. Now it dove for U'Brea'Sua, wings back and beak out, ready to skewer the young unblooded. Easily the size of an ooman, the interesting creature went silent.

U'Brea'Sua was foolishly oblivious, spending his time searching to the right and behind him. Never once did he feel it was important to scan overhead.

T'U'Sa spun and leaped, shoving the plunging riftwing to the side. They went down, but their fall was planned and he rolled to an upright stop, propped on one knee, wristblades deployed. The riftwing landed in a cloud of dust, tearing up plants, screaming as it rolled and rolled until it crashed against one wall of the rift.

As he began to stalk it, the riftwing clambered to its feet, staggering, one wing broken and another appendage twisted at an impossible angle. It turned, saw the Yautja approaching it, and reared up with one wing flapping. Before the creature could get its bearings, T'U'Sa darted in and sliced it—up, then down, then across. He then stepped back as it separated into three pieces, its internal organs spilling in every direction. Dead.

T'U'Sa turned and glared at U'Brea'Sua. "It was coming for you," he ground out. "Remember, death can come from any direction."

He motioned for them to follow. Moved down the rift floor, quietly pleased at how the three unblooded stared at the riftwing with interest rather than fear. They moved stealthily for another few moments, then T'U'Sa grunted in approval as he heard the recognizable sounds of juvenile Xenos. He rotated both shoulders.

"Two juveniles up ahead," he said to his team. They stopped and stared hard, but their vision could not compete with his technology at hand. "Wait a moment, and I will show you how to kill."

"What about us?" T'See'Ka said in a hushed voice. "I thought this was *our* blooding."

"Crawl, walk, run," T'U'Sa whispered. "Newborns don't learn how to run. They crawl first. Now you are walking. I will show you how to run."

The first Xeno moved into view from around a corner, tail whipping, walking on all fours, head jerking left and right, searching, wanting…

"Stay here." T'U'Sa eased forward, hands at his side. His wristblades were back in their sheaths, but he didn't feel it necessary for him to use them. At least not yet. "The thing about the juveniles," he told them, "is that they are all aggression and all need. They have no thoughts of caution or tactics. They come right at you."

As if on cue, the juvenile Xenomorph saw him and stiffened. Its tail went straight, and then it screamed and shot toward him. It covered the distance between them faster than one would believe, then leaped.

"When they leap, they lose all of their ability to react," T'U'Sa said calmly while the Xeno was still airborne. He stepped to the side and grabbed the creature's front legs, helping it to adjust its course until he released it and it slammed into the side of the rift. "The same goes for one of you. If you leave your feet, you lose the same ability. Remember this."

The Xeno hit the wall and spun, coming at him again as if nothing had happened. This time, T'U'Sa deployed the wristblades on his right hand. The Xeno leaped and the hunting captain bent to one knee, slitting the juvenile from stem to stern, yellow blood and acid exploding from the wound. Some fell on T'U'Sa, but he just shook it free, letting the acid splatter and burn through the spare foliage nearest him.

The Xeno fell like an empty sack of exoskeleton, devoid of anything that made it move, think, or need. Born hours ago, seemingly for the sole purpose of dying. Dead now. Had it known it was nothing more than a teaching tool, it might not have cared, but that's all it was. An experiment.

A demonstration, just to be killed.

INTERLUDE

Each world was chosen for something that made it a unique challenge to a blooding party. Some planets were superheated, and required the hunting parties to adapt or succumb to the environment. There were opposites, of course, but weather was an easy modification to work around. Yautja armor was the result of an ancient and magnificent technology specifically created to allow their species to hunt and survive in even the most extreme surroundings.

As a result, they had to strategize for second and third orders of reaction, such as hostile fauna, or flora, or occasionally warlike creatures. Ar'Wen remembered one blooding party, when he had placed the Ovomorphs in the midst of a battle between hordes of eight-legged creatures. This had been done more as an experiment, and it hadn't been long before the facehuggers had overwhelmed the indigenous creatures. Then there were hundreds of drones waiting for the nine inexperienced unblooded whose mission it was to eliminate them.

When the senior hunt leader was provided the readouts prior to landing, he and the other two leaders agreed that sending the unblooded out would be nothing short of a suicide mission. Their only option was to nuke the planet and move on, postponing the blooding until they located a more suitable world.

That had been something of a disappointment.

Here on LV-363, Ar'Wen climbed back down into the rift and observed the local fauna, seeing how the planet interacted with the indigenous creatures. This world had a mature relationship with its flora and fauna, likely developed over millions of years. Introducing the Xenos was going to have a cataclysmic effect, both in the rift and up top, since once the Xenos grew larger they would expand their territory.

The Yautja younglings would have their challenges, but if they kept to their teachings they would survive and learn, as if this were any other planet.

On the rift floor, a Xenomorph drone moved from side to side. Young and still not adjusted to the weight of its own head, the bullet-shaped skull tapped along the ground as it used all four legs to ambulate, pinging off rock and dirt alike. It was difficult to tell what local animal had been used for the gestation. Ar'Wen dropped the last several meters, coming to a stop in front of the Xeno.

He became visible.

The creature lifted its head and noted his presence. Still a little groggy from its birth, it shook itself and in doing so, finally came fully out of its daze. It made a noise only Ar'Wen could hear and charged him much faster than one would think such an infant beast could move.

Ar'Wen caught the skull with his hands but was propelled by the momentum, falling onto his back. He held the head and watched with excitement as the mouth extended, then extended again, snapping multiple times at the air as it fought to get to him. He wanted to play with this one. He could kill it with ease, but it was meant for the unblooded. To remove it from the game would be to cheat on their behalf.

Still holding the creature's head, he climbed to his feet. He lifted the Xeno into the air and swung it around so that it gained enough momentum that when he let it go, it flew into the side of the rift, where a sharp, jutting rock slashed its skull. Ar'Wen sprinted away from it at full speed, toggling his invisibility.

Despite its young age, this one now had a scar on the side of its head. He would track this drone and see which unblooded might have survived, had Ar'Wen himself killed it. Not much of a game as games went— then again, he had little choice in the way that he accomplished his mission.

He checked the time. There were three days before he was scheduled to leave this rock and be on his way to intercept another egg carrier. His mandibles clicked in anticipation. A lot could be done in three days. He definitely wanted to participate in what was about to transpire. After all, it wasn't every day that an enemy became available for comeuppance.

Watching them prepare for their first excursion into the rift, Ar'Wen wondered if she was the same as she had been back when they were unblooded together. Would she even remember?

Would she even care?

9

In the office part of his tent, Murray slouched on the chair in front of his desk. "Desk" was a pretty stupid description, since in reality it was a beat-up metal card table that had a distinct lean to the left rear. He kept sticking wadded-up pieces of paper under that leg, but somehow they always slipped out, ending up useless. Instead of fixing it, he was starting to compensate by propping the table up with one knee while he sat in front of it.

Pathetic, really, considering the money this operation brought in.

Murray never thought he'd end up some punk-ass middle manager for a corporation, but that sure as shit was what he'd turned out to be. In his visions of the future, *he'd* been the boss, with unlimited credits in his accounts, private retreats on vacation planets, and expensive bling. Yet here he was: the boss, all right— in charge of crap like supply requests, inventory, production schedules, and assholes like Shrapnel and

Margo. Just making sure they didn't kill the addicts was hard enough, but now they had some kind of creature making dinner out of their workers.

They had more than enough addicts to replace any who died—there were always more—but despite what his mercs thought, they weren't simply disposable. It took time and money to find the ones who were so whacked out they'd do anything, give up anything, to keep their highs going. There were too many ways to get caught in human trafficking, and lately the legals had come down on that shit way harder than on the drugs.

That meant the cartel had to find willing harvesters, and the price of Khatura pollen was as far out of reach to the street druggies as those private retreats. Yeah, Murray had been to a couple of those, back when the cartel was trying to entice him to ditch his previous employer. It had been a big step up, and Murray knew it, and they *knew* he knew it.

They had been generous… in the beginning. Nowadays the generosity was still there, but behind it were the subtle threats, implied actions that might involve Murray or the few people in the galaxy he actually cared about—his mom, his little brother. He'd gotten too fucking good at his job—his crappy middle management job—and as a result, the times he could get away to enjoy those retreats was getting as scarce as Khatura pollen on Earth.

Muttering to himself, Murray swiped at the layer of dust coating his computer screen, keyed into the secure comms, and began typing. Despite the almost tropical environment, that shit came out of the ground everywhere. All the machinery was covered, it settled into the crevices of everyone's clothes, even somehow got into his damned mouth. Murray couldn't wait to get off this shithole, and hopefully the message he was sending would do the trick.

There weren't a whole lot of places that the Khatura flower grew, but the cartel could damn well find a location with indigenous animals that didn't kill off people.

```
//date withheld//
//Location: Montana//

To: Scar Face Major
From: Montana 1

Request immediate withdrawal of green ore quarry
development to fresh location. Current situation
unstable and treacherous due to newly discovered
predatory and carnivorous animals. One worker
deceased. Will commence packing and prepare for
departure.

Please advise new locality.

//Montana 1 out//
```

Murray hit "send" and tipped his chair back on two legs, staring at the smudged screen, as if that would somehow make a response magically appear. It wasn't like he was top of the hierarchy, but he wasn't on the bottom, either. He couldn't recall ever requesting that an operation be moved mid-harvest. So—

The computer made an irritating noise that Murray could never quite identify—something between a high-pitched bell and a long fart. Obviously not a notification sound he would have chosen, but the cartel seemed to think it was different enough that it wouldn't be ignored. He had to admit they were right.

//date withheld//
//Location: withheld//

To: Montana 1
From: Scar Face Major

Request for immediate withdrawal denied. Current
quarry conditions profitable. Continue and complete
development. Worker supply unlimited. Defend
location as needed.

//Scar Face Major out//

"Oh, you blood-sucking, greedy bastards," Murray said. "Like you fuckers don't already have so much money you could burn credits for fuel!" For an instant all he wanted in the universe was to swing his open palm across the miserable, cockeyed table and empty it of everything—the dirty little computer, the paper printouts they insisted were safer than digital worksheets, the schedules, and all the bullshit that came with it. They probably spent more on those old-fashioned tree shavings than they paid him.

Ultimately Murray lowered his hand, even if he did ball it into a savage fist. He could destroy everything in this tent and it wouldn't make a damned bit of difference. He could even have everything packed up and loaded on the transports... except the fucking cartel wouldn't send a ship for them to rendezvous. Yeah, he could get the harvesters out of the rift, but they would have his head for disobeying.

They were stranded here until Scar Face decided to come for them.

Sitting there for a few minutes, he mentally went over what needed to be done. He'd been on LV-363 before, several times, with zero problems. Always during harvesting season, obviously. Arrive, do the job, make sure everyone else followed orders, then get out. Go enjoy life somewhere for a couple of weeks, even if he always knew the cartel could pull him out of whatever temporary paradise he'd found.

This time, however, it was a whole new playground— one that included an unknown player, or possibly two.

Sure, harvesters died all the time; they got their masks off and overdosed, they didn't fasten the safety lines and fell, they didn't bother to eat when they were supposed to, and the lack of potassium stopped their clocks. But having some unknown... *creature* kill a guy and—what had that worker claimed? *Eat* him?

Murray wanted to call bullshit on the whole thing, but the guy *was* gone, and there didn't seem to be much of a body left to bring up.

Shit.

He flicked on his comms, overriding anything else on the channel.

"Montana one to all personnel," he said. "Put all harvesters on hold fifteen minutes before descent, and report to central tent for briefing."

* * *

As ordered, Shrapnel and Margo and the other eight mercs arrived at the tent before the next shift of workers went down. Murray could tell from the expressions on their faces they were pissed about being called—probably felt too much like the military or a prison. He didn't give a shit whether they liked it or not, just as long as they were there. Whatever their background, here they felt free to bitch and moan, and while there was a lot of that going on right now, Murray wasn't in the mood.

"All right," he said, voice loud enough to cut over the complaints. "Listen up."

Most of them quieted, but the mouthier ones kept talking among themselves. Murray gave it a full ten seconds—a *lot* for him—then slammed an open palm on the metal table in front of him. The metal reverberated, and if it didn't exactly sound like a gunshot, it was loud enough to finally get their attention.

"I said, *listen up.*" There were some surly looks, some surprised ones, some unreadable ones. "I'm sure the news of what happened to one of Shrapnel's harvesters has already made the rounds. By now, it's probably blown out of proportion, because fuckers don't know how to keep their mouths shut."

Murray glanced at Shrapnel, but the jerk only lifted his chin. "People got a right to know what might be out there," he said defiantly.

Murray grimaced. "Sure they do. When *I* say so—and I don't remember doing that." Shrapnel started to open his mouth, but Murray held up a finger. His expression was dangerous. "Don't."

"It was that woman," someone said from the back. "Edith or whatever her name is."

"Enid," Shrapnel said sullenly.

"I don't care if her name is the President," Murray retorted. "Since when do y'all *not* have the brains to ignore the ravings of an addict?" Most of them suddenly found their boots very interesting. "Yeah," he said. "That's what I thought." His gaze swept the space. "Just in case it wasn't just a riftwing attack, I contacted the main base." It was always good to make himself looked concerned to the employees. "Just like I thought they would, they said to stay put. There's way too much money to be made—for *all* of us—out of this harvest." He gave it a moment, then continued before their mutterings could grow into arguments.

"If there really is anything to that druggie's story, other than a far-out exaggeration of a riftwing attack—and I'll tell you right now, that's what it is—then just be fucking ready, okay? Make sure your weapons are cleaned and loaded—"

A couple of voices started in, but Murray cut through them.

"Shut up. I've *seen* how some of you don't take care of your shit." He let the silence fill the tent. "And carry extra ammo. If you want heavier firepower, fine. Just don't be jackasses and start shooting each other or the workers. We've got extras, but the supply isn't endless." He turned his back on the mercs. "Dismissed."

They muttered to one another as they filed out, a concoction of words made of threats and bragging and bullshit. It just never ended. Enough of this; he had paperwork—always—to get to.

"Boss?"

Murray glanced over his shoulder and saw Shrapnel standing there.

"What now?"

"What about the other thing Enid saw, you know—the two-legged thing?"

"What about it?"

"If it's—"

Murray spun to glare at the merc. "And that's the million credit question, isn't it? *'If.'* She's a fucking *addict*, Shrapnel. She lives, breathes, eats and shits Khatura pollen."

"But—"

"But *what?* You ever done that pollen? Of course not. If you had, you'd be hanging on one of those harvester cables, cuz that drug don't let go. It don't give take-backs. Those harvesters are batshit crazy, man. A sane person can scare his own pants off staring at a dark room when they don't know what's in it. It's dark as hell in the rift. How much worse do you think these junkies are?"

Shrapnel pressed his lips together, then shrugged.

"Yeah, you're probably right."

"Of course I'm right," he ground out. Murray gestured toward the tent's opening. "Now, get the fuck outta here and go back to work."

1 0

Movement, above. Light.
Go up, over edge. Too open.
Food moving. Too many, outnumbered.
Not seen, hide.
Watch.
Want solitary food.
Wait.
Want mother.
Watch.
Wait.

1 1

"Margo, get the hell over here," Shrapnel said.

He tapped impatiently at the ground while he waited. His face was hot with the dress-down he'd received from the little man, Murray. If this had been an alley on one of the stations or a corridor in a mining colony, that asshole would have been plastered all along it, his begging filling the space as much as his blood.

"Margo, where are you?" He turned toward their tent. She hurried out, slinging her rifle over her shoulder and straightening her shirt.

Shrapnel felt his aggravation rise. "Were you taking a nap?" He glanced around in disgust. "After all that's going on, you were getting your beauty sleep?"

She grinned, her scarring making the effort anything but pleasing to the eye. "All the beauty sleep in the world ain't gonna help me." She stopped in front of him. "You know how it is. You catch a nap whenever you can."

"That was in the marines, not on guard duty," he growled. "You sleeping on duty is why we lost one of our harvesters."

"That's not fair." Her grin disappeared. "He wasn't mine to watch. He was your—"

"Enough excuses," Shrapnel snapped. "Murray wants you to find Khaleed's body. See what happened. Your harvester Enid claims there's a monster down there."

"And you want me to go instead of you?" she asked, raising an eyebrow.

"We can afford to lose you, but not me." He pointed to the rift. "Get going."

* * *

"Beauty sleep, my ass," Margo muttered as she turned and left Shrapnel. He was nothing but a coward. "It's not a bad thing to be afraid," she told herself. "Fear's what keeps people alive—but let that fear sink its grimy claws into you, keep you from doing your job—well, that's when you oughta retire."

She approached the rift's edge and stared into it. Glancing at the sky, she figured they only had about twenty minutes of sunlight left inside it, so now was a good time to descend. She went to Khaleed's cable and found it loose, devoid of weight. Either he'd fallen, or something had ripped him free.

She checked her M41A pulse rifle and noted that

she had ninety-seven rounds remaining. Snugging her helmet into place, she pulled on her gloves and prepared to descend. She'd never been afraid of heights, but she did have a thing about the dark. She didn't want to be anywhere without light, if possible.

Grabbing the auto descenders from her belt, Margo affixed them to the cables. She snagged the remote for the power pulleys and released the tension. Her descenders allowed her to lower herself slowly enough that she could keep an eye on the rift walls and down in the rift itself, in case one of the riftwings decided it wanted to take a bite out of her.

So far the riftwings had pretty much left them alone, with only a few early attempts to attack. A few well-placed shots and the creatures had learned that humans were a worse target than anything else in the rift. These days they approached the guards and even the harvesters with a lot more caution, flying around them like human-sized bees.

The usual flora hugged the side of the rift, roots digging deep into seemingly impenetrable walls so that the plants could grow outward and try to reach the sun's short blessing. A variety of insects, most of them pollinators, moved from plant to plant, largely ignoring her as she descended. A few birds, riotously colorful, zipped among them, snatching slower moving bugs and caterpillars from branches.

What she didn't see is a monster.

Fucking Shrapnel.

He was the kind of soldier who'd quit the military and gone in search of something easier, because serving was too hard. The kind who, when things got tense or there was even a hint of danger, shoved someone else in harm's way.

Fuck that guy.

Margo lowered herself a little more, and saw the first signs of blood. It began as a splattering of red across the many greens of the moss and flora, but quickly devolved into a mass of red meat, flies buzzing madly as they dove and tasted and digested what was left of Khaleed.

Then she spied his head.

His face still was covered with the mechanical mask. Already worms and beetles had found his eyes and were making a fine meal of them. She saw the lips trembling and, for one insane moment, thought he was going to speak to her, but they parted gently. A red millipede scrambled out and across his sunken cheeks.

One thing was for sure. He didn't just fall. So, what took him out?

Margo descended further, hyperaware of her surroundings. What sort of creature were they dealing with here? She was about two-thirds of the way to the rift floor when she realized that something was different— *off*. The surroundings had changed in subtle ways she didn't quite understand.

The insects were still ever-present and the slight wind

moving through the rift stirred the flora, but strangely, there was no *sound*. What had in the past always been a low, constant cacophony of birds and small animal noises was missing.

Then Margo heard something new, directly below her.

The sound of something moving… *dragging*.

Then there was a chittering sound, the movement of long legs through the weeds and stunted trees. She thought of activating the pulley so it would propel her back to the top, but curiosity got the better of her. She needed to know, so she hung on with one hand and leaned out to scan what she could of the shadowy canyon floor.

Nothing.

Then she spotted movement. While the rest of the saplings leaned in one direction, one of them rustled in the other. Margo stared at a shadowy figure until it passed into the light, then couldn't stop herself from gasping.

It had four legs, the rear ones larger than the front. It might have been an animal, but the bullet shape of its head was all wrong. The body was strangely ribbed, as if the shiny, pure black skin was stretched over the bones because it was starving or something. Each limb ended in claws, and the tail had a tapered, almost blade-like end. It whipped back and forth, and she could imagine it tearing through human skin.

Where the hell had this thing come from? She'd been to LV-363 several times over the years, and had never seen or heard of this kind of predator.

Suddenly, it turned its head upward. It had no eyes, yet somehow it focused on her. Without hesitating, it leaped for her cable and missed. For a too-long moment, Margo's pulse hammered in her chest and she froze.

It leaped again, and missed again.

How many tries before it succeeded?

Getting a grip on her fear, she almost felt like taunting it as she watched it pace back and forth beneath her cable, trying to work out how to get to her. Still, Margo didn't feel quite *that* safe, and when it started clawing at the side of the rift, trying to climb, all thoughts of stupid fun vanished.

Shit. Shit. Shit.

Margo actuated the pulley and it began to tug her toward the surface. *Too slow!* The walls of the rift were hard, and footholds among the moss and Khatura flowers difficult to find, but the creature wouldn't give up. It scrambled around beneath her until it managed to climb just enough to leap and catch the cable beneath her, sending her swinging wildly. Margo and the beast rocked together on her cable, each trying to make the other lose their grip. As they bumped to a stop, Margo kicked downward, trying to dislodge it.

It swiped at her boot and she kicked again, catching it in the jaw. At that moment, she saw how much of an actual monster it was. Its mouth opened, revealing two rows of silvery teeth, many of them pointed and dagger sharp, all of them dripping with seemingly endless lengths of drool.

Another kick, and finally she dislodged it.

Margo pressed the emergency button, activating the pulley again, and brought up her rifle, trying and failing to get a bead on the hideous thing. The pulley sped up and she began to rise, leaving it below. She glanced up, seeing the freedom of the sky and begging in her mind for it to get closer faster.

Then she felt a tug.

Then another.

Then another, like she was a fish on the end of a line.

Full stop. The hoist system screamed above her as too much weight again forced it to a stop. Margo stared in horror as the creature tried to scramble up her legs. She could feel each grip of its claws digging into her boots and scraping her skin through the heavy canvas of her pants. The tail, whipping back and forth, was almost mesmerizing. But its mouth…

It opened wide and then another, smaller mouth snapped out, filled with oozing, needle-like teeth, trying its best to fasten anywhere on her leg.

Something jolted in her brain and she realized she still had the rifle in her right hand. She brought it up and just unloaded, her screams overwhelmed by the *barraaaatt* of the rifle and the inhuman shrieks of the creature. She watched the red indicator light count down the rounds she expended, and didn't care if she fired all of them. But when it hit fifty-something, pain scorched through her lower body.

The creature's blood—a volatile green—was like acid. It was eating through her clothes *and* her skin.

The last flood of adrenaline jolted through her and she kicked desperately at the monster, fighting against the fiery pain that threatened to blot out everything. With one last kick, Margo knocked it free and watched as it plummeted to the ground below. Then the pulley jerked back into motion, lifting her into a heaven where light was as present as the pain.

1 2

Ca'toll had everything set up and ready to go in the ship's lab when she keyed into the comms and called in her team of unblooded Yautja. She had placed the Ovomorph within the largest isolation cube, where it was sitting in the open, resting on a cooling table that kept it in a deep freeze.

She'd left the entrance open and motioned them all to come inside the fairly roomy area. Hetah, Ptah'Ra and Sta'kta kept a respectful distance, as she expected of them, never taking their gaze off the cube as they circled it carefully.

"It's an impressive example of biology," Ca'toll told them. "Very complicated. Research indicates that some of these eggs—Ovomorphs—can remain viable for hundreds of years, perhaps longer. They are laid by a queen, although the Xenomorphs are supremely adaptable. In the absence of a Queen they can multiply via an alternative known as eggmorphing."

"Do the eggs ever die?" Ptah'Ra asked.

"Eventually," Ca'toll answered, "but there is no reliable data as to *when* that happens. Remember that, because if ever you are hunting in what appears to be an uninhabited or expired environment, you may come across one… or more. In such an instance, exercise extreme caution." She moved past the unblooded, stepping up to the cooling table. She could practically feel her students' nervousness.

Good—they have every reason to feel that way.

Although she'd told them there was no need to wear their armor, she remained fully protected.

"Note that, even in stasis, there remains an attempt at the Ovomorph's instinctive response." Without wavering, she reached out a hand and drew the tip of a sharp fingernail from the top of the egg down to the middle. Although the temperature was too low for it to open, there was still a… *shiver* of sorts that ran through the entire form. The sounds her unblooded made were a healthy cross between fascination and anxiety. "When an Ovomorph senses an approaching organism that might make a viable host, the four triangular pieces at the top peel open to release its facehugger. If the target is near, the parasitic creature will launch itself at its victim. Alternatively, if its objective isn't close enough, instinct will tell the facehugger to hide and wait for a chance to strike."

Ca'toll stepped back and motioned at her team. "Everyone outside the quarantine area," she ordered. She waited until they obeyed, filing into the corridor, then keyed the command to close off the entrance. They could watch her through a large, impenetrable window. Off to the side was another sturdy table, this one with a smaller but functional isolation container. The lid was open. A flip of a finger opened the comms so her words could be heard in the corridor.

"Now I'm going to show you how an Ovomorph awakens, and what to expect when it does," Ca'toll said. She pressed a series of controls along the edge of the cooling table, then stepped around it and unlocked the failsafe on the opposite side. The lower half of the platform began to transform, going from cold silver to a soft, orange glow as it heated up. Through the speaker she could hear their mandibles chitter involuntarily, an apprehensive reaction. Good; there was no relaxing around a viable Ovomorph.

The display on her helmet revealed that her own vitals had increased substantially in response to what her brain knew was coming. Ca'toll slowly circled the platform, never taking her gaze away from the rapidly warming egg.

"Witness my body's reaction to what my brain knows is about to happen." The three unblooded remained silent, entranced. "My normal response is anticipation," she continued. "However, I will not allow myself to forget that, when you are dealing with an Ovomorph or a Xenomorph in any stage of life, anything and everything can change in an instant."

The table's computer gave off a series of warning chimes; soon the egg would be fully thawed.

"For instance," Ca'toll continued, "what if I hadn't done proper reconnaissance, and came upon this Ovomorph without warning?" She glanced quickly at them, noting with approval that all were paying close attention, then refocused on the Ovomorph. "And what if..." She dragged out the sentence, then was pleased when the top of the Ovomorph shuddered and fissures appeared. Her timing was perfect.

The petals folded back until they were fully opened.

The facehugger exploded from the top of the Ovomorph and launched straight for her face. Despite its terrifying speed, Ca'toll's gloved hand shot out and snatched it in mid-air. Outside the quarantine area the unblooded jerked involuntarily. More than one gasped. The spider-like creature thrashed wildly in her grip, and even though she was helmeted, she kept it well away from her face.

"What if this had been a hyperfertile egg?" she continued calmly. "In that case, the Ovomorph might have released multiple facehuggers, and my situation would become immediately dire." Ca'toll turned her wrist so that her team could see the creature's proboscis, furiously trying to find an opening into which it could bury itself, while its tail lashed furiously in every direction.

"The facehugger's goal is to impregnate a host with a Xenomorph embryo. Once this takes place—and it will be rapid—it will subdue the host with chemicals that both paralyze it and suppress any immune system response, so the hosting body does not attempt to attack the developing embryo. The paralytic substance is secreted by the proboscis itself as well as the flesh surrounding it. Once the facehugger has settled over the host's mouth, the struggle is over. Impregnation is almost instantaneous and the host is beyond saving."

Ca'toll let that sink in, then used her other hand to grasp the creature's flailing tail. It continued to fight as she stretched it out so they could glimpse the full length.

"If the host manages to keep the facehugger from inserting its proboscis," she noted, "its goal becomes to wrap its tail around the neck of its victim. In that manner it will cut off circulation to the lungs and brain until the host becomes unconscious and can no longer resist." She carried the facehugger over to the smaller isolation container, then slammed the creature into it. When the weight of its body landed on the container's bottom, a blast of cryo-cooled air from side vents stunned the creature just long enough for Ca'toll to yank out her hands and slam the top shut, where it automatically locked.

An instant later the facehugger was battering nonstop at the walls of the container. Ca'toll stepped back and stripped off her gloves, then turned to face her watching team.

"You've been trained to be the best warriors you can. Even so, I can't stress enough that you must *continue* that training and, in particular, pay extra attention to your reflexes. A single response, if it is a half-second too slow, could cost you your life."

As she spoke, T'U'Sa stepped up behind the unblooded to watch her presentation. Ignoring the other hunt captain, she keyed in the sequence to open the quarantine area's door and stepped out. Continuing five meters down the corridor she flipped a switch, and a panel slid up, revealing one of LV-363's local animals. To her knowledge, no one had ever bothered to categorize the local fauna, so there was no scientific name for the medium-sized quadruped. On the oomans' home plant, Earth, it might have been labeled a species of deer, although there were distinct differences in the feet of the animal and its long, split tail.

It also had a double row of short, flat plates that ran from just above its oversized eyes to where the base of its skull stopped. Ca'toll wasn't particularly interested in animal evolution, but the logical conclusion was the creature was prone to head-butting. As if to support this, the creature lowered its head and grunted as it shuffled its feet. Before it could do anything, however, Ca'toll snapped an electronic rope around its neck and tightened it, then pulled it out of the compartment.

At first it resisted. Then when it cleared the doorway, it tried to run, but as much as it was firmly muscled, it was no match for Ca'toll. She easily dragged it over to the quarantine cube and forced it inside, then withdrew the rope and reclosed the entrance.

"Watch carefully," she instructed, "and you'll get a firsthand look at how a facehugger attacks and incapacitates its victim so that it can implant the embryo."

She took off her helmet. There was a smaller keypad on the wall below the one that controlled the entrance. Opening it, she rapidly keyed in a code, then paused. "Look away even for an instant, and you'll miss it." She hit the final number.

The lid of the smaller cube suddenly flipped open. The facehugger's response was instantaneous—it hurtled toward the animal so quickly, it was only a blur. It fell short, however, and with a low, terrified sound the quadruped jumped sideways, crashing into one of the tables. It tried to scramble away and almost lost its footing, then found itself backed against the wall just to the right of the rapt team.

The facehugger skittered toward it and in an attempt to protect itself, the mammal lowered its head and jumped *toward* its attacker.

It was a bad move, and the perfect example of what not to do.

The facehugger leaped from the floor and landed squarely on the quadruped's short muzzle, wrapping its bony legs and tail around the animal's nose and mouth. The creature reared and shook its head. After a few moments it went down on its forelegs, and was still.

"See how quickly the facehugger's paralytic agent goes to work," Ca'toll told them. She keyed open the entrance to the quarantine area and stepped inside, motioning at them to follow. They did so with intense caution, and when they were in a circle around the still animal, Ca'toll extended one of her wristblades and prodded at it with the tip.

The mammal didn't move, and she pushed harder, piercing its exterior; the wound released a milky goo. The facehugger didn't move at all. "At this point," Ca'toll said, "the facehugger cannot be extracted from its host without killing them both." In an instant, both Ca'toll's serrated wristblades were out and she impaled the parasite from two different angles, running the blades through it and into the brain of the quadruped.

Neither creature moved as they died.

Her unblooded were silent and thoughtful, and Ca'toll was pleased. There was a lot to be absorbed here, and they would discuss it among themselves while they prepared for their next incursion into the rift.

Meanwhile, T'U'Sa stood in his original place outside the quarantine area. His gaze met hers and he gave a low, mocking laugh as he turned and strode away to get his team ready for their turn in the planetary gash. Ca'toll scowled and watched him go.

1 3

Murray was in his tent going over the supply requests. *Fucking paperwork, again.* It just never ended. He stared at the documents and absently scratched at his arms. Everything on this planet seemed to make him itch. It wasn't the Khatura pollen, but who knew what other kind of shit was floating around in the air from thousands of other flowers? While the cartel had tested for and found Khatura, however many years before, there's no way they'd looked for stuff that might cause allergies.

Like they even gave a flying fuck.

Finally he swore aloud and pushed back hard from the stupid, crooked table, then stood and went over to the storage box next to his cot. He keyed in his personal code and the lid popped open, giving him a view of the only thing that brought him any relief on this fucking nowhere rock—a smaller, cloth-lined case holding a bottle of vodka. It cost a helluva lot of credits to get it from Earth, but who cared? It wasn't like he could go shopping.

Careful to make sure he had a good grip on it, Murray lifted the bottle out of its case with one hand, then reached with his other and snagged the shot glass next to it. It wasn't actually *glass*, just a shot cup, and it seemed like a fucking crime to pour the prime vodka into a battered piece of round aluminum that had seen way too many trips to harvester planets.

He poured anyway.

To Murray's eyes, the vodka looked like liquid from heaven, crystalline and pure, as it filled the cup to just under the rim. Oh-so-carefully he set the cup on the ground, then recapped the bottle and stowed it away. Then he picked up the aluminum chalice full of nirvana and passed it under his nose, inhaling.

Mmmmm.

The edge of the cup had just grazed his lip when Shrapnel's voice blared out of his comms speaker, loud enough to make Murray start and his hand jerk. A good half of his precious vodka sloshed out and onto the dirt floor. Shrapnel's voice had been so loud and irate it hadn't even been lucid, and anger made Murray's face go instantly red. In one, fast move, he lifted the cup and poured the rest in his mouth.

Not enough—not *nearly* enough.

He thumbed on his comms as his fist curled around the aluminum container.

"What the ever-loving-*fuck*, Shrapnel?" he bellowed. "I can't understand a damned word coming out of your shit-filled mouth!" He could feel the last of the spilled vodka evaporating on his hand, and he didn't know if he wanted to scream—which he could do any fucking time he wanted—or go and cut the merc's throat.

There was a garbled mashup of sound and static, then Shrapnel's voice slowed enough to be clear, even if it was still at volume twelve on a ten dial.

"Need you to come to the harvester launch area, stat."

Murray's teeth ground together. "What the fuck for?" he demanded. "I got better things to do than—"

"It's important!" Shrapnel practically shrieked through the comms, making Murray wince. *"You gotta get over here and see! You gotta—"* The rest was powered out by garbled sounds from other people, and maybe... screams?

"Fine," Murray said. "I'm coming, damn it." He thumbed off the comms so it would stop giving him an earache, then put the now-empty aluminum shot "glass" back into the case with the bottle of Elit. Next time, he told himself, he'd make sure there was nothing around to interrupt him. He had hardly any time to himself, and almost nothing enjoyable on this trip. He wouldn't be fucked over again.

After the storage box was locked, Murray buckled on his weapons belt, jammed a dirty hat on his head, and headed out.

* * *

The space the mercs had set up to lower and raise the harvesters was a real shitshow. Murray got paid relatively well because he'd always run a clean and orderly operation, and if anyone from the cartel decided to do a drop-in right now, all those years of effort might as well get tossed into the rift they were yammering about.

First off, they were supposed to run patrol shifts for security, making sure this weird-ass planet hadn't spawned some new kind of animal that would somehow get past the perimeter traps. At that moment, though, it looked like every merc on the mission was here, which left zero personnel on watch.

Secondly, a bunch of the harvesters were milling around when they oughta be getting ready to go down the cables. Instead they were all google-eyed and slack-mouthed, ignoring the protein packets they were supposed to ingest and tripping over the tangled piles of nets and cables. Murray *hated* it when his carefully planned logistics were so fuckingly ignored that everything descended into chaos. It would take hours to get this mess back to normal.

And last of all—well.

That was the worst.

Margo was sitting on an overturned cargo box. Her lap and the ground around her were piled with bandages splotched with blood and some other kind of green goo. Shrapnel was hovering over her like a nervous bitch while Jackson, an old merc who'd been a medic in some long-forgotten asteroid war, was gloved up to his elbows in acid-resistant butyl. He poured some kind of grainy white liquid all over her legs.

Murray didn't know what the hell Margo had gotten into, but as he strode forward, tough as he was, he felt a twinge in his gut as he scanned the damage to the female merc's lower body.

The legs of her work pants hung in ragged strips, singed around all the edges. Had she caught on fire down in the rift? If so, how the hell? Where Jackson hadn't yet covered her with white gunk, Murray could see open, wounds festering between the strips of fabric. As he covered the last of the distance to her, he realized her chest was heaving and Shrapnel was holding her in place by clamping down on her shoulders.

Her head was thrown back and her teeth were clamped on the thick plastic handle of a hunting knife. Even so, Murray could hear guttural, agonizing sounds coming from deep in her lungs. He stopped just short of where Jackson was working, just in time to see the guy jerk a syringe out of his belt and slam the needle into the side of Margo's neck.

It took a good five seconds, then her body relaxed… not unconscious, but not fighting, either. They could still hear her groans, but the volume had dropped by a good seventy-five percent. Even so, they were enough to raise the hair on Murray's neck.

Shrapnel looked up from where he was holding Margo tight and spotted him.

"What the ever-loving *fuck*, Murray?" Spittle flew from his lips as he screamed. "Look at this shit, *look at this shit!*"

"I see it, Shrapnel," Murray said in his best professionally calm voice. Calm didn't even belong in the same brain category as what he was really feeling, but the truth wouldn't help anything. Damn it, this was bad. "Jackson, bring me up to speed."

"It looks like some kind of acid." Jackson kept working and didn't look up. "I'm neutralizing it, but it did some first-class damage before we could get her out of the rift."

"You gotta get us the fuck outta here, Murray," Shrapnel bellowed. His voice was loud enough to be heard on the next planet. "I don't know what's down there—"

"Monsters." Margo's voice was thick around the blade handle, but everyone around could still understand her."

"*Fucking A!*" Shrapnel continued at the top of his lungs. "Monsters! Enid told you about them, she told you—and you didn't listen, you asshole. Now look at Margo, man, look at her! All these burns, she's gonna have scars!"

It's not like she doesn't already, Murray thought. Thankfully a moment of self-preservation kept that tidbit from coming out of his mouth. It wasn't the time for sarcasm, and he knew that in the past Shrapnel and Margo had been more than just coworkers. Share some alcohol and fuck a couple of times, and you always had a bond, whether or not you couldn't stand the sight of each other ninety percent of the time.

"I heard you the first time," he said. This time Murray's voice boomed over Shrapnel's, the voice of the guy who was in charge even in a fucked-up situation.

"She's out for the rest of the operation," Jackson said. "Gonna take months to get fixed up from this shit. Debridement, bio-grafts, induced coma to handle stress to the organs, the whole med program."

Murray had a flash forward as to what the cartel would have to say about this when he told them, and he grimaced. Their first reaction would be about cost—profits always came first. This would cut deep into what they'd make by staying here. When Murray had tried to get them to pull out, they should've done what he'd asked—but they hadn't, and that was that.

There would be no sympathy, and there would be no waste of profits on extensive medical bills and rehabilitation and crap. They would tell Murray just to find a way to get rid of her.

"We're not going anywhere," Murray told Shrapnel. "I already asked if we could scrap the job, and got a no-fucking-way in response. We—"

Murray wasn't ready for how fast Shrapnel was, as he was hauled off his feet and slammed against the trunk of the nearby thing that passed for a tree on this dump planet. The air went out of him, but only for a moment. He might be a pencil-pusher, but he stayed in shape.

"You get us off this shithole," Shrapnel brayed. The merc's face was right up into his. Spit and probably the remains of whatever he'd eaten at mess spewed from his lips. "Unless you want me to—"

"Do what?" Murray asked. His voice was low and dangerously cold. Shrapnel's words cut off in a gasp and he blinked, then very carefully he set Murray back on his feet. He didn't step away, just stood there, his posture stiff.

Tucked deep into his right armpit was the razor tip of Murray's favorite knife, the one everyone ignored because it hung off his weapons belt and no one had ever seen him use it. He loved being underestimated.

"What are you going to do, Shrapnel?"

"I—I—I'm sorry, boss. I lost my temper." Shrapnel flinched as Murray let the blade slip, just a little. It was nothing for it to part clothing and ease into the merc's skin, so very close to the artery there.

"I don't like people who can't keep their heads," Murray said, "and I don't like being threatened by an *employee*."

"I understand. I swear it won't happen again, honest to God, I'll never—"

"Shut up."

Shrapnel did.

Keeping the knife in his right hand, Murray reached up and placed it flat against Shrapnel's broad chest. The back of his hand was tattooed in deep black ink on the pitted skin, the head of a viper. The inky image twitched as if it were alive and couldn't wait to strike. Murray lowered his voice so that only the merc could hear him.

"Don't fuck with me, Shrapnel. If you do, I'll kill you." Murray looked Shrapnel straight in the eyes, making sure to keep his expression smooth, almost pleasant. "And you won't see it coming. We clear?"

"Yes, boss," Shrapnel whispered.

"Good." Murray closed his hand into a loose fit, then stuck out his forefinger and oh-so-gently pushed the merc away.

There was no resistance.

Shrapnel turned without a word and made his way back over to Margo. The shot Jackson had given her had quieted her somewhat, but Murray figured it would only last for a quarter of an hour at the most. She'd have to be taken to the med tent and dosed up solid.

"I want everyone to shut up and listen up," he yelled. "Eyes and ears on me, no exceptions." There were a couple of harvesters hanging around, and he glanced at them hard, stopping them before they could skulk away. They were masked, but he could still make out Enid and Fetch.

"You addicts, too," he continued. "Take the news back to your friends, and don't fucking change a word. Get it?" They nodded.

"All right, then." Without looking, Murray slid his knife back into its place on his belt. "Obviously we got a problem here, a big one. I don't know what it is, but we're gonna handle this." He looked around, catching every one of the other mercs in his gaze. "I told all of you before to make sure your weapons were at the ready.

Now I'm telling you again, plus some. Clean your guns and pack 'em with the maximum load. Then go to the armory shack and get *more* guns, as many as you can carry, with as much extra ammo as you can carry. The cartel won't let us out of here.

"So we stay put and make war with whatever the hell is in the rift."

1 4

Stea'Pua followed the others into the rift. He was enjoying himself more than he thought he would. Throughout the journey here he'd been worried that he would be too scared. He didn't want to let his family or his elders down. He was destined for greatness, they said, and to achieve it he would have to become blooded like the rest of them.

He was still limping from the fight over the combistick.

T'See'Ka carried it proudly, both a trophy and a weapon to be wished for.

Stea'Pua had hesitated. That he knew. He hadn't meant to, but he did so nonetheless. And now their hunt captain, T'U'Sa, thought worse of him, suspecting that the young unblooded was soft. Stea'Pua was far from soft, and was already devising ways to win back the prize.

Each of them rappelled down on their own cables, and Stea'Pua was eager to reach the bottom. He'd watched T'U'Sa destroy Xenomorphs and was ready for his turn. Though wearing only light armor and his wristblades, he'd trained with them enough that he felt as if he would be able to take down any predator this planet could devise.

U'Brea'Sua hit the rocky bottom first and spun left to check for danger, sliding into the foliage along the rift wall for concealment. Stea'Pua landed next, spinning right, ensuring no danger would come unnoticed from that direction. T'U'Sa and T'See'Ka followed, setting down softly between them. T'See'Ka twirled the combistick, earning him an angry glance from the hunt leader.

The rift was as silent as they'd yet heard it. Normally, they would expect to hear the cries of birds and the whirring of insects. Even the air seemed to have stalled and was no longer slipping past the leaves. It was as though the land knew something was coming, and was waiting for it to happen.

Stea'Pua had an unsettling feeling in his stomach. He stepped further to the side and peered into the encroaching gloom. If a Xeno attacked, he'd only have a second or two to react. So he searched for the movement of a whipping tail or the jerk of a long black head. He looked for so long that, when T'See'Ka tapped him on the shoulder, he jumped.

"What the hell?" Stea'Pua said.

"Just checking to see if you were paying attention," T'See'Ka said.

"You watch your own sector," Stea'Pua said. "I'm paying attention to mine." He gave a hard glance at the combistick, and wanted to say that having it wasn't the same thing as being the leader, but looked away instead. He didn't want to give T'See'Ka the satisfaction.

T'U'Sa toggled all of them on the comms. "Now is the time. Before the day is over, one of you will be blooded. I can feel it. Can you?"

Stea'Pua felt his own blood warm as he flexed his wristblades. Of course he could feel it. The sizzle in the air. The anticipation of what was to come. His brothers had told him about how all great warriors could sense violence from the taste of the air. Not that he could taste anything different, but he could feel something, something *different*—

A Xenomorph exploded from the brush, heading straight for them.

Stea'Pua shifted to a fighting stance, but the Xeno leaped against the hillside and bypassed him, launching itself at T'See'Ka. Before there was time to extend the combistick, T'See'Ka swung and caught his attacker on the side of the head. The Xeno tumbled in the dust as it rolled uncontrollably. Then it found its footing and twisted, coming back toward the four Yautja.

Stea'Pua let his knees sink in a tactical squat, flexing his wristblades, ready for the attack, while T'See'Ka extended the combistick so that it was a double spear, capable of slicing or pinning the alien. U'Brea'Sua held back in the shadows, unknown and unheard, waiting for an opportunity to attack from behind. His wristblades were flexed and ready, but his stance was that of a statue where he held as still as he could until his target came within reach.

The Xeno paused and shook its head, saliva raking the leaves next to it. It was closest to Stea'Pua, and gave him a predatory tilt of its eyeless head. Stea'Pua sunk deeper into his stance, fully ready to leap left or right if he was charged. And that's what the Xeno did. It charged—barreling toward him with teeth telescoping and snapping at the air.

Stea'Pua brought a hand up to claw it as he leaped to his left, but suddenly found himself falling sideways as he was pushed away. T'See'Ka had shouldered him aside, knocking Stea'Pua to the ground as he set the spear ready.

The Xenomorph came on, unable to stop, impaling itself on the staff, its blood searing everything nearby with the smoky tendrils of its death. The spear penetrated all the way through its back, jutting past the creature's spine.

"T'See'Ka, you *pauk-de*!" Stea'Pua growled to his feet. "That was my kill!"

"I'm blooded now," T'See'Ka rumbled in response. "You're not."

"Because you stole my kill!"

"It's not my fault you leaped out of the way. Your fear got to you."

"My fear—" He felt his face redden. "I didn't leap anywhere. You shoved me."

"You fell," T'See'Ka said, smiling sadly. "I don't know why you won't admit it."

"Enough fighting, you two," T'U'Sa commanded. He turned to T'See'Ka and punched him hard enough in the chest to send him flying on top of the Xeno's corpse. "And you! Where is your honor? That was his kill!"

T'See'Ka rolled off the body of the alien, his back smoking from contact with the acid blood, but he kept quiet. It was clear he wanted to say something, but he held back. He'd crossed the line and he knew it—had been too eager for the kill.

Stea'Pua glared at him. As dishonorable as he was, T'See'Ka was the only one of the crew who thus far was blooded, and the unfairness of it was remarkable. Still, he wouldn't have a glorious tale to tell. Whenever he would be asked how he became blooded, T'See'Ka would know he cheated. His honor was forever besmirched. Stea'Pua granted himself that.

When he was blooded, he'd be proud of the moment. If his blooding was great enough, he might even create a song about it, to sing to members of his clan. He was destined for great things and his honor demanded that the greatness be constant.

There was a loud rustling behind them. They all spun and saw something unimaginable headed toward them— from above.

It was a riftwing.

Except it wasn't.

This was something new, a combination—a Xenowing. It had the head and tail of a Xeno on the body of a riftwing, including the *wings*. It crashed heedlessly through the greenery over their head as it dove toward its prey—*them*.

Stea'Pua and the others somersaulted out of the way as the Xenowing touched down on the rift floor. It prowled around the dead Xenomorph, then spied T'See'Ka and leaped for the newly blooded Yautja. But T'U'Sa wasn't going to let that happen. He pegged it with his shoulder cannon, three beads of red light on its torso, and fired.

Inconceivably, he missed.

The Xenowing was nowhere to be seen.

T'U'Sa and the other three Yautja studied the area around them. The creature had to be close. They couldn't let it get away—no one had ever seen such a creature, and it would provide an amazing trophy. Stea'Pua was aware from his teachings that sometimes a Xeno could take on some of the characteristics of the creature in which it incubated, but he'd never heard of one with wings before. The idea was terrifying.

Pauk, it wasn't an idea.

It was there in front of them, somewhere…

U'Brea'Sua screamed as a tail whipped out of the darkness and grabbed his leg, snapping around it and yanking him toward the brush. Stea'Pua leaped forward and sliced at the tail with his wristblades, his jaws open in a silent warrior scream. The tail separated, spewing acid blood everywhere.

A few drops hit Stea'Pua's arm, crackled against his skin. He clicked his mandibles in pleasure and knew that a story had just been created. He grabbed the end of the Xeno's tail and shook it until most of the blood flew off, then wrapped it around his belt. T'See'Ka might have stolen his first kill, but Stea'Pua would be known as the first Yautja to ever wound a Xenowing.

He turned to T'U'Sa to show him the trophy, then jerked. Another Xenowing was above them, diving and gaining momentum, tail straight and arms and legs held back to gain the greatest possible speed. The thing's teeth led the way, as if it were a missile fired from a spaceship.

The Xenowing smashed into T'U'Sa before anyone could warn him, shattering his back and crushing him against the ground. As it landed, it opened its wings, wrapped them around the hunting party leader, and began feeding, tearing into T'U'Sa's flesh.

Stea'Pua was the first to shake himself free of the horrible sight. He dashed forward and sliced at the Xenowing, his wristblades cutting one of the wings to ribbons. In his peripheral vision, he saw T'See'Ka already fleeing, hurrying up the side of the rift, the combistick strapped to his back.

U'Brea'Sua was right behind him.

Stea'Pua swiped again at the Xenowing, then barely dodged out of the way as it turned and snapped at him, jaws dripping saliva and blood. The beast was too large. He needed reinforcements, heavier weapons. He needed *help*, but the other two had left him with their dead leader. As much as he didn't want to retreat, to stay would mean suicide.

With a wail, he backed away from the body of his leader and the creature feeding on it. He scaled the rift wall behind his fellow team members, halfway hoping to be snatched into the air so he could be rid of the despair he felt.

1 5

T'See'Ka sprawled on the ground amid a circle of his peers. The sun was approaching the horizon, so the light was beginning to fade.

They had all removed their helmets. Half of them were in shock. The other half looked at one another as though they couldn't believe one of the hunt leaders had been killed. Such a concept seemed impossible.

Ny'ytap towered over the newly blooded Yautja. Rage made his voice so deep it was barely understandable.

"What do you mean you left your hunt leader behind?" T'See'Ka started to rise, but Ny'ytap shoved him back down with a booted foot. "You never leave anyone behind. Have you not learned *anything* about honor?"

The others backed away at the violence rising in Ny'ytap's voice. The elite captain kept his foot on the young Yautja's chest and turned to U'Brea'Sua and Stea'Pua.

"And what of you two? Why did *you* leave?"

"T'See'Ka was blooded. We weren't." U'Brea'Sua lifted his head. "With T'U'Sa dead, T'See'Ka became the leader," he continued. "He left so we followed. Were we wrong?"

Ny'ytap snarled and almost lunged at U'Brea'Sua. The younger Yautja flinched. Then the senior Yautja noticed Stea'Pua hanging his head.

"What say you?"

"What he said is correct," Stea'Pua responded. "I tried to fight it, but the creature was immense. It wasn't like a normal Xenomorph. This one could fly and—"

Murmurs from the other Yautja overran his words as they all considered what he said. Ny'ytap stepped back and allowed T'See'Ka to climb to his feet. Ca'toll stepped forward and addressed the entire circle, staring each Yautja in the eyes as she spoke.

"We never leave any one of us behind. Ever." Her words were measured. "We die first." She reached out to T'See'Ka and said, "Give me your weapon."

T'See'Ka's head lifted. He puffed out his chest and held his combistick firm.

She glowered at him.

"You will give me your weapon, or I will shove it in one end of your miserable, cowardly body and out the other." Again she held out her hand.

Ny'ytap watched in approval as T'See'Ka conceded and handed the weapon over to her. Ca'toll might be the smallest of the leaders, but she was well versed in the honor of the hunt. She knew the old ways, and T'See'Ka would be wise to listen to her. She turned to Ny'ytap and offered it to him, but he shook his head.

"Give it to Stea'Pua. He, at least, showed bravery."

Stea'Pua shook his head. "I don't need it." He held up the tail in one hand and flexed his wristblades with the other. "I am more than proficient with these. Give the stick to someone who needs it."

Ny'ytap opened his mouth in surprise, then rumbled in approval. He liked this unblooded. He had spirit, and had what it took to understand the ethos of an elite hunter. He was also from a senior clan, yet he was acting with generosity and respect. If he survived his blooding, he would go a long way.

"Tell me about this flying Xeno," Ny'ytap ordered.

Stea'Pua stood straight and described what he had seen. The other unblooded had varying reactions. Some gasped. Some stood stoic, but all of them looked thoughtful with the possibilities of this new threat and what it might mean to defeat it.

When Stea'Pua finished, Ny'ytap nodded, then his face darkened as he turned in the circle and glared at the students. He saw their fear and dismissed it. There was no place here for such nonsense.

"We will choose a crew to go back down and retrieve T'U'Sa. His body never should have been left as *food* for that creature." At least the younger Yautja had the good sense to hang their head in shame. "Let's go."

* * *

The sun passed beyond the horizon, and all they were lit by the stars and the twin moons of the planet. That was enough. Nine young Yautja stood around Ny'ytap while he still fumed. Ca'toll stood in the background, holding the coveted combistick. Like his, her face showed her anger, but she held it in check. If he hadn't been in charge, he had little doubt that she would still be ripping through the young ones.

Ny'ytap pointed to Ba'sta and Stea'Pua.

"You two will accompany me to retrieve T'U'Sa's body. The rest of you will return to the ship and set up a perimeter. There are oomans on this rock, and we don't need their interference. Ca'toll will lead you." He paused his glare at each of the young bloods. "What you witnessed was not only a foolish battle, but entirely useless. Each of you will be given a combistick for use in battle."

T'See'Ka looked as if he was about to say something, but Ca'toll's head jerked toward him, braids whipping around with her movement. Wisely, he decided to keep whatever thoughts he might have to himself. They donned their helmets in silence. Ny'ytap strode to the edge of the rift, grabbed one of their cables, and leaped over the edge, diving forward and into the darkness below.

As he dropped, he flipped on his heat vision and let it guide him. When the cable went taut, he slung his feet back to the rift wall and rappelled the rest of the way to the dark floor.

The sound of insects and animals had returned with the emergence of nocturnal creatures. It died, however, with his presence, as if they knew that an apex predator was nearby. Waiting for the others, Ny'ytap scanned his surroundings, taking in the different shades of heat and translating them. Some readings were just residue from the heat of the day, but others indicated small animals in hiding, silent, waiting for him to pass.

Ba'sta and Stea'Pua landed on each side of him, making more noise than they should have, but now was not the time for a teaching lesson. The two unblooded activated their night vision, as well. He ordered both of them to watch the sky, and be wary of any movement.

The three of them moved several meters, then Ny'ytap spied the still cooling body of T'U'Sa. He moved quickly over to it, but knew by the fading color that there was no life left in the body. T'U'Sa's face had been ripped into shreds, and from the way he was twisted it looked as though his back had been broken. Unfortunately, the hunt leader had never fired a shot. With the possibility that such a creature could ambush so perfectly, they needed to be extremely wary.

Ny'ytap put his arms beneath T'U'Sa and lifted him, then detected movement to the front. The heat signature was weak, but it was there, and in the shape of a juvenile Xenomorph. He targeted three lasers on the creature and fired, satisfied when he heard squealing and the rustling of its retreat. They would have time later to return to the rift and kill all the Xenos, but for now, they would bring T'U'Sa back to the surface.

Ny'ytap ordered Ba'sta to rise first, then he followed. Stea'Pua took up the pivotal position at the rear. When they arrived at the top of the rift, they carried T'U'Sa, walking side-by-side back to the ship in formation. T'U'Sa deserved their respect. He had been a great fighter who had been overwhelmed by a new species. He had died so that the rest of them would live.

They needed to learn from it.

They needed to realize it.

And because of it, they needed to change the way they did battle.

1 6

At the bottom of the rift, the Xenomorph crouched in the dark by the base of a small tree and watched as the two-legs climbed back into the air.

One had three lights.

Three lights danger.

It slunk farther back into the darkness until it could barely be seen.

Danger.

Avoid.

Find place to stop.

Sleep.

Wait.

Mother.

1 7

Shrapnel hated that he'd backed down from the old man.
He could have taken him. He *should* have taken him. It
wasn't like he didn't have the balls to do it. It was just
that the cartel had put Murray in charge, and if Murray
ended up dead there would be some explaining to do.

Yeah. Big explaining.

To add to the indignity of it, this was Margo's shift. Had
she not gotten wounded, she would be pulling the guard
duty for which she was scheduled, instead of shamming
in bed with barely a scratch. Well... there *were* the burns.
Those were real enough. But how the hell had she gotten
burned to begin with? There hadn't been any fire or heat.
Shrapnel didn't know much about chemical combinations,
but he had serious doubts there was anything on this
planet that could have caused those injuries.

So what had *really* happened to her?

Monsters, she'd said. Jackson said the wounds were
made from acid. Monsters with acid.

Shrapnel shuddered as he leaned against a tree,

scanning the landscape through his NODS—the multi-spectrum night observation device. Now that he thought about it, Enid had said the same thing—monsters. He didn't believe there actually were monsters, but there was certainly *something* out there. There had to be. Enid and Margo hadn't been injured by spontaneous combustion.

Then there was Khaleed. He hadn't removed his own head. His torso had looked like the used part of a candle, dripping and scorched.

A thousand monsters flashed through Shrapnel's mind, and he felt a sudden chill. The darkness wasn't his friend. Maybe they didn't really need a guard by the Khatura. Maybe everything would be okay. He could head back to the camp, slide into his bunk, and no one would even know it.

Yeah, that's what he was going to do.

He turned to go, and heard rustling behind him.

Shit. Shit. Shit.

He spun, putting his back against the tree and sinking the butt of his pulse rifle into his shoulder. Was it Murray checking up on him? Maybe Jackson?

"Who's out there?" he rasped. Then, with more confidence, he raised his voice. "Show yourself."

The rustling came again, as if something was climbing out of the rift.

It couldn't be.

Shrapnel felt his pulse start to race as heat filled the skin on his face. His mouth went dry as he tried not to think of monsters with acid, but as much as he wanted them to be nothing more than a figment of his imagination, when the first one crested the edge of the rift a dozen meters in front of him, Shrapnel gasped.

It didn't move like any animal he'd ever seen. Instead of smooth and steady, this one stepped forward in fits and jerks, its head going left, then right. A predator for certain— four legs and a long, spiny tail that whipped viciously side to side. It didn't go in a straight line, either. It crept, its body close to the ground, accentuating the length of its legs.

Then it stopped.

Shrapnel held his breath. Barely moving, he flipped through the spectrums of his goggles and decided to keep the sight on night vision.

The twitching stopped and he realized the creature was actually staring right at him. Yet it didn't have eyes…

Then it charged, impossibly fast.

Shrapnel barely had a chance to pull the trigger, but when he did, he held it fast, watching the counter go from 99 to 50 before he let up. With his back against the tree, he had nowhere to go. Thankfully, he didn't have to. The creature or monster or whatever it was nosed into the earth, arms and legs limp, tail dragging.

Dead… or at least it looked like it.

Shrapnel realized he'd automatically gone into a tactical crouch. He straightened slowly. That hadn't been hard. He grinned to himself.

In the end, guns would always win.

1 8

High in the tree it watched.

Two-legs and fire.

Egg mate down.

Not alive.

No breathe.

No find mother.

It began to uncurl from the branches it was on, and its tail wrapped around the trunk as its jaws opened, dripping saliva.

1 9

Something hit the top of his head. Shrapnel reached up and rubbed at it, his hand coming away with a thick goo. He smelled it, then jerked his hand away. Like ammonia, but not quite.

Another drop hit him.

He glanced up and through his NODS saw movement in the tree. He tried to make out the details but could only see an arm... and then a face—teeth, then more teeth, then clear goo-like saliva.

HOLYFUCKINGSHIT!

He backed away and fired the remaining fifty rounds into the tree, trying to keep from screaming as he unleased all the hell he possibly could.

Limbs and leaves exploded into the air, obliterated and falling like nature's own hail. Then came the creature, sliding inexorably down the trunk until it fell to the ground, a hard, tangled mass of black appendages. A mirror image of the one he'd just killed. Except when it fell, it splashed droplets of blood on him, and where it hit he burned.

Acid.

Here were two of the monsters.

Shrapnel realized he was hyperventilating. He struggled to control his breathing as he dropped a magazine and slid another one into place. Some of the fabric of the uniform on his arms and legs burned away. It hurt like hell, but he'd survived. He wanted to simultaneously scream at the pain and jump for joy.

He did neither. Instead he ground his teeth.

Crouched, he swept the rifle across the area in front of him. He waited for several minutes, assuming his fire would have drawn attention—waiting for another one of the acid-dripping monsters to climb out of the rift. After ten minutes, he realized it wasn't going to happen. If there were more of the creatures, he must have scared them off.

Finally Shrapnel stood and slung the rifle over his shoulder. Then, careful not to get any more of the acid blood on himself, he grabbed each creature by the tail and began dragging them back to the camp. It took twenty hard-pulling minutes before he made it, sweat pouring down his face, out of breath, and burning in places as if the fire would never go out.

The others were awake. They—along with Murray, Margo, and Jackson—had formed a perimeter. Margo, finally back on her feet, scowled at him.

"We heard gunfire. What happened?"

Shrapnel answer, his voice flat. "I killed the monsters." He jerked his catch forward and dropped the bodies of his kills in the middle of their circle. While they all stared at the dead things in front of them, Enid poked her head out of a tent. After a moment's hesitation, she came over. When she saw the creatures, she covered her mouth.

"Are these what you saw?" Shrapnel demanded. She looked from him to the monsters and then back. Her mouth worked but no sound made it out. He sharpened his voice. "I asked if these are what you saw, *addict*?"

Enid swallowed, opened her mouth, but couldn't speak.

"Are they or aren't they?" Shrapnel's eyes narrowed. *"Say something."*

"It might have been," she whispered, "I don't know. His chest... There was so much blood..."

Fucking useless. Shrapnel's head jerked back and he stared at the dead monsters. How many of these things were there? The damned addict had to be in the midst of withdrawals. He grinned and shook his head.

"Yeah, right." Dismissing her, he headed toward his tent.

"Hey, what are you going to do with these?" Murray called after him.

Without turning, Shrapnel shrugged. "Not me, someone else. My shift is over."

When he got to his tent, he sat down on his cot and started to shake. It was a long time before he was able to stop.

2 0

Thirty feet above the floor of the rift, three winged insectoids circled a large Xenomorph that was trying to climb the slick wall. They searched instinctively for the best angle of attack as the Xeno dug its claws into a strong clump of greenery rooted deep in a crevice.

Finally ready, the riftwings dove as one, wings flattening along their bodies for maximum speed. Their screams—

JAI-REEE! JAI-REEE! JAI-REEE!

—split the air when they converged on their target. When they struck, another sound rolled in with theirs—a horrific mix of screech and growl. The battle went on for half a minute as everything else in the rift went silent with fear.

Then it was finished.

* * *

Things in the air.
Fast.

Attack prey.
Defend.
Not prey.
Predator.
Feed.

2 1

Well, here she was again.

Hanging from a cable, Enid shifted her position on the grid. The air she breathed through the mask was stale and hot, stifling. She thrust her harvesting vacuum at an open Khatura bloom, her movement jerky enough that she hit the side of the flower. More pollen sifted down than went into the opening. Wasteful—that's what the bosses would say—but they couldn't see her, they couldn't feel what she felt.

She wasn't sure why, but the smooth buzz in her bloodstream from this morning's quota of Khatura was almost gone. Usually it was plenty enough to last through her time slot and past lunch, when she and the other harvesters were required to eat the slop masquerading as food. If they didn't eat, they didn't get their mid-afternoon fix—that was the rule. No one in Control made any effort to make the so-called food palatable. The only prerequisite was that it contained the bare minimum of nutrients needed to keep them alive.

Truth be told, they were never hungry anyway.

At least not for food.

Now her veins felt itchy, like tiny insects were crawling inside them. It wasn't debilitating—yet—but it was damned uncomfortable, and just a little pollen could alleviate it. Knowing that was enough to drive her crazy.

Her gloved hands found the mask and yanked at it. No good—it was locked in place. If she could only move it a little, just enough to get a single, pollen-dusted finger between it and her skin… but no. Clayton was an old hand at suiting up her harvesters. None of her workers would ever come off their shift high.

Fetch was about twenty feet to her right. Ever the compliant addict, he was dutifully harvesting, moving his vacuum slowly around the pollen-swollen flowers as though he was hypnotized. Hell, he probably *was*—still high from his morning dose, going on autopilot. He might be bigger than her, physically, but he was also younger. A baby addict who hadn't built up the tolerances that a hardcore user like Enid had.

It wasn't hard to remember when she'd been like that. Even wearing the hated mask, with a buzz in her system, Enid had loved watching the red pollen swirl from the center of the bloom and into the nozzle of the vacuum.

Now…

Now all she felt was the addiction, a sort of hot swelling that started in her chest and spread through her system, growing into fire the longer she had to go between doses. As time passed, the periods between these attacks grew shorter, her addict's body responding with chills, spasms and shakes bad enough to make her drop the vacuum. Yeah, there was a backup attachment, but now and then the yanking motion would disassemble the vacuum and the container of pollen would drop into the rift—a serious enough offense, but a supreme infraction if it was full of pollen.

The cartel was like a mother doling out treats to her brats. Always providing, but holding out until the last minute, the equivalent of waiting until the kid was screaming and twisting on the floor.

Enid swallowed and tried to focus, despite the sweat pooling along the inside edges of the mask and making the skin of her face itch mercilessly. Another full dose would only come if she managed to fill at least half of the vacuum's container, and she still had a ways to go.

Fetch had been lowered at the same time, and she could see that his vacuum's basin was bright red a third of the way up its side. He was showing her up in a big way: if she didn't catch up, she'd pay for it up top when Clayton measured the load. She just needed to find a rhythm like Fetch had, and if she didn't have the high to fuel it, she'd just have to manufacture one. An old song, maybe, something catchy that her arm could—

In the blackness below, the rift exploded with sound.

A maelstrom of noise, almost indescribable—animalistic screams, shrieks so high-pitched they made her eardrums sing with pain. Somewhere in the mix was the familiar screeching of riftwings, but there was something else, too, something new and… unspeakable.

Enid gasped and her whole body jerked on the cable, her hand instinctively closing tighter around the handle of the vacuum. She twisted and tried to see into the darkness, but it was too far down. The cacophony had broken through Fetch's ridiculous fascination with his task, and he was lurching wildly on his line as he tried to figure out what was happening. He'd lost his grip on his vacuum and it dangled precariously at the end of its safety cord, banging into his thigh every time he turned.

There was no sense trying to yell at him about his vacuum, since their comms weren't connected— harvesters weren't allowed to talk to each other while in the rift. The cartel thought there was too much of a chance they'd work out a way to reach each other, and find a way to dislodge their masks.

Right then, Enid was a whole lot more concerned with whatever the hell was happening down on the rift floor. She wouldn't have thought it possible, but the level of noise increased, spiraling, up and up and up as if the devil himself had turned up the volume on Hell's own symphony.

The desire to clap her hands over her ears was almost as strong as the desire to get the fuck out of here. The 'get the fuck out' urge finally won. Turning her face upward toward the daylight, Enid fought the need to look down, to see what kind of beasts were below. Instead she smacked at her comms.

"Clayton!" she cried. "Clayton, get us out of here! There's—"

Enid could just make out the merc's silhouette, moving to the edge of the rift about ten meters overhead. Clayton's response was immediate and harsh.

"Get back to work, addict."

"No! There's something going on below us! Ask Fetch—he'll tell you!"

But Fetch was useless. As she'd feared, his thrashing had caused the base of his vacuum to come loose—it was gone, probably shattered on the ground far below. The idiot had somehow managed to get himself thoroughly twisted in the cable. Snagged like that, there was no way it would retract—one of the mercs would probably have to come down and cut him out of it.

She didn't waste time thanking God that she wasn't him.

"There are things fighting with each other down there," she shouted into the comm. "What if they decide to come up? You've seen what they did to Margo! What if they want to eat us? Can't you *hear* them?"

"Yeah, yeah, yeah. I hear," Clayton snapped back. "The riftwings are fighting—big fucking deal. Let 'em kill each other. You stay where you are and keep working, or you can twist and sweat all night in your cot and go down tomorrow sober as shit. Got it?"

Enid glanced below again, but couldn't see a damn thing. She looked up, straining her neck as though that would somehow get Clayton to start reeling in her cable.

"Please," she begged. "I don't want to die down here. Please, pull me up."

When Clayton answered, her voice was thick with sarcasm. "Oh, I see. The same shit you claimed about Khaleed. Monsters again, right? Well, I'm not that simple-minded, not like that loser Shrapnel, so you can just—"

Whatever Clayton was going to say ended in a wheeze as something with a body three times as thick as a riftwing and a wingspan twice as wide blotted out the sky behind her.

Then it—along with Clayton—was gone.

2 2

On the rift floor, another Xenomorph—the largest and most mature—lifted its elongated head as the battle between the two winged creatures and the smaller Xenomorph above came to its bloody conclusion. It had waited all this time, listening and learning about its environment, and finally, it was ready to hunt.

Stirring, it shifted and unfurled its long, ink-colored body. That triggered more movement, and a whole group of shining black forms unrolled from the shadows and crevices where the rift wall met the ground, gliding around and over each other until the creatures covered the rocky bottom like a pit of oily snakes. In the end there was nowhere to go but up, and when the alpha started to climb, the others instinctively followed.

The walls were slick and hard, and their first attempts saw the Xenomorphs simply slide back down, their razor-like claws unable to puncture the hardened rock. The alpha tried again, this time more carefully. Scattered along the surface of the walls were areas of low-growth foliage where seedlings had taken root and stubbornly held on. Not bushy or thick, but resilient enough to stretch beneath the weight and movement of the winged creatures that had perched there.

The Xenomorphs were heavier than the winged creatures, and as they stretched and clawed their way upward, so too they learned—often the hard way—to test each grip before trusting it to bear full weight.

Halfway up, with a bright slice of sky widening above them, one of the Xenomorphs on the edge of the group caught the scent of fresh food not far away. Its enormous head turned in that direction, searching for a way to get to it. The food was hanging, but out of reach, with almost no usable vegetation on which the Xenomorph could climb. It would have to go above and drop, so it continued its measured ascent with the rest of its kind.

The alpha, too, sensed the presence of food. It began to angle toward the prey's position, the rest of its kind intuitively moving with it. The thick mesh that held their prey would provide a much better opportunity to climb than the walls, and although the greenery to which they clung was taking them around and over it, anticipation was producing excitement. Focused on what they perceived to be a meal, they were overhead and ready to leap...

The winged creatures attacked.

They were outnumbered, but they treated the Xenomorphs as prey. Their assault was fast and brutal, but so was the response—a vicious defense that quickly turned offensive. The winged creatures clutched at the thrashing black forms and tried again and again, without success, to stab and puncture with their proboscises.

In turn, the Xenomorphs lunged at the winged attackers, jaws snapping and tails lashing. They tangled in the web and the strands that hung from above, bodies thrashing and wings beating as they fought and slammed repeatedly against the walls.

Every hit showered thick, red dust into the air, every flailing appendage swirled it around the combatants. In a matter of seconds, the bodies of the winged creatures and Xenomorphs were dusted with it.

The winged creatures seemed to show no effect from the red dust, but the alpha Xenomorph became disoriented, off-balance, enraged, and confused by its own loss of coordination. So did the others, and they lashed out at anything within reach. Their attacks doubled, tripled, tails slashing and sharp, dripping teeth seizing whatever flesh it found. Xenomorph turned on Xenomorph in uninhibited violence.

Their broken bodies struck the chasm wall, spraying everything around them in green, liquid pain, and all the while the winged creatures dodged and probed and tried to feast. But the blood accomplished more than the fight, searing holes in the wings and bodies of the predators.

Then the disorientation began to abate, and the alpha's rage began to calm. Around it, a half dozen of its kind were dead. Where their broken bodies had struck the wall, the caustic blood pitted the surface.

With the retreat of the winged creatures, the remaining Xenomorphs turned again to the fading slice of light above and began to climb.

2 3

Enid was going insane with fear.

She was trapped in a swarm of monsters on two sides, and they were *fighting*. Most were black and shiny, like huge mantids—all head and elongated legs—with tooth-filled, dripping mouthparts. The rest were riftwings, nothing short of giant mosquitoes with four enormous, leathery wings that supported their weight and tube-like tongues that could break through a fragile human body with one good lunge.

She twisted this way and that on the harvesting net, wailing uselessly into the comms. But who would hear her? Clayton had been taken by… *something*, and the mercs never tuned in to any of the harvesters except the ones assigned to them that day. Unless someone had seen Clayton snatched off the ground, her absence would go unnoticed until the pollen collected by the addicts was unpacked from the vacuums, weighed, and reported. The best hope for that was an hour or two from now, when her boxes and tallies on the end-of-day record were supposed to be reported.

Enid wasn't stupid. She'd be dead long before then.

She wanted desperately to go up, get to the surface and run the fuck as fast as she could away from the rift. She yanked frantically on the cable, but with Margo gone there was no one to activate the lift mechanism—she was stuck here, like a fly in the biggest web in the universe.

Red Khatura pollen spun around her, shaken free by the creatures smashing against the blooms as they fought. It seemed to be causing some kind of reaction among the bug-things with the big, stretched heads—they were fighting the riftwings *and* their own kind, dying as they lost their grips and fell, lifeless, to the rift floor. Where they landed, the ground steamed.

Maybe the pollen would kill them all.

Then her hopes were dashed as the monsters seemed to shake off its effects. The ones that remained alive stopped fighting. If the pounding of her heart wasn't overwhelming enough, Enid wanted to faint with the realization that, at any second, she would become the center of their attention.

Fainting wasn't an option—if she did, she would die all the sooner. Hanging from her cable and gasping behind her mask, she looked up but found any chance of freedom in that direction already blocked by a mass of struggling monstrosities. Even if someone was on the surface to operate the lift, Enid couldn't go that way—in fact, she needed to get the hell *off* this cable.

Sideways on the net would be impossible: the cable kept her from going left or right, and even if she could, there was nothing beyond the net that would hold her weight.

The only way she could go was *down*.

The harvesting method wasn't rocket science. Each merc masked up their addicts and dropped them down to a few feet below the top of the cable grid in their sector. From there, the workers moved along the netlike grid, harvesting Khatura pollen as they went. Although each cable was fixed to the grid on one side, it would allow workers to shift their positions so they could reach the swollen blossoms below them.

Forcing herself to move slowly, trying not to catch the attention of any of the monstrous lifeforms, Enid worked the cable's release switch. The oiled mechanism limited her control, but let her glide silently downward a couple of feet at a time. She kept sending quick looks upward above to see if she was being tracked, but even as the conflict up there began to subside, she sunk deeper into the gloom.

The cable ended about a yard beyond the last level of the rope grid, at a point where a worker could vacuum the scrawniest of the Khatura blossoms. Enid had never been this far down before, and to her surprise she realized there was no safety stop at the termination of the cable— it simply ended. She saw it coming and figured there was maybe five meters between it and the rift floor, enough of a drop that she could end up seriously hurt.

Enid almost laughed.

Seriously hurt?

How about seriously *dead* if she didn't go for it? She wondered if she could just hang down here on her cable until the monsters either killed each other or got tired and went away. Then she felt the cable tremble. It went all the way to the top of the rift—had one of them just bounced against it?

The cable moved again and this time it was a hard jolt, like something had grabbed it.

That forced a decision.

She thumbed the lowering apparatus all the way to OPEN, then gripped the cable as tightly as she could with one gloved hand, praying the ribbed, rubbery palm would hold. With her other hand, Enid quickly released the safety carabiners on her harness, one at a time. When she was hanging precariously by the last one, she adjusted her hold on the cable a final time, then undid it.

The drop happened faster and sharper than she expected, but she still managed to snag the cable with her other hand. For a long moment she just hung there, but her thin shoulders and arms began to throb with pain. Gritting her teeth, she loosened her fingers just enough to let herself slide down the cable until she saw the ragged metal ends.

Looking toward her feet, Enid could barely make out the ground, but she could tell it was uneven and rocky. It was going to be a hard landing, but at least nothing was moving down there. Stretched as far as her body would allow, she let go.

The impact traveled though her legs and all the way

to her head. She folded up in the dirt, wheezing and trying to breathe through more pain than she had ever experienced outside of waiting for a fix that was way overdue. Everything in her body was in agony, and the pulsing in her skull was the least of it. Most of the shock had been absorbed by her hips and lower back, and that entire area was an oval of mangled nerve endings. Fire pulsed along the neural pathways like drummers in the devil's own marching band.

Her upper back and arms had had hit hard against the rock-strewn bottom. It was difficult to consider herself lucky right now, but nothing seemed actually to be broken... just hellishly battered.

Panting, Enid unrolled her limbs and tried to sit up. She wouldn't have thought it possible to hurt more than she did, but new pain skittered across her bruised muscles. Without thinking, she slapped a hand across her mouth.

Her mask was loose.

Fighting not to groan with the effort, her fingers scrabbled at the metal covering her nose and mouth. The device was cracked diagonally and, although the two pieces were still joined, the amount it moved told her it couldn't hold. Enid pried at it, trying to be methodical in her movements when what she really wanted to do was claw at her face until she was fucking *free*. She got enough space between the mask and her skin that she could work a couple of fingers from each hand under each side, then pull, pull harder, and then—

The mask she detested with every fiber of her being fell away.

Precious time ticked past while all she could do was sit there and stare at the two jagged-edged pieces in her hand. Then she flung them as far away as she could, cringing at the sound they made when they bounced off a rock. She inhaled, drawing the hot, moist air of the rift's bottom as deeply as possible into her lungs.

Jaw set against the misery that ran through her body, she looked up and forced herself first to her knees, then fully to her feet. Wobbling, she tried to see what was happening above, but from down here the sky was nothing but a faint blue slit in the middle of two dark black silhouettes broken by terrifying shapes flashing across it. The cable was entirely out of reach—not that she'd want to climb it anyway. There would be no escape, but she had to believe that eventually, once the mercs had taken care of the fucking monster infestation, they would come looking for her.

In the meantime, she had to find a place to hide and wait.

Without a flashlight, she couldn't see much in the gloom—harvesters never ventured so far down they'd need one—but there were darker spots, some no more than shin high, and others half her height, here and there where the walls of the rift met the ground. Holes? Caves? Definitely openings of some kind. Enid stumbled toward one of the larger ones then winced as something banged against her aching thigh. When she looked to see what it was, she froze where she was.

Her vacuum.

Years ago someone had slipped bleached Khatura pollen into her line of old-life cocaine at what was supposed to be a "safe" travel saloon. From that one incident, Enid's outlook on life had devolved into pure pessimism—a fatalistic trap in which she'd become snared. Now, however, picking up the hated device, she remembered what it felt like to be the happy optimist she'd once been. Picking it up, she used the strap so that it hung at her side.

Her stumbling gait increased and she pinballed to the wall. Heart hammering, she peered into what, indeed, was the narrow entrance to a cavern. Haltingly, she wriggled inside and found where it opened into a larger cavity. Running her hands along the walls, she estimated that it was at least seven meters deep, but only a little more than the width of a person. Gasping with relief, she backed up and found a spot where her back was against the wall. She sat there, facing outward.

Nothing was going to make her move. All she could see was the uneven gap she'd used to get in here, and how it was much too small for either of the horrible lifeforms to fit through.

For now, she was safe.

With no mask around her face.

And a vacuum basin that was half full of Khatura.

She smiled. *Half full.*

There. Hints of her old optimism.

2 4

"Line up."

Standing to one side, Ca'toll studied her new team as they obeyed. Six now, double the number of unblooded to train. A large team but still well within the realm of manageability. What made the task unpredictable, however, was that the new half of the group had started under another hunt leader's school of thought...one that did not entirely mesh with her own.

T'See'Ka, in particular, was going to be a challenge—he had some of T'U'Sa's attitude, the strutting and ego, but other habits that did not speak well of his hunting prowess or techniques. He clearly thought more of himself than he should have, based on his now-deceased hunt leader's account of how T'U'Sa had become "blooded."

Normally such an act—stealing another's imminent kill—would be cause for severe punishment, or worse, abandonment. T'See'Ka was lucky that T'U'Sa had chosen not to do that, but Ca'toll could not honestly say that she would have been as lenient. Evaluating the youth now, considering himself fully blooded and apparently feeling no remorse for his past actions, Ca'toll wasn't sure T'U'Sa's leniency had been a good idea.

Be that as it may, here they were. She decided that was the first thing she would need to address to her new double-sized team.

"As you know," Ca'toll said, "I will be your hunt leader from this moment on." She walked in front of them, checking their armor. The six of them stood straight and stiff, and the feeling of competition among them was palpable. Hunt leaders were used to that between teams, but having it surface within the same group was unfortunate. Unblooded who had been training and practicing together knew their fellows' predilections, and were comfortable around one another, ready to stand with their own.

"We are all equal here," she said. "We are all together. We will be there for each other and for the group. We will hunt together and train together. We—"

"I am not their equal," T'See'Ka interrupted from his place at the end of the line. He inhaled so deeply that it made his chest armor puff out. "I am blooded and they—" he swept a hand dismissively toward the others, "—are not. I have accomplished my goal, and finished my training with these *unblooded*." His sarcastic tone made it clear what he now thought of his prior peers, and they broke their training stance to turn their heads and stare at him in disbelief.

"In fact," he continued, "I don't need to be *here*."

T'See'Ka started to step out of line, then drew up short when he realized Ca'toll stood in his way.

"Yes," she said. Her words were calm, flat, and cold. "You do need to be here. And you will stay."

The newly blooded Yautja youth looked down at her with disdain.

"Step aside, Ca'toll. I am your equal now."

Ca'toll hit T'See'Ka on the side of his face so hard he flew off his feet and landed four meters down the corridor. Before he could rise, she was standing next to him. She slammed a heavy, booted foot down on his chest shield and pinned him to the floor. He began to push himself up, but suddenly her wristblades—notched with curved hooks and twice as long as those allotted the younger Yautja—were pushing against his throat.

Then she *laughed* at him.

"When you are as fast as me, when you are wise enough to train the young, and when you have made as many kills as me—and not the dishonorable one you stole from Stea'Pua—then you *might* be my equal. Right now you are nothing more than a shameful, deceitful braggart." She leaned over him, pushing the deadly blade tips into his flesh until it broke and green blood trickled out. "You are a lucky *child*, T'See'Ka, to have had T'U'Sa as your hunt leader. Had you been one of mine, I would have cut you loose and told your family the truth about your actions." She retracted her blades and stepped off him, then shoved him sideways with one foot.

"Or maybe I would have simply killed you."

Deliberately turning her back on him, she returned to where she stood in the middle of the line. She didn't look at T'See'Ka, but she heard him shove himself upright, then return to his former position with the other unblooded.

"I do not tolerate disrespect or disobedience." She let her gaze stop on each of her charges, let it linger the longest on T'See'Ka. "I don't care if you kill a dozen Xenomorphs. You are not blooded until I say you are. You started with a different hunt leader, but he is dead now. He cannot advise you, he cannot correct you. Do not forget his teachings, but put mine first. And I will tell you all again...

"You are all equal here."

2 5

Fetch's eyes were so wide he felt like he ought to be able to see behind himself. Clayton was gone. Enid was nowhere to be seen, and these monsters had come from nowhere to fight the riftwings. Some were more like humans or apes, could appear and disappear like phantoms.

Others were pure insect-like evil.

Even now one of the new gruesome creatures jittered up the side of the rift wall and leaped atop a flying shape, both of them plummeting to the ground far below as they screamed at each other in impossible octaves.

He was frozen in place. He'd been so involved in the harvesting that he hadn't even noticed when the battle had begun. But wasn't that always like him? He had the ability to concentrate and tune everything out, which was why he was such a great gambler. He could count the odds and keep track of what had already been played. The house never liked it when he was around, not because he always won, but because he made all the calculations inside his head and they couldn't prove anything.

In fact, last time he'd been aboard a Weyland-Yutani space station, he'd almost bankrupted the house, winning pot after pot until they sent coolers after him. But even the coolers couldn't stop him, because it wasn't about luck. It was about math. It was about being able to calculate in his mind as fast as a computer. He wasn't born with much. He'd never win a beauty contest. He wasn't particularly tall. He had a gut on him that wouldn't go away even when he lost a ton of weight. But he could calculate.

So, what had the casino done?

They'd fucked him.

They spiked his non-alcoholic drinks with Khatura over a period of three days, and when his mind slowed, they'd won back most of what they'd lost to him. After seventy-two hours, he was hooked. The heady rush, the loss of reality, the sparkle of the universe, was all because of the new drug—and he wanted more. He paid for it until he had no more credits, then he paid again, trapping himself in indentured servitude.

As they said, the house always wins.

Even when they cheat.

Even when they turn a high roller into an addict.

The sad thing about it was, because of the nature of Khatura, he didn't mind. All he cared about now was the drug. Being close to it, harvesting it, seeing it in its natural state, that was all total Zen for him. The mercs had dropped him on the harvest cable over which he had no control, but they hadn't needed to. He would have stayed without ever considering running away. He did agree, though, that it was a good idea to cover his nose and mouth with the mask, because if it was up to him, he'd be inhaling the luscious drug every moment of every day.

A screech brought Fetch back to the here and now, and he watched another monster attack a riftwing. In this case, the riftwing had managed to grab the monster and drop it from way up high. The shiny black creature plummeted to the rift floor far below, where it went *splat* and most assuredly died.

Watching the battle was one thing, but realizing that he might be in danger was another. Enid had slid into the blackness below, and now a monster had attached itself to her cable. It was scrambling over to the harvesting net. Its avenue of approach would take it close enough to Fetch that it could reach out and kill him. It didn't take a rocket scientist to realize it would probably be a good idea for him to not be here when it arrived.

He glanced around feverishly, searching for a way out. He put the soles of his boots on the rift wall and pushed out with everything he had. He left at an angle, away from the danger. When he hit again, he pushed out, but instead of staying away from the danger, the angle of the cable above brought him right back to it. His legs actually straddled the outstretched arm of a monster as it climbed along the many flora and the net attached to the rift wall.

Fetch pushed again, then let the cable pendulum him back to the side as far away from the threat as he could get. This time, instead of pushing out again, he grabbed with both hands, getting fistfuls of Khatura vines to hold him in place.

The monster turned toward him. Its mouth opened and another mouth shoved out, snapping at the air like it was tasting with its teeth. Drool dripped from the extension—drool that Fetch knew was meant for him. The creature looked hungry, and he'd been designated as its next meal. It began skittering toward him along the side of the wall.

He flexed his knees and pushed off with everything he had, barely missing the outstretched claws of the creature. He ended up where the creature had been and the creature halted where he had been, a crazy game of switch. Fetch grabbed hold once again and held himself in place. He was already out of breath. Not from exertion, but from fear. He couldn't keep going on like this. The creature would catch him in no time at all.

Even now, the monster seemed to be examining the net. It reached out and ran a claw down it, and Fetch winced when the movement made a sound like fingernails on a blackboard. Then it jerked on it hard enough to make the net wire audibly go *ping*. Somewhere in the not-drugged part of Fetch's mathematical brain it registered that the wire on which the monster hung loosened, just a bit.

The creature reached out again and swiped at it, and this time its deadly claws sheared the metal wire in two. The longer of the pieces wrapped around one of its arms, the weight pulling down on the monster, while the upper piece drifted away until it was out of reach.

With the thing unable to swing toward him, Fetch began to climb. His breath hitched. His pulse tripled. He grabbed, using the Khatura vines to pull up on one side and slid his grip on the cable above him with the other, hauling upward with all his might. He dared a glance behind him and saw the monster fixed on him, chittering like a bug, mouth opening and extending again. He felt his luck returning. He was going to make it. With one last heave, he dragged himself to the top of the rift and climbed over the edge, then crawled across the ground like a huge insect until he was at the base of the closest tree.

Fetch's breath came fast and heavy. His legs were almost too tired to move. He used the tree to get to his feet, then hid behind it.

Please, he thought, *don't let the monster track me down.*

He counted to three, then peered around the tree.

Nothing.

He exhaled, tried to slow his racing heartbeat.

He counted to three again and checked again.

The monster was coming over the edge of the rift and seemed to be staring directly at him.

Fetch looked at the tree. He knew he couldn't climb fast enough, and even if he could, he'd seen how that thing zipped up vertical surfaces. He had no choice but to run, and he'd never been much of a runner. Still, he was Lucky Fetch, and he counted on the universe to come to his aid. He lurched to his feet and took off.

He heard the sound of brush breaking behind him.

Then a sizzle.

A scream.

He spun in midstride and fell to the ground. He tried to stand, but he was snared in fallen branches and vines. He twisted in the brush, but the weight of his metal facemask kept pulling him down. He finally got free and into a sitting position, then saw the monster limping toward him. It had a wound on its side and was staggering. What could have done that? Every other step, it would stumble and almost go down.

But it was still coming, a living nightmare.

A huge head with telescoping jaws.

A tail whipping back and forth, angry twitches like a monster-sized whip.

Clawed feet digging into the soil as easily as they would his own flesh if it was able to get to him.

And again… that monstrous, eyeless head that was so much larger than was probable.

Fetch scrambled to his feet. He searched desperately around and saw a tree with branches low enough for him to climb. He limped to it and pulled himself up and onto the first thick limb. Then he realized he'd trapped himself. He had only one way to go, and it was up. He glanced toward the ground and saw that the creature was almost at the base of the tree. All Fetch could do was climb.

So he climbed.

All the way to the top.

Ten meters, until the limbs were so thin that even a breath would make them sway.

The monster still came.

At this point all Fetch could do *was* scream, and he did—like a madman inside of his mask. Over and over, his voice cracking as it pelted and careened through the breathing holes.

Still the monster came.

When it was a meter from him, lightning from the heavens took it.

A *SHOOM*, followed by a *CRACKLE*, and the monster was cut in half by a beam of red light.

One moment it stood facing him, the epitome of all evil, and the next it was toppling to the ground in pieces, bleeding blistering liquid that scorched everything around its body. Then there was a *CRAAAACK*.

The tree limb he was on broke in two.

Fetch fell and landed hard. He tried to pick himself up, fell, tried again. On the third try he succeeded, then he ran. Without realizing it, his feet led him to the edge of the rift and he went into it face first, grabbing the cables, the harvester rigging, and whatever vines he could until he crash-fell down the entire nearly sheer wall.

Khatura plants, small animals and plants whipped by his vision, slowing but not stopping his fall. Fetch didn't care. He needed to get away. Whatever had fired the red laser light might come for him next.

He landed in a curled ball of curses and pain at the bottom of the rift, then bear-crawled to a low-hanging bush. He pushed himself under it as far back as possible, then gulped air, struggling to catch his breath despite the mask that still clung to his face.

Damn, he was lucky to be alive.

Still Lucky Fetch.

But now… what?

Now watch. And wait.

2 6

The darkness on LV-363 was complete as both moons spun their light on the other side of the planet. Clouds blocked the glow of the stars, wrapping the entire atmosphere in a solid gauze. The air was filled with the sounds of nocturnal creatures, especially insects and mammals, including the primates that remained unseen during the day.

The Yautja had constructed their forward operating base in a wooded area, far enough away from their craft to dissociate it. It was their only way off planet, and had to be protected at all costs. Experience had taught their predecessors that the best way to do that was to conceal it, and leave it alone.

Ptah'Ra was on perimeter guard. When he'd been younger he would have hated it, but on this planet, carved like it had been sliced into by the gods, he looked forward to it. His duty was to make sure everyone was safe.

Ny'ytap told them the oomans had a motto for what he was doing. In their crude language, it was, "*Guard*

my shift from flank to flank and take no shit from any rank."
At midnight, with him in charge, it fit. He was here to
protect everyone.

No. One. Else.

Still, some of his fellow unblooded had remained
awake for a time, describing the kills they'd seen. They
were so immature in the way they approached things. He
supposed that was to be expected. After all, they hadn't
been blooded yet. They'd just heard all the stories about
it, about the glory. Certainly, they all said they *wanted* to
be blooded, but Ptah'Ra had seen them when the Xenos
showed up. He knew the fear the creatures could inspire,
if one surrendered to it...

Which they had. He could smell it on them.

Not Ptah'Ra. He was from a strong family where all the
males were hunt leaders. He would never let any malformed
Xenos haunt his dreams. No, he would kill them.

Even now he wore the shoulder-mounted plasmacaster
of his elders, used on many worlds to fight countless
different alien life forms. Here, he was only allowed to
use it for guard duty, but once he was blooded, his hunt
leader would decree that Ptah'Ra could carry it forever.

This one had been carved with the names of the planets
and moons where it had been carried in battle. Letters
scored into the metal, to remind the wearer of the pride
he should show when carrying the familial weapon.
Ptah'Ra's dream was to become blooded while using it
to kill, thus proving its magnificence.

He'd seen the plasmacasters carried by Ca'toll and Ny'ytap. Theirs were nothing—flat black and barely used, while his, gifted to him by his family clan, was a true artifact of warrior greatness. He knew—

A sound came from his left.

He spun. Waiting, he heard nothing.

The nighttime cacophony had gone silent. Ptah'Ra activated the visual sensors on his bio-helmet and zoomed in, switching through the various image intensifier settings, to no avail. His optics were auto-gated to shut off as needed, so he wasn't afraid he might be blinded if there was someone with a powerful light.

Another noise, this time from his right.

Again, his left. Distinct now.

Sticks breaking, brush crackling, from two different directions—

And a third, this time from behind him.

Was he being surrounded?

Standard operating procedure was to wake the hunt leaders. Ptah'Ra hesitated for a moment, wondering if he could take out the approaching enemy on his own, then his training kicked in.

For many reasons the Yautja were the greatest hunters in the universe, and perhaps the first of those reasons was that they knew how to follow procedure. Ptah'Ra hurried to the middle of the camp where the rest were sprawled, sleeping, and nudged Ca'toll awake. When she sat up, he used sign language, and pointed to the three locations.

She nodded but made no sound, then gestured for him to wake the others. Strapping on her plasmacaster, she woke Ny'ytap. After a short and silent exchange, he shrugged on his weapon as well.

Within moments, everyone was awake and ready. All of them faced outward, backs protected as the three plasmacasters pointed equal distances apart. The unblooded were spaced between them, combisticks and wristblades ready. Ptah'Ra felt his chest swell with pride. Yes, they were about to be attacked, but they were *ready*.

As if to punctuate the moment, one of the LV-363 moons began to rise, its thin illumination breaking through the shadows of the night, filtering through the branches of the trees.

What he'd mistaken for bushes earlier were Xenomorphs, adults and juveniles; there were too many to count. Absent a queen, they had continued to multiply through the process Ca'toll had called "eggmorphing." The creatures faced them without moving, as though waiting for some kind of signal, proving they just might be more than simply creatures of instinct.

The Yautja were surrounded, but it didn't concern them. Being in such a tight formation would allow them to concentrate their fire without fear of being attacked from behind.

The species stared at one another, time stretching between them. The Yautja stood tall and proud in armor and bio-helmets, while the Xenos hunched on four legs, tails twitching, heads jerking, mouths extending in what seemed like anticipation. Moonlight glinted off of their midnight carapaces.

Another long moment—

—and they attacked as one.

To call the battle a frenzy would be wrong. It was more like controlled chaos. Although the Yautja could not dictate when and where the Xenos came from, they could regulate their rates of fire and their ability to inflict damage.

The plasmacasters did so repeatedly, but needed time to charge. In the between moments, the hunt leaders were protected by their unblooded, whose combistick spear points quickly were dripping with the acidic blood of their attackers. The battle felt like it took hours, when in reality it was over in a matter of minutes. Once the Xenos attacked, the Yautja defenses rapidly cut them down.

Then an immense form landed directly into the center of the Yautja circle.

It must have been moving through the trees overhead, the noise of its movement camouflaged by the battle. Ptah'Ra spun and found himself face to face with a monster that towered over him. Its black surface glistened in the moonlight, teeth gritted and dripping with drool within an arm's length of his own face. Ptah'Ra's heart rate felt like it tripled. Remembering his heritage, he tried to spin his plasmacaster to fire, but it had less than one bar. It needed time to recharge.

Time he did not have.

The others in the circle were hammering the surrounding Xenos with fire, so it was up to him to take care of this one. Before it could snap at him, he dove and somersaulted out of range. When he came up, Ptah'Ra had his wristblades extended. The simplest of weapons that pups learned to use while they were sucklings, they were all that stood between him and death. He whirled—once, twice—the blades flashing beneath the creature's jutting chin and severing the Xeno's rippling neck muscles.

It screamed as it died, a hideous, deafening screech, flicking its tail and sending a rope of acid through the air. It hit his body armor but sloughed off. Had he not been wearing it, he'd have ended up with a scar like old Ny'ytap.

Ptah'Ra twirled, ready for another battle, bellowing with battle fervor.

This was what he had been created to do.

2 7

The Xenomorph attack was over in minutes. Blasted bodies surrounded Ca'toll and the others, acidic blood scorching the dead leaves and branches that littered the ground. Three Yautja bodies lay among them.

Even so, those who remained had fought well, and killed well. A quick glance showed no major injuries, although all of them likely had been peppered with the creatures' blood. Those wounds would be deemed insignificant and likely not even acknowledged.

All of the young ones were now blooded, and she was particularly proud of Ptah'Ra, who'd faced off with one of the largest Xenos and destroyed it. Leaping into their midst as it had, the creature could have destroyed them, but her ward hadn't hesitated to step in. He was, indeed, an excellent student and now an apt hunter.

However, they hadn't killed all the Xenos. Some were injured and retreating, others appeared unhurt but still working their way back into the native fauna, trying to strategically blend back into darkness rather than face overwhelming odds and certain death. One of the things, twice the size of the others and even larger than the one Ptah'Ra had killed, was leaking blood from a couple of small but inconsequential wounds. It leaped high into the trees and crashed away with no attempt at stealth.

This would make the creature easy to track.

Just because some of the Xenomorphs had given up the fight didn't mean the Yautja would follow suit. The glory of the hunt would continue. Ca'toll and Ny'ytap led the way, with all the newly blooded young ones following. Without being told to do so, each automatically made sure the creatures along the path were dead. If they weren't quite there yet, they sent them the rest of the way without comment.

The Yautja moved silently, although they needed not have bothered. The largest monster was still hurtling from tree to tree above them, headed away from where they had attacked. The way it was moving, with no attempt to conceal itself, it didn't seem to be fleeing, but… *irate*. Was it tracking something? Ca'toll had never witnessed such behavior in the species, but Xenomorph biology was disposed to evolve rapidly, depending on the nature of its host.

Ny'ytap and Ca'toll glanced at each other, then motioned to the others behind them, instructing them to keep going. It didn't take long to reach the edge of the woods. Thirty meters beyond the trees was the ooman camp, and a rapid left-to-right scan revealed exactly what had pulled the surviving Xenos away from their combat with the Yautja.

Three dead Xenomorphs hung from makeshift structures.

The bodies had been strung up a couple of meters from the tents, the carcasses ravaged and split open. At first, Ca'toll thought the oomans might be trying to learn from the corpses, but no—there was too much damage, most of it clearly uncontrolled, as if the result of a revenge beating. Only oomans would be stupid enough to take their anger out on a dead thing that couldn't feel it, and thus could offer no satisfaction.

Ca'toll held up a hand, and the others halted behind her.

There had been no opportunity to count the number of Xenomorphs that had attacked back at the forward operating base, so there was no way to know how many that had blended into the trees and brush. Ahead of them, the few Xenos who were out in the open crept forward, like an advance guard for the ones that couldn't be seen. From previous hunts, Ca'toll knew how capable the Xenos were at stealth, how they could stretch along walls and ceilings and tree limbs and wait for hours for just the right moment to attack their prey.

This time, however, they didn't bother.

Without a sound, they attacked.

Ooman screams mixed with the Xeno shrieks, while the snap of gunfire sliced through the afternoon. Ca'toll and the others watched for a few seconds, then she turned and motioned for them to follow her back to their own camp.

"This is not our fight."

2 8

Shrapnel screamed like he'd never screamed before. The attack came fast and furious. The creatures he'd seen before leaped in waves from the trees surrounding the camp. He opened fire with his pulse rifle and bellowed for the other mercs to grab their weapons. There was no time to aim at anything. He was just spraying and praying.

The tents emptied as men and women lurched out and tried to process what was going on. One guy was taken down before he was able to straighten; another was dragged back into the woods. The creatures had already overrun their location.

Shrapnel had been on this dreary piece of rock many times before, but had never seen creatures like these. The sheer number of them and the ferocity they exhibited was beyond comprehension. They were *everywhere*—he found himself whirling and firing, again and again, and when his pulse rifle was empty he tossed it aside and grabbed one from the body of a dead merc. Then it was all rinse and repeat, firing again until the rounds digited down to zero. Luckily he laid such a concentrated amount of fire that nothing was able to touch him.

Yet.

At one point Shrapnel thought he might have hit one of his fellow mercs, but she was jerked off her feet and pulled into the trees by a monster before he could be sure.

Responding instinctively, most of the mercs had come out blazing, rifles jerking in their hands as they took aim and let loose. Whether or not they had ever seen this kind of creature, they were experts in the art of killing— and knew how to defend themselves. The noise pounded through the air and the stink of gunfire filled their nostrils as they fired and reloaded, giving it everything they had.

Still, like ants from an enormous underground nest, the enemy kept coming.

Suddenly an immense monster with a bomb-shaped skull dropped from a tree, right into the middle of their crew. Shrapnel and the others retreated, trying to watch their backs *and* the invader, knowing instinctively that if they fired they'd hit one another. Before any of them could figure out what to do, the beast lunged at one of the mercs and took him down, its jaws snapping out and through the man's skull. When its teeth retracted barely a second later, the skin and brains around the hole in the guy's head began to sizzle and turn to liquid.

Fuck no, Shrapnel thought. *I didn't sign up for this.*

Out of the corner of his eye, he saw Murray dash out the back of a main tent and head in the direction of their ship.

Oh, hell *no!*

He wasn't about to let that weasel of a boss take off and leave them behind. He snatched a charged weapon up from the ground and fired his way through the melee, hurtling past the trees and after Murray. Anger made him push his legs to their limit, but the smaller man was fast—faster than Shrapnel because he didn't have a weapon and an equipment belt to weigh him down. Plus Murray was running for his life.

Shrapnel's breathing turned ragged, but he could still hear the man crashing through the forest, crying out as he bounced off trees. If the situation hadn't been so fucked up Shrapnel would've laughed, because Murray squealed like a pig when some kind of animal crossed his path.

That small bit of humor was gone in an instant as he struggled after the cartel boss. If only he'd listened to the harvesters. For all he knew, the others back at camp were dead by now, and he and Murray were the sole surviving humans on LV-363. What he *did* know was that when he caught up with that fucker, he was going to make Murray pay for his piss-poor leadership and his cowardice.

He tore through the last of the overgrowth and into the clearing just in time to see Murray dive through the ship's open door. Before he could cover the distance, the metal hatch slid silently closed. Shrapnel just managed to halt his forward movement before he slammed into it.

Out of breath and sweating in the night air, he slapped his palm against the keypad, but nothing happened.

The bastard had locked the controls from the inside. Knowing it was useless, Shrapnel tried again anyway, then yanked his pistol from its holder and hammered on the door with the handle.

"Murray, you son of a bitch, open this fucking door!" he howled. He beat on it again, then heard another sound behind him.

One of the monsters crashed from the tree line and came straight for him.

Shrapnel spun and opened fire with his pulse rifle, barely taking it out before it was on top of him. It was close enough that its blood splattered his legs. The pain made him want to scream, but he bit back the sound, knowing it would only attract more of them. *This* was what Margo had experienced. The agony was excruciating, and made him stumble along the side of the ship.

Murray was never going to open the door—hell, if their places were reversed, Shrapnel wouldn't have, either. He stayed there for a moment, chest heaving as he tried to suck in air and breathe around the agony in his legs. Circling the ship, he approached a cargo door in the back, tried tapping in a code.

Nothing.

That fucker.

Despite the tears leaking from his eyes, he kept his pulse rifle aimed at the darkness in the trees, ready to fire at the smallest movement. Then he glanced down at the readout, and realized there were only two rounds left.

Two.

What a fucking joke.

Less than useless.

Disgusted, he threw the weapon aside and took off at the closest thing to a run he could manage. All he had was a knife and his pistol, neither of which was worth a freefall shit against this kind of enemy, if he was attacked. Then he laughed.

If he was attacked?

When he was attacked.

He'd never been much of an optimist *or* a pessimist. He just believed in reality.

Shrapnel headed at an angle away from the ship, pushing through the foliage. He was making too much noise and knew it, but he was fighting panic. All instinct would let him do was keep pushing forward while he hoped the monsters that had finished at the camp were distracted enough by the ship to buy him some time. He ran with his pistol in hand, knowing it was foolish to put it back in the holster.

He was surprised—actually *amazed*—when he made it to the rift unscathed. His forward motion almost took him over the rocky edge; for an overlong moment he teetered on the edge, arms pin-wheeling as he threw himself backward and fought to regain his balance. When he finally did, he had an instant of pure terror.

What now?

A fast glance backward showed nothing coming out of

the trees after him—yet—but he had nowhere to go that was safe. No place—

Wait.

Shrapnel's eyes focused on the cable boxes spaced among the boulders at the rift's opening. He ran to the closest one and peered down. Of course! The descent cables. He holstered his pistol, knowing he couldn't do what was needed with only one hand. Then he gripped a cable and thumbed the controls.

It wasn't a fast ride and he alternated between trying to see what waited in the darkness below his feet and what might suddenly come over the edge above him, a line against the star-filled sky that was growing dimmer by the second. Eventually the cable reached its limit and stopped. Since he couldn't go back up, Shrapnel let go of the controls and went hand over hand down to the very end, hanging there by one hand.

Looking down into the darkness, he tried to remember how far the cables went, and figured he was maybe four or five meters from the floor of the rift. Enough to break a leg, or even his back if he landed the wrong way, but what other choice was there?

He dropped.

And hit the ground with just enough of a twist to cause a lightning flare along his left hip. He straightened his back and clenched his teeth when pain ran down his leg, then forced himself into a crouch so he could turn and evaluate his surroundings. Gradually his eyes adapted to the gloom, enough that he could see vague shapes. There wasn't much down here but more foliage and... what was that? Almost shaking with fear, he forced his physical pain to the back of his mind and crab-walked toward a darker area about five meters away.

A cave.

He was a big man and it was a tight fit, but he managed to work his way past the entrance until he could tell by the feeling of the air that it opened up somewhere ahead. He thought he heard something make a squeak behind him. Probably some kind of local vermin—he could live with that. All he cared about was that the opening at the front of the cave was too small for one of those monsters.

He went down on his belly in a sniper's position, pistol out and aimed at the opening. Lying there, he realized he was barely breathing, and let himself inhale deeply. He had a flash of a moment when his mind registered a feeling of graininess in his mouth and throat, then he exhaled, making a sound like an overworked machine.

It resonated strangely in the small space.

And then Shrapnel realized that, somewhere along his descent, his face must have brushed against one of the Khatura blooms.

Suddenly the cave and its entrance came alive with lights in all shapes, colors, and sizes. His eyes lost focus and the gun dropped from his fingers as every muscle in his body relaxed and the pain in his legs melted away. Mind spinning, all he could do was gawk at the cave's small entrance as it opened and closed like the mouth of a great, psychedelic worm.

He heard a sound behind him—a small, frightened sound and a scrabbling as if something was trying to move away from him. Then his attention returned to the mouth, opening, then closing.

Shrapnel had escaped monsters that wanted to devour him, only to be trapped by an evil wearing a very different disguise.

And he embraced it.

2 9

The war whoops echoed in the darkness.

Back at their ship, the two remaining Yautja hunt leaders watched as the newly blooded youth celebrated. They'd returned with the bodies of Cau'dki, Hetah, and U'Brea'Sua, all of whom had been nearly torn to pieces by the Xenos. Their corpses were laid in an evenly spaced row in front of the ship, but there was no sadness among the survivors—only pride in the fighting spirit and the effort the dead young bloods had shown. Not that they were envied in death, but they were honored for the personal courage they represented, and their sacrifice to the hunt.

Ny'ytap felt the pride surging through him. The moment they had been attacked, his hunt team and Ca'toll's had moved as one, establishing their battle lines and protecting themselves and one another. The intense training they'd been through, all of the preparations before and since their arrival, had paid off. He removed his helmet and held it up to the starry night sky like a dark and deadly fist.

The young bloods cheered and began to pump their weapons in the air. When he glanced over, he saw that Ca'toll was doing the same, her body movements taut with elation.

She had taken out several Xenos herself, in a deadly spin of combistick and wristblades, slicing and carving up the creatures with barely any effort. He had to admit that she was among the best hunters he had ever seen—perhaps even the best. Her smaller size and stature meant she might never make it to battlemaster, much less elite, but she should find herself leading many hunts in the future and gaining much honor.

Allowing himself to live in the moment, Ny'ytap was proud. The Yautja were few, in the greater scheme of things; across all of the systems, in all of the galaxies, he was one of the select hunt leaders whose mission was to take the young of their kind and transform them into warriors. Like a paramilitary alchemist, he mixed the right combination of traits to produce the superiority of their species.

He plunged his combistick into the ground, and stood tall to address the young bloods.

"We stand here to say *n'dhi'ja*—farewell—and honor our lost," he proclaimed. "Cau'dki, Hetah, and U'Brea'Sua, and the first dead, T'U'Sa. Yet during these difficult battles, the rest of you stood fast. You faced the beasts and were strong, deadly. All of you fashioned your battle language like the warriors of the ancient writings, who understood the essence of what they had been taught. Who absorbed those lessons into the very fibers of their beings. My pride for you is unbounded. You have learned well here." His mandibles spread for a moment, then he continued. "It's time for us to leave this place and return home. When we arrive, all will know—"

Without warning, a riftwing dove into their midst, as stealthy and silent as where the wind began and ended. With its wings pulled back and body flattened to enable it to angle through the tree branches, it struck with extraordinary speed, far deadlier than should be possible.

Before the big Yautja could react, the creature dug sharp claws into the hunt leader's unprotected neck, and dragged him into the air.

* * *

Snapping into motion, Ca'toll registered everything that was wrong about the attacking riftwing. It was some kind of mutation, both riftwing and Xenomorph...

A Xenowing.

The young bloods stood frozen, staring after it as if mesmerized. Blooded or not, they were still hardly more than children, only a step above amateurs in a deadly game of survival.

Ca'toll jammed her helmet back in place, then whirled and shoved the closest young one to break their stance.

"Weapons up. Now! *Ka'rik'na*—let's go!"

Ca'toll looked to the sky, tracking the Xenowing's flight as she and the young bloods began to move. Ny'ytap was big, and heavy, so his attacker was struggling to gain altitude and speed. The hunt leader was still alive, hammering at the flying monstrosity with his fists as he tried to make it release him.

Like a riftwing, the creature had the insectoid eyes and an extra set of legs along its midsection—now those were tipped with Xeno claws that gripped Ny'ytap solidly around his torso. He opened a wound near one of its eyes and, as with a Xeno, acid dripped from it. Ny'ytap writhed and attempted to twist away from the liquid.

Then the Xenowing took him into the night in the direction of the rift.

Ca'toll crashed through the woods with the younger Yautja scrambling behind her, the red letters of her helmet's optics flashing across her vision as she watched for any indigenous lifeforms or oomans that might be obstacles in the path. Moving this rapidly through the trees and thick underbrush was dangerous, especially at night. Falling into upturned dead limbs could yield severe injuries, and there was the rift to consider. In some places the tree line simply ended at its edge, with no clearing to prepare them to stop.

The night vision on Ca'toll's helmet showed Ny'ytap still fighting in the Xenowing's tight grip. The initial attack must not have injured him too badly, and his mid-air struggle demonstrated how great a warrior he was.

She glanced back to track the young bloods, and could see fires of battle thick in the way they followed her at full speed.

Then they were at the rift.

* * *

Ny'ytap felt like a prey animal being carried to a nest. He was furious at himself for letting his guard down, and not being on watch at all times.

Even though his helmet hadn't been connected to his suit, it had remained in place when he was yanked off the ground. Now he pulled it off his head and used it as a bludgeon, beating as hard as he could on the pair of limbs that held him in its grip. Over and over again he struck the beast—better to fall than remain a victim.

Rage at his own actions fueled him—how he'd strutted around and joined in the proclamations of their victory, celebrating as though the entire planet had been cleared when he *knew* better. How he hadn't protected his hunting team while this creature flew out of the sky and snatched him up like it was the easiest thing to do. Such idiocy wasn't even close to befitting a Yautja of his stature.

Suspended in the night air, all he could do was strike, again and again, at this—

—*damned*—

—*flying*—

—*aberration*.

As he fought, more acid dripped onto his unprotected face and he fought the urge to scream like a cub. The pain was beyond incredible. He would never get this thing to release him—it was impervious to his blows, seeming to feel no pain at all. Pounding on it was useless: finally he let the helmet drop into the trees below.

Instinct made his mandibles spread wide, but he couldn't bite—the thing's acid blood would eat right through his face. His body swung wildly as the flying Xeno pumped its wings. At the same time, its second mouth kept snapping out; the needle-sharp teeth made it look as if it was grinning in anticipation. Silver drool whipped behind them in the wind.

Scanning the surface below, Ny'ytap saw a darker slash along the ground and realized where it was taking him.

The rift.

Dimly he heard the sounds of Yautja calling for him. Ca'toll and the young bloods were running along the edge of the crevasse. Their efforts would be futile, though. The mutated Xenomorph would pull him into the darkness and devour him... or worse, expose him to an Ovomorph that would implant his body with another of its kind.

No—he wouldn't die like that, staining his honor by succumbing to this creature and leaving his memory blanketed by shame, an embarrassment to his clan. They would remember him for his bravery, his skills and his brutality. Not his ignominious death.

He'd lived and would die as a hunt leader.

With a scream of fury, Ny'ytap snapped out his wristblades, plunging forward and up with both hands, catching the flying Xeno's throat on either side. At the instant the razor-sharp blades punctured its black body, he yanked outward.

The flying monstrosity screamed and spun in midair as acid blood sheeted onto Ny'ytap. It coated his body armor, the sheer amount of it eating through the protection like it was nothing. He bellowed in agony and drove his wristblades up again, aiming for the gaping wound, going for its innards. Even though he felt as if he was burning alive, triumph shot through him as the insectoid's head sheared off.

They hung there for an instant, suspended, then plummeted into the black depths of the rift. The last thing Ny'ytap saw was the night sky filled with a billion stars. One of them shone its light on his home planet, and he wished he were back with his clan.

INTERLUDE

Ar'Wen wasn't distressed to witness the demise of the hunt leader. Ny'ytap had been a bully who had risen to great heights despite his lack of care and unwillingness to work with others. The elders of his family were high in the Yautja social structure, however, and memories of past deeds still held weight.

Thankfully, not every hunt leader was like Ny'ytap. He reveled in victory and ignored defeat, which was why he had given in to celebrating, even though he'd lost three of the wards who had been placed in his care.

This placed Ar'Wen in the kind of dilemma he'd experienced before. He lived and worked alone, so the only feedback he had was his own. To say that he operated within his own mind would be an understatement. His was a universe where most of the time he was the sole occupant, and because of that, he was cognizant of the fact that his way of thinking might be archaic.

He'd never led a hunt team, nor would he ever.

Still, Ar'Wen found it difficult to accept that the care and concern for a hunt leader's wards should be left to the vicissitudes of an often-maniacal universe. How was an unblooded to learn the intricacies of the hunt if it wasn't by watching, then following the example set by his or her elders? To thrust an inexperienced ward into a deadly situation solely based on the strength of their training, seemed capricious.

Once Ar'Wen had found a way to escape his captivity and return to the embrace of his own kind, he'd shaped his own destiny. He liked to think that in the forging of it, he'd created something closer to pure—especially when it came to the idea that unblooded simply could be replaced.

The Yautja were an exceptional and unique species, and any loss—particularly one that resulted from poor leadership—came at extraordinary cost to the species.

To lose so many only meant one thing: they were led by the wrong hunt captains. The fault, he believed, lay with the elders as much as it did with Ny'ytap and his ilk. The elders had chosen the hunt leader in the classic way. As the oomans were known to say, he walked the walk. He talked the talk. He looked good in armor. He came from the right family. To overlook him would appear absolutely wrong, so they had selected Ny'ytap.

And they had been so very wrong.

Not only had Ny'ytap allowed three unblooded to die, but he'd met his own demise in much the same fashion, leaving Ca'toll as the senior hunt captain. It aggravated

Ar'Wen to admit it, but things had turned out for the best. She would perform admirably, unless it came down to saving herself or her charges.

Ca'toll's history spoke for itself. If the odds were turned against her, she would prioritize her own wellbeing over that of other Yautja.

Still, better her than Ny'ytap.

Even before he became Xeno food.

3 0

Ca'toll ordered three young bloods down into the rift to retrieve Ny'ytap's body. When Vai'ke, Stea'Pua, and T'See'Ka stared into the slash along the ground and hesitated, she responded with a deep-throated growl that spurred them into action, swiftly fixing temporary cables into place so they could descend. She adjusted her helmet's optical display, but still couldn't see all the way to the bottom.

The situation had gone from an assured victory to something far less positive. Ny'ytap had always been the best leader among them all, but he knew it, and that was the problem. He acted the part. Sometimes it seemed as if the Yautja didn't have a word for *humility* in their lexicon, but they did know how not to tempt fate. What he'd done with the early celebration had gone against all of her instincts, though she had to admit that she'd been caught up in the thrill of the moment.

They'd prepared for one thing, and had encountered another, far worse. They'd lost warriors, but without loss there could be no gain—and now, by all of the elders, they were about to learn.

She was in charge. Ny'ytap's mistakes—inattention and overconfidence—had proven fatal. She knew better than to replicate his conduct. Ca'toll would be ready.

"Position yourselves to guard us from the woods," she ordered the rest as the trio disappeared over the edge, "and don't forget to look to the skies. There are certain to be more of those flying demons, and we must never again let ourselves be susceptible to such an attack. Those closest to the rift must watch for anything coming up that isn't Yautja."

Her plasmacaster was spun up and ready. Even split between the sky, the rift, and the woods, she kept her attention sharp.

Five minutes passed, then ten.

Finally, Vai'ke, Stea'Pua, and T'See'Ka pulled themselves out of the rift—but they were empty handed and breathing heavily.

Vai'ke fell onto his back and heaved.

The other two, hands on hips, sucked air.

"Where is Ny'ytap?" she demanded. "Where is his body?"

"We saw him," Vai'ke answered dismissively, "but he didn't survive the fall."

"Didn't survive the—" Enraged, Ca'toll backhanded Vai'ke, then kicked the other two hard enough to take them off their feet. They landed flat on their backs, staring up at her in shock. This was a mistake she had made before, and she never would again. "We *never* leave a warrior behind! Did you learn *nothing* from T'U'Sa's death?" She spun to the others, her rage making her crouch and hiss. "Did you hear that, young bloods?"

Nodding warily, each still carefully focused on the perimeter. This wasn't what they expected, and it showed. The death of their hunt leaders had demoralized them. At a moment when they should be celebrating, they were mourning—something intrinsically wrong with the way things were meant to be.

They needed to snap out of it, lest they be next in the death lottery.

She turned back and grabbed Vai'ke. Although he was almost as large as she, he still didn't have decent battle acumen, and they both knew it. There was a code to be learned here, despite the danger of losing more newly made young bloods.

"We will go back in," she gritted. "This is a *hunt*. The goal is battle leader Ny'ytap's body. This planet is trying to take him, and we cannot allow that. There have been many ill-made decisions during this trip, and those choices have caused disgrace and loss of life. We will *not* bring further shame on this bloody excursion." As she stressed the word *shame*, she pointedly glared at Vai'ke.

"But he's dead," the new young blood protested.

"Is that what you want to tell the elders? That he was dead, and you were too miserable and lazy to bring him back?" she said, challenging him to admit his cowardice. "Or is it something worse? Do not tell me that fear is pushing the words out of your mouth."

The young blood flinched, then growled. He moved again to the edge, casting his cable down the side of the rift, and waited for the others to follow.

Ca'toll admired his spirit and let him go without further comment.

Still, she hated his momentary weakness. She would deal with him later, once they were off planet. Until then, he'd jump when she said to do so, and ask only how high.

3 1

Every cell in Enid's body was screaming for her to wail aloud.

Something was in the cave!

Instead of screaming, however, she jammed her fist between her teeth and bit down until she scraped against bone. Bad enough that those... *things* had been outside, that she'd seen the one that attacked and slaughtered Khaleed. And then the brutal melee, so many ghastly creatures that she couldn't get out of her mind.

And now...

Which kind of monster worked its way through the opening? she wondered. It was right there, between her and the only way out. She'd thought she was safe, that none of those monsters could fit through the small fissure, but she'd been panicked, frantic to find safety.

The Khatura pollen had tamped down her fear for a while, but she was coming off a high that was a lot shorter than it should have been. It was ruined by the adrenaline that fear pumped through her bloodstream.

Enid swallowed as the fog in her brain cleared enough for logic to set in.

The monsters had been huge, larger than humans—

But nothing was born full size.

When she'd been a little girl, there had been few things beautiful in the bottom of a space station, so a she'd had to find them where she could. Her father, before he disappeared, had drawn her a picture of a flower and explained to her what it was.

"This is the germ of creation," he explained. "Every plant in the universe comes from a bloom of some sort. This is your flower, Enid. I hereby dub this the Enid Rose." He'd drawn it on a piece of paper and pinned it on the wall by her bed. As inexpertly as he'd done it, with blues and purples and yellows and reds, it was still clearly a flower. During those many nights when she'd been especially scared or missing her father, she'd stare at the Enid Rose and imagine a breeze rippling its edges.

As a little girl she'd found secret places to hide, nooks and crannies where no adult could fit. She'd taken her picture with her, keeping it close to reassure her. Flowers that always held the promise of safety.

Later, when she was grown and able to walk the upper decks, she'd discovered that the station had an arboretum, a separated and specially controlled area where plants and flowers from across the known systems were cultivated. One of the first things she had seen when entering for the first time was an immense flower, much like the Enid Rose. The rapturous smell enthralled her and made her want to touch it, to caress it, to take it away for her very own.

One evening, feeling overly brave, Enid had, indeed, touched it. Only barely and with just the tip of her forefinger. Two things happened: an alarm sounded, and the petal died instantly from contact with her body oils. She had cried as she watched the brilliant hues turn to black and the petals fall to the ground.

The arboretum's guards took her away and punished her then, but there was nothing they could do that would make her feel worse than she did already.

When she had spied her first Khatura flower, the Enid Rose memory came barreling back. Here was a flower she could be a part of—not only could she touch it, but she could make it part of her by inhaling the essence of its ethereal beauty.

Muted noise came from across the cavern, something adjusting, a grunt and raspy inhalations. Did those creatures have lungs? Did they breathe like people? She didn't know, and she didn't want to find out. She made the mistake of trying to imagine the life cycle of the thing that had skittered and climbed along the cables and the rift wall like some kind of hellish lizard with teeth.

And then the flying one—so close to a gigantic, deadly hornet that as she pictured it she had to stop herself, again, from crying out. Which adolescent version was in here with her, this very second?

Muscles as tight as fitted cargo straps, Enid waited for her invisible killer to make its move. But the minutes ticked past without incident, each feeling like a small eternity. Her breathing was shallow and she struggled to keep it silent—any kind of noise would draw attention to herself.

Her high was completely gone now, her mind as clear as an addicts, could be at the pivot point between *no longer stoned* and *loading back up*. If she swore to the universe that she would never use the pollen again, would it step in and rescue her? She'd never believed in a greater being that could be all-knowing and all-seeing, manage everything in existence like some kind of supreme puppet master. Yet if she promised, if she vowed on her life to get off this world and do something—*anything*—to help others, would someone magically come down and save her?

If she'd dared, Enid would have laughed out loud.

What a stupid idea.

There was only one way Enid could think of that would guarantee that she didn't make a sound, one that wouldn't catch the unwanted attention of her cohabitant. Moving incredibly slowly, desperate not to make a sound, she opened the vacuum pouch and quietly reached down with her first two fingers, lifting a generous portion of the pollen to her nose.

If she died anyway, she wouldn't feel a thing.

3 2

Other die, fall.
Fly down.
Find nest.
Others still small.
Some fly, some not.
They follow.
Swarm.
Attack food.
Attack good.
Attack now.

3 3

The attack came swiftly and without warning. One moment, Vai'ke, Ptah'Ra, and Sta'kta were slipping easily down their cables; the next, the air around them was filled with Xenowings. At the same time, more attackers scrambled up the spotty foliage on the walls and leapt for them. Some fell short, but tried again and again until they managed to trip and clamber within range of the three suspended young bloods.

From her vantage point at the top, Ca'toll spotted the incoming adversaries, but their arrival was so rapid and so dense that the display warnings were little more than a blurred sequence of red and yellow flashes across her optics screen. Crouched at the edge of the rift with Ba'sta, Stea'Pua, and T'See'Ka, she snapped out orders at the same time she slammed the fastener of her own drop cable into the ground.

"Secure your cables and head down," she said. "Watch on all sides and above. Watch for yourself *and* your comrades." Ca'toll ensured her voice would be loud and clear through their comms, leaving them no need to ask questions. "Get down there and fight!"

The first to swing into the rift, she skimmed downward fast enough to make smoke rise where her gloves connected with the cable's alloy surface. Within seconds she was in the midst of the carnage, surrounded by a horde of gleaming black carapaces and darkly tinted wings. The noise was tremendous—the shrieks of the Xenomorphs and Xenowings went from high to low, making her teeth vibrate in her mouth. Even the cable thrummed: she couldn't tell whether it was caused by her descent or the racket the animals were making.

What seemed to take eternity was in reality only a few seconds, but by the time she was a few meters from the first of the young bloods—Sta'kta—communicating with her charges was rendered unfeasible. None of them could hear the comms. She hoped they had been paying attention to their rigorous training and strategic routines, *and* to her oft-repeated warnings about remaining aware of the entire combat zone, including above and below, because there were creatures coming from every direction.

Ca'toll scanned the scene. About two meters below and off to her right, Ptah'Ra struggled with a Xenowing almost twice his size—the creature may have chosen him because he was the largest of the young bloods in the fight. It probably didn't see Ptah'Ra as a worthy adversary, though, but simply the most abundant of the meals available.

Because he was handicapped by having to grip the cable, Ptah'Ra's formidable size was turning out to be a hindrance—size meant weight, and gravity made his own body mass pull hard on his supporting arm. Add the weight of the gigantic Xenowing trying to pull him free, and he was bound to lose—especially given the creature's added attempts to connect its second mouth at his face. All Ptah'Ra could accomplish was to wrap one oversized hand around the flying horror's neck and hold it at arm's length.

Even from where she was, Ca'toll could see his arm shaking with the effort. Silver drool flew everywhere and he wouldn't be able to keep that position much longer— if he didn't lose strength, the slimy liquid was sure to make his fingers slip.

Ca'toll braced herself to kick off the wall, intent on angling in Ptah'Ra's direction. Suddenly an adolescent Xeno landed on her, slashing at her neck and face. The claws grasped for purchase but slid uselessly off her helmet. Before the creature could get a grip on the helmet's edge, she wrapped both legs around the cable, then rotated until she was upside down. Not the best position, but she needed both of her hands.

Reaching out with her left fist, she seized the thing by its neck. It snapped at her arm, but before it could bite her she punched its teeth with her right fist. Over and over she pounded, even as its jaw telescoped outward as if it were a separate tooth-filled adversary.

Ca'toll had fought Xenos on many planets, and especially enjoyed battling them at this stage of their growth. Although still too young to exhibit even the most rudimentary, instinctive strategy, what they lacked in tactics they more than made up in the desire to kill. Something in their chemical building blocks necessitated the need to feed constantly.

At this age, they would attack anything that moved.

They were also quite pliable.

She let it snap at her again, then gripped its main upper and lower jaws in her gloved hands. Grunting as her muscles bunched, she began to force its jaw apart.

Then something lunged across her vision—the Xenowing attacking Ptah'ra.

Her gaze tracked the movement and she watched Sta'kta let go of his cable and land between the creature's thrashing wings. She realized the edges of the wings were as sharp as blades, and slashes—dozens of them— started appearing all over the young blood's body where it wasn't protected by armor. When he roared, she heard irritation in the sound, not pain, and inside her helmet her mandibles snapped in appreciation.

Sta'kta's grip started to give way, but Ca'toll was still struggling with her own Xeno.

Ptah'ra, Sta'ka and the Xenowing were a jerking, battling cluster, and anything Ca'toll tried to do would only make it worse. She had to finish here, then move on to where she was more useful.

3 4

Shrapnel thought of a thousand ways to die, and ten thousand ways to kill Murray. He could just see some of the horrendous battles taking place outside of the cave.

If he ever made it out of this rift and off this alien-riddled planet, he'd track down the drug dealer and bury him neck-deep in the soil of Rigus 4, where the army ants could strip the flesh off of him, bit by tiny bit. They were known to go first at the eyeballs, sucking them free of fluids before severing them and taking them to their anthill. Then, as the victim screamed, they would march into his mouth and chew on the uvula until it was nothing more than a calcified nub.

Next, they'd flow into the upper stomach, trigger the duodenum, and pack the large and small intestines with eggs provided by the queen. For twenty hours the eggs would gestate, subsisting on the flesh along the intestinal walls.

In that, there was no pain.

At least not right away.

As the eggs gestated, they'd pump endorphins akin to Khatura into the surrounding tissue. At worst, it might feel like a stomachache… until the eggs began to hatch. Then the hatchlings would eat their way out. Once they pierced the epidermis from the inside, they'd carry the soft tissue back to the queen for her to consume. At this point, the ants would have made it into the brain and quieted the pain sensors. The victim could see what was happening, but there was nothing that could be done.

Couldn't move.

Couldn't scream.

Destined for a minimized existence as the ants removed all the parts necessary for life.

Once the "food" was dead, the queen, escorted by battle ants, would leave the hive and travel to the victim's neck, stabbing it with her proboscises and sucking the blood until she was as engorged as a tick. Then she would crawl back into the depths of her own hymenopteran warrens.

Shrapnel envisioned it all with relish.

Then again, it might be too good for Murray.

Still, the vision of the queen straddling Murray's neck as the man's body gave a final death rattle momentarily warmed the aging mercenary, at least until the next round of weapons fire lit the entrance to the cave. It replayed in his mind like a vid, stuck on repeat. He shook his head, but it wouldn't go away—the vision of Murray being eaten from the inside out.

He scooted back a little further.

The new kind of creature was a merging of old and new. Shrapnel had seen the riftwings ever since he'd arrived at this godforsaken rock, had shot his fair share of them, protecting their junkie harvesters. But the riftwings had merged with something else, something far more hideous—a murderous creature that came out of nowhere. Where the original species possessed elongated legs more akin to a butterfly, the new version had multiple sets of jaws and steel-hardened claws. If he'd seen and felt correctly, they had some sort of acid in their veins that could melt nearly everything.

They had wings, too.

Fucking Murray.

How could he leave Shrapnel on this planet?

Shrapnel had lived the life of a cat. He'd almost died seven different times in his life. Once at birth, when the cord was wrapped around his neck. The next when, as a baby, he'd pulled a pot of boiling water off the stove and onto his back. The third time he'd fallen thirteen meters from scaffolding in the bottoms of Ganymede Mining Colony Number 5, where he'd been spray-painting antigovernment slogans with his new crew.

During his first enlistment with the military police, he'd been overwhelmed by protesters and beaten into a coma. He'd called for help from his fellow MPs, but they'd retreated and left him to die. That's when he'd switched sides. He'd never been one for governments anyway.

Two months later, after he'd recovered from his wounds, he'd defected and pooled all of his money to travel into deep space where he could make a fresh start. His fifth near-death had been when his cryopod had malfunctioned and he'd been forced to waken an old woman, knock her out, and place her in his broken-down machine while he took hers. He felt no remorse. After all, she'd already lived a life, and he still had a long way to go.

Or so he'd thought.

Four months later he'd signed on with the mercs to protect a mining platform on the outer rim. Pirates had been coming weekly for their cut and the owners of the mine were tired of it, so they'd pooled their money and signed a contract with Anodyne Mercenary Corporation. When the pirates arrived, they'd ambushed them, killing all who'd dared to disembark. The rest escaped in the ship and returned eight days later with three times the muscle.

AMC repelled these attacks, too, but not without significant losses.

Shrapnel got his nickname then, stumbling into a L-shaped ambush and triggering a pair of anti-personnel mines that had punched six dozen holes in him. If he hadn't entered the battle injected with hypercoagulants, he would have died a sixth time. But the pre-battle med cocktails that AMC provided kept him alive long enough for an orbiting hospital to use magnetic resonant enhancer tools to remove the hundred-plus metal objects inside his body.

Then came the seventh.

They said no one could survive a dropship crash.

They say it was impossible to survive the Gs and the trauma associated with such a collision, but among his twelve merc comrades, he'd ended up in the middle. The bodies beneath and atop him cushioned his fall so that he was actually able to walk away. The impact had sent his brain slamming against the inside of his head in such a way that he'd experienced amnesia for a week. He could never remember what he ate or drank, but he was neither dehydrated nor starved.

When he made it back to the crash site, animals had been at the bodies, tearing flesh from bone, eating all the fingers and toes and noses and ears, even genitals, before they satiated themselves with the meat and fat from the stomachs.

That was when he realized he could no longer be a merc. He needed something safer. Here, in the dubious safety of a hole in the darkness, Shrapnel laughed aloud—but quietly—at the idea of *something safer*.

Just then, one of the two-legged hunters with a monster wing attached to it crashed a couple of meters away. Neither made a sound or showed fear. The two had become one incredible beast, joined in combat.

He ducked instinctively and listened to the hiss and *brrrrrrp* of firing, the screams of the dying, and the yawps of the living. For the moment, Shrapnel was happy to be here where it was relatively safe.

Relatively.

As long as he remained still and silent, he would be fine. But for how long? The fighting had to end sometime, and probably soon. After that, he had no plans to just sit here and die of thirst or hunger. No way.

Not before he had a chance to seek revenge against Murray and the rest of the godforsaken cartel.

3 5

Sta'kta felt every cut as the edges of the flying Xeno's
wings savaged him. None were shallow, and his blood
glowed like a thousand rivulets in the shadows of the
rift. Each one a prismatic rainbow of pain that couldn't
be seen but was surely felt. His body registered that it
hurt, but his mind refused to acknowledge it.

He frankly didn't care what was happening to him.
True to the hunt leader's instructions, his only concern
was Ptah'Ra, and the overwhelming desire he had to see
his fellow young blood survive.

Sta'kta found an area on this Xenowing onto which he
could latch, some kind of spiky bulge between the wings.
He was able to get his fingers under it. A line of them ran
all the way down and past where he hung, likely going
to the tip of its tail.

Like everywhere else on his body, his fingers were
bleeding.

No matter. First, he would take care of these *pauk-de*
wings.

Sta'kta flicked his wrist to free his wristblades. The blades weren't as long and formidable as the hunt leader's weapons, but they were still sharp enough to cut through carapace and flesh. With a roar he thrust his hand forward and down, digging deep into the Xenowing's body between the pointed lumps where its wing were attached. He didn't stab—such a primitive movement—but *carved*, ripping down the Xenowing's with all his power.

He jerked his head sideways as acid blood sprayed his arm and torso, bellowing in furious pain as he turned his wrist at the end and forced the shining, black carapace to part from the tissue that held it in place.

The Xenowing's scream split the air as it bucked, then it screeched again as Sta'kta drove his wristblades into the newly opened gap and slashed until only a few tendrils of sinewy flesh still held the piece in place.

The monster tried to claw at Sta'kta with its back legs, but was blocked by the hanging section of its own body. Everything in Sta'kta's vision swayed wildly, but he still caught a glimpse of how Ptah'Ra's hold on his cable was being pried away. All his efforts, all his *agony*, would mean nothing if both of them died as a result of this combat. Neither would have any glory or honor, and the only thing they would be remembered for was their failure to defeat this primitive beast.

The truth revealed itself.

Only one of them could survive.

Still holding on with one fist, Sta'kta pushed himself as far forward as he could, raised his other hand and rammed his bloody wristblades into the Xenowing's head. It bucked again beneath him and shrieked, finally releasing Ptah'Ra as it twisted and bit at Sta'kta with its second mouth, telescoping outward almost faster than he could move out of the way.

Acid blood belched from the wound, sheeting his hand and arm, but Sta'kta was past feeling any more pain, riding an endocrine high like none he had ever experienced. As he and the Xenowing dropped, the dank and fetid air of the rift rushing past him, Sta'kta pulled back on his wristblades and prepared for the killing blow. The Xenowing's oily-looking head parted in the middle like a bloated carcass and Sta'kta gave a fierce, final battle cry.

There would be tales of his honor and bravery, and Ptah'Ra would tell them.

* * *

Fetch was pleased to see that the monsters had such a dedicated enemy. He was also quite thrilled that all of this hadn't just been in his mind. As he lay entombed by the thick branches of the bush and the tall grass beneath it, he'd begun to wonder if the monsters weren't some irrational, chemical-created monstrosities his mind had brought to life, fully formed to terrorize him. Perhaps the Khatura had found a better way to ensure that he returned to its sweet embrace.

No Khatura, no peace.

On the flipside, this also meant that the monsters were real, and that meant they'd be coming for him soon. He wondered if they could detect his trail, and realized he'd peed his pants somewhere along the way. As predators they could surely smell the acrid taint of vinegar-tinged urine. They'd probably come fluttering down the side of the rift, run across it, and locate him beneath the bush.

There were sounds of combat, but he couldn't tell how far away it was. Nothing was visible from his vantage point.

Fetch shook his head, the weight of the mask making the movement difficult. He hated the imagination he had when he wasn't high on Khatura. It glorified the possible and rarified the impossible. If only he could be like most everyone else and flit through life, not bothering to worry about anything and oblivious to the dreadful things that could happen.

Suddenly he spotted movement, and wanted to wet his pants all over again.

It looked like a wet, tan crab with an exceptional long tail. Fetch stayed as still as he could, watching as it skittered along the bottom of the rift, searching... for what? Food? Its body went right, then left, then right again, and all the while its tail whipped about as if it had a mind of its own.

Then it halted and became as still as a statue.

Suddenly it spun in his direction, and with an insane squeal it loped toward him on small, ungainly legs, its carapace barely above the ground, its tail straight into the air.

Now it was Fetch's turn to scream. He wanted to flee, but there was no place to go. He tried to scoot backward, but the massive roots of the bush had gone between his legs and he was stuck with one on either side.

He lost sight of it and had a single, brief moment of victory, feeling as if he'd escaped. Then the hideous creature was on the ground in front of him and launching at his face.

It grabbed at him but slid off the metal facemask and back to the ground. The sound of its claws were like a devil scraping for his soul. Tiny talons slid through his eyeholes and almost got his eyes.

Fetch tried to grip the body of the hideous little creature, but its tail wrapped around his wrist a full four times, solid and tighter than he could have imagined. He shook his hand to make it release him, but it refused to let go. It was like trying to throw away something sticky: no matter what he tried, he couldn't get free.

Changing tactics, Fetch hammered his hand against the ground as hard as he could, over and over.

The creature squealed, but the grip only tightened.

If he didn't do something soon, he wouldn't have any feeling in his fingers. Already they were becoming numb. Then he remembered his harvesting tools. He reached down to his belt with his free hand and pulled out the small, curved knife. The blade was on the inside of the curve, but the hand shook. He fought to keep it still, terrified that he would cut himself.

He placed the blade against the tail and slid it beneath the appendage where it touched his skin. Once he felt the coolness of the metal, he pulled up hard and the blade sliced through the tail.

Then Fetch screamed.

The thing's blood was made from some kind of acid, and oh, it burned, so *fucking* hot! He shrieked again, begging anyone who might hear him.

"Make it stop! Please, make it stop!"

But no one came to his aid.

The lower part of the tail split away and began to flop side-to-side without a brain to guide it. The part that was still attached to the crab-like creature flailed wildly, slinging acid blood with each swing.

Fetch forgot all caution and stabbed at the back of the creature, impaling it on the curved harvesting knife, then tossing the creature and the knife clear of the bush. It rolled and landed on the floor of the rift a few feet away. Meanwhile, his skin bubbled and blistered, and spots dotted his vision as he wiped his wrist savagely against the grass. The stalks sizzled and blackened, but he managed to get most of it off.

Rocking back and forth, he glared at his wrist. The flesh was vividly red and puckered with ugly, suppurating burns. All Fetch could do was squeeze his fist and grit his teeth at the pain. He dragged it against the grass one more time, then stared out from his hiding place. Things had been peaceful, just another day in the rift, until those two-legged aliens had come. Now there were fucking land crabs with acid-filled tails and who knew what else.

The sounds of fighting continued unabated, but he still couldn't see what was happening. He shook his head again, as hard as he could, to make sure he wasn't having some kind of Khatura fantasy gone bad.

But no, the dying creature was still flopping in the short grass.

3 6

Murray had spent time—way too *much* time—recovering from his flight from the camp to the ship. There was no escaping it, he was the oldest person in the group, and yeah, the most out of shape. By the time he'd made it through the hatch, his lungs were burning.

Most of the mercs, especially Shrapnel, thought he should've been aged out of the job years ago, but he had a thing or two to teach that bastard. He thought he'd given Shrapnel a clearer picture of where he stood in the pecking order in the command tent, when he'd shown up with a bunch of gripes—what with Murray's knife poking a hair's width away from the axillary artery under the man's arm—but apparently not.

Men like Shrapnel never learned. They just pissed and moaned and turned into violent fools who thought they could solve everything with their fists and their guns, but couldn't find a brain to use if it was inside their heads... which were always empty.

So there was no way in hell Murray would have

considered opening the door and letting Shrapnel onto the ship with him. Murray was ready to cut his losses. He could tell the bosses anything. He'd never been late. He'd never siphoned product. He'd always brought back more Khatura than he'd been ordered to harvest. He was the model employee of an intergalactic drug organization, and he'd be damned if he was going to let some third-rate mercenaries and worthless addicts get the best of him.

He sure as hell wasn't going to die for the cartel. He wouldn't fight for it, and he sure wouldn't be killed because of some planetary turf war. One moment LV-363 was a lush planet with a drug-filled gash, the next it was a battleground for monsters. He'd have nightmares about those teeth. What fucking joke of a god would create such a creature? And what good was it anyway, besides being the perfect killing machine?

Finally Murray felt like he could breathe.

He'd watched on the exterior display while Shrapnel had circled the ship, tried to get in, then fought for his life— despite his age, the man was damned good at fending for himself, not so good at helping others. Then his pulse rifle was empty, and the merc took off into the darkness.

The ship hadn't been used in far too long, and the engines would take time to power up enough to escape the pull of gravity. For a while the black creatures that had swarmed the camp had investigated the clearing around the ship while Murray tried to monitor all the camera displays at once from the commander's seat, his lips pressed together with tension. There were half a dozen screens showing the majority of the areas around the outside, and every time one of the beasts slipped out of vid range, he double checked his stats, making sure all of the hatches were tight and stayed that way.

It felt like hours, but finally the vids cleared and nothing moved on any of the screens. He programmed a series of alarms according to a grid that corresponded to each area, making sure he'd be able to hear it no matter where he was in the ship. Like any good worker bee, he was blind to the knowledge of the cartel's home location, and it would take some time to get to a planet where the cartel would at least send a representative.

After the alarms were activated, he started programming in the calculations to get to the first stop, sending out notification that he was pulling out immediately. They were gonna be pissed, but maybe his follow-up message—that he was the only survivor— would shut them up. It wasn't like he could harvest the damn Khatura by himself.

And again, he refused to fucking die for them.

Murray was a third of the way into the star map when he thought he heard something. He was bent over a portable computer pad logging path numbers into the computer. He lifted his head and waited, his brain trying to grasp the sound that had slid into his ears.

It sounded like something sliding across the floor, which didn't make sense because the floor had a deeply textured surface to prevent the crew from slipping. Things that dropped didn't roll—they simply stopped.

So what—

There it was again. Quiet, but absolutely real.

Frowning and pushing himself out of the chair, Murray was uncomfortably aware that his pulse had climbed and the muscles across his back had tightened since his run. He stood where he was, listening, turning over possibilities in his mind. None of the hatches had opened; he'd made sure they were locked and sealed, ready in pre-liftoff mode. And no one was walking around inside—the alarms would be screaming like a wounded banshee if anything had broken any of the infrared beams.

The beams started at knee height and stopped about the same distance from the ceiling, both spaces too small for anything to pass without detection. Something smaller, then—one of the weird local animals. Not a riftwing or a bird—if either had been flying around, it would have set off the alarms.

There were stories of a rat-like thing with six legs, called a jivening, down in the rift. He'd never seen one—management like him didn't go down into that fucking hell—but if he remembered correctly, that was the place they were only supposed to have been found.

He remembered school lessons from old Earth, studies that said rats had come to the United Americas island state of Hawaii via ships, and rabbits were brought to Australia for food and hunting. Both species reproduced wildly, causing environmental cluster-fucks. It wasn't inconceivable that a jivening, maybe a young one, had found a way to hitch a ride on a cable or a harvesting net, or even one of the harvesters themselves.

Damned rodents always somehow found a way onto ships.

The seconds crawled past, the silence around him competing for the *thud* of his heartbeat in his temples, something he remembered from stress migraines ages ago in his office days. Murray wasn't sure how long he stood there, listening. He felt like he'd been holding his breath for a long time—too long—underwater, and now he was finally able to surface. The air he pulled into his lungs wasn't sweet and fresh, but it was okay; ship-modulated, perfectly balanced humidity and temperature and...

Something else.

Murray inhaled again, slower this time.

Something heavier, like dirt.

Yeah, he thought, *one of those fucking rat-things got in here somehow.* His hand slipped to his right side. His old M4 pistol, strapped there for a little extra protection, slid noiselessly out of its holster, fitting into his hand like it had been grown there. He would take care of the filthy thing now, before it could squeeze out a bunch of babies and spread its joy to other parts of the system.

He eased the pistol up and—

All the alarms in the ship seemed to go off at once.

Murray gasped and instinctively jumped backward.

At the same time something black fell from the ceiling, missing him by inches. He had a second to wonder if anyone had known jivenings could climb like that, then he actually *saw* the thing in front of him.

It was one of the monsters.

Small enough to crawl above or under the infrared beams.

A fucking *juvenile* monster.

Murray screamed and lurched to the right. At the same time, the thing went for him. He fired at it as fast as he could, but he'd never been a decent shot and it leaped side to side, too fast for him to follow and coming closer.

"How'd you get in here?" Murray bellowed. It hissed and reached for him, so Murray threw a computer pad at it, hitting it smack in the face. Too bad his gun aim wasn't that accurate. He dodged behind the copilot's chair, swiveling it to keep the creature's attention as he tried to figure out his next move. It must've already been in here when he closed up—the hatch had been open when he got there.

How many things had come in and out?

The monster tried to slip around to Murray's right, and he fired at it again, then again—

—and he was out of ammo.

He had no backup clip. Having the gun on his belt to begin with had just been a comfort thing, what he'd thought of at the time as being a stupid just-in-case move to make himself feel safe.

That sure as hell hadn't worked.

Despite what the mercs and addicts thought of him, Murray wasn't one to give up without a fight. The little fucker tried to lunge at him. He flipped the gun and whacked at it, ignoring the scorching pain along his palm from the impact. He was able to crack it a couple of times, just enough to make it back off.

This wasn't going to work forever, though—the thing's crazy, elongated head snapped to the side each time the M4 connected, but the alloy grip didn't so much as leave a dent. He hammered at it a couple more times, then turned and ran.

He passed three mini-stations before he was able to stop and take a scant three seconds to input the override code for the doors. He just needed to get farther along the ship so he could open the hatch, get out, then turn and close it again so the thing couldn't follow him. If Shrapnel was off in the bushes waiting for him, then fuck him—Murray would let the creature out and they could do their own little death dance.

A crash came from around the last turn, a few feet away—no stealth now—and he took off, giving silent thanks for the textured flooring that was the only thing keeping him from landing on his ass every few feet. He didn't know why the monster couldn't keep up. Maybe it was trying to crawl along the too-slick walls or the ceiling, which would never hold its weight. Murray made it about as far as he figured was safe. Stopping at an exterior hatch, he keyed in the passcode and a ten-second auto-close.

The door was open only a foot when he tried to squeeze through—

—and the nightmare that was hunting him fastened onto his left leg.

"No!" he screamed. Pain, hot as lightning and twice as fierce, zinged up his thigh muscles and into his chest. He was still gripping his pistol as he fell on his side, beating at the creature as he tried to pull the rest of his body out of the ship. Despite Murray's efforts, the mini-monster managed to get its head through the opening. The agony in his leg began taking its toll, dragging at his reflexes and winnowing away at his strength, and he could feel himself slowing.

He *had* to get free.

Even as he thought that, the M4 hit the creature on the side of its head, then went flying away. Fighting for air, Murray got his left hand under the thing's neck, holding its head away from his face while his other hand hunted for his knife, the one that had saved him more times than—

Inches from Murray's mouth, the creature's lips pulled back to show silvery, blunt teeth, framed by twice-as-long fangs on each side. Murray screamed and tried to pull his head back, even though he knew the thing couldn't reach him.

Then it opened its mouth wide.

A second tooth-studded jaw snapped out and fastened on Murray's face.

3 7

Monsters were everywhere, enjoined by a cacophony of battle rage and pain.

There were too many, and the Xenowing mutation was a new variation she had never fought before, never even *considered*. Ca'toll had not imagined that the heavy, clumsy Xenomorphs would ever go airborne, nor had any other Yautja she had ever known.

Such an idea was unthinkable.

Inconceivable.

Yet it had *happened*.

The Xenomorph's rate of reproduction was fast but predictable. The Ovomorph seeding of this planet had been carefully planned, and much consideration had been put into the lifeforms the Xenos would use to incubate their young. Yes, there were larger animals here, some of them mammals, but they were slow and simple, non-predators that lived on fauna and weighed far too much to be an asset beyond nutrition.

How *ignorant* it had been of the Yautja to fail in their projections, to miss the potential for Xenomorphs to take advantage of other lifeforms that possessed desirable attributes. Above all, how reckless had they been to not research what kind of insectoid organisms existed on LV-363. Such short-sightedness threatened to be the end of them all. Even so, it would be their honor to overcome this malfeasance of planning and nature, and be the first to take down airborne versions of their longtime nemeses.

Sta'kta and the Xenowing—the largest she'd seen so far—had fallen into the depths of the rift. Ca'toll had witnessed Sta'kta's final assault along the creature's elongated head and knew it would be dead before it hit the rift floor. It was unlikely the young blood himself could have survived the fall, much less the cascade of acid that had sheeted the entirety of his body. Likely he suffered the same fate as his opponent, and never felt the impact.

Another of the young bloods dead.

Ca'toll flung herself down the cable, at the same time yanking the combistick free of her belt. A glance told her that Ptah'Ra was recovering; he was headed toward the rift floor, but was still far enough away that none of them could see the bottom. With one hand she extended her spear, leaned out, and disemboweled a Xeno that was clambering toward her. When it toppled away, she jabbed another that was slinking behind, piercing it in the throat and pulling sideways. It, too, fell into the blackness below.

To her left she saw T'See'Ka fighting for his life. He was

pinned between two almost-grown Xenomorphs. They were clinging to flora on a wall, circling him, cautiously staying just beyond where he could reach them with his wristblades. One would slip in to slash at him then back away again, and the other would launch a similar assault.

Abandoning her cable, Ca'toll retracted her spear and sprang for a clump of vegetation growing along the side of the rift. She grabbed onto it with one hand and it held, if only long enough for her to find a stronger outgrowth slightly farther down. She made her way toward T'See'Ka, moving as fast as she could with all of the handholds she could find, until finally the Xeno above him realized it had turned from hunter into prey.

Instantly it twisted to face her and lunged in her direction, its narrow limbs shooting out. As it stretched forward for a final leap in Ca'toll's direction, it was an easy thing for her to snap out her wristblades, severing both of its front limbs. It gave a primal scream when it realized its back legs couldn't hold it, and the planet's gravity took it down.

Confident T'See'Ka could handle himself against the other Xeno, she turned away, checking to see if any of the other young bloods were being overpowered.

Vai'ke spun on his cable and disemboweled a Xenowing, only to have an unchanged riftwing drop on him from above and try to pull him free. Ca'toll grimaced, but she was too far away, and would never get there in time to assist him. Even so, she still tried to visually map a way toward his position, then realized she wouldn't be needed.

Vai'ke managed to loop the cable around one foot so that it supported his weight, and while he still couldn't release his hold, it gave him a substantial increase in stability. With a hefty battle cry, he punched upward with one wrist and pulled, twin incisions appearing across the riftwing's thorax. An instant later his arm was drenched in viscous liquid. The riftwing fell away, its body careening into several Xenomorphs that had been heading up the wall toward the conflict. They were knocked free and plummeted into the gloom.

It still wasn't enough.

Ca'toll scowled and wondered if there had been an error in calculations during the Ovomorph seeding, but dismissed the thought as quickly as it occurred. The Yautja in charge of the preparations would never make such an egregious error. Whether this somehow was the result of eggmorphing, or resulted from the melding of the Xenomorphs with a previously undocumented species, they were vastly outnumbered. That was all that mattered in the here and now.

Something flashed on her display screen, and she realized Ba'sta had used his netgun and trapped a young Xeno against the rift wall close to her. It screeched and struggled, but Ca'toll didn't bother to finish it off—it would be dead soon anyway, forcibly separated into small, acid-dripping cubes as the net drew back into itself. Instead she balanced herself on a strong but stubby growth of brush and unhooked the plasmacaster from her shoulder. After a quick set of adjustments to the controls in her helmet, she did a fast scan and determined the locations of all the young bloods.

"T'See'Ka," she barked into her coms. When the young Yautja turned his head to look at her, she tossed the weapon to him. He caught it without hesitation. "Pass it to Ba'sta, below and to your right."

He obeyed instantly. Ba'sta's arm shot out, his training taking over where his reticent personality might've failed him. He scanned below, trying to determine the next recipient.

"To Stea'Pua!" Ca'toll ordered, and Ba'sta complied. Stea'Pua caught the plasmacaster, but was still too far above the rift floor to do what she wanted.

"Ptah'Ra, how far are you from the bottom?" she asked. Even as she asked the question, her display found and marked his location as a few feet above where she wanted him to be. Beneath her helmet, Ca'toll's mandibles flared in anger. He was the one whose size and stature would benefit them the most, but not where he was. "Stea'Pua, pass it to Ptah'Ra, who will descend and plant the plasmacaster in the soil, *h'ka-se*—now!"

Neither young blood hesitated. She had barely vocalized the order when Stea'Pua flung the weapon and Ptah'Ra snatched it out of the air. Ptah'Ra then dropped down the cable at a nearly dangerous speed, and Ca'toll followed.

They descended into darkness.

3 8

Somehow Shrapnel had managed to fall asleep. It must have been the backlash of all the adrenaline that had been released while he'd been fleeing. His body had shut down on its own. He woke with dirt in his eyes and blinked it away, still afraid to move. He also smelled the sweet, alluring scent of the Khatura--was he becoming an addict?

Outside the small cave he could still hear violence— the sizzle of powerful weapons, the cries of the dying, victory whoops from the living.

The bipedal hunters, whatever they were, had come prepared for a fight—maybe they were doing it for some sort of sport. He didn't see how *anything* could be worth this sort of shit. Somehow he and Murray's cartel had managed to get between the hunters and the hunted, which apparently meant they were fair game. For at least the hundredth time, he wanted to punch Murray into the next system for leaving him behind. Shrapnel understood cowardice better than most—

it could save your life—but he also knew there was strength in numbers.

Right now he had an even bigger problem.

Say he was able to get out of this cave alive, and say he was able to avoid contact with all the new nasties that called this shithole of a planet home. Say he found a way to climb all the way out of the rift without the riftwings, the bug-creatures, or the hunters noticing him.

What then? What was left?

There was no way off this damned pile of dirt, and he'd be marooned like the old stories he'd heard about wild men on barely breathable planets who went nutso and attacked rescuers when they finally arrived. Shrapnel didn't want to be that sort of lost cause. He wanted to have a future. He wanted to get back to the main belt where he could gamble and party, then get a shot for whatever ailed him the next morning so he could up and do it all over again.

There was a disgusting squirming in his ear, and he swiped away a millipede-like thing that was trying to dig in there. Fucking bugs. He *hated* bugs. A memory surfaced through the mire of his depression and he laughed quietly, remembering the first time he'd ever seen a Carcozian spider. How he'd grabbed a flame thrower and not only fried it to a black smudge, but burned down the tent and one-tenth of their stock of Khatura.

Fun times.

Suddenly there was a sound from somewhere behind him.

He quieted the voices in his head and listened.

Ten seconds.

Twenty.

A minute.

Nothing.

It must have been all in his mind.

Was he high on Khatura again?

Shrapnel was ready to dismiss it as nothing, when it came again. Not so much a sound as a displacement of air.

"Who's there?" he whispered, immediately feeling stupid for even asking the question. Then something lightly touched his leg. He kicked out and was rewarded with a screech.

A screech?

It sounded human, so it couldn't be one of the monsters or one of the hunters. So who was it?

He kicked out again.

This time there was a hiss of pain.

"Stop!"

"Enid?" He couldn't believe it. "Is that you?"

"Please." Her whisper was thick and garbled. "Don't tell them."

Shrapnel almost laughed. Like he was going to tell anyone where they were? The irony of the situation didn't escape him. A guard and a harvester hiding in the same damned hole, on a planet large enough for them to get lost and never find each other again. Talk about fickle fucking fate.

He shook his head, although she probably couldn't see him, and kept his voice low.

"Don't worry about that, Enid," he said, keeping his voice down. "We're in the same boat."

"What *are* those things?"

"Your guess is as good as mine." His next question was automatic. "Are you okay?" As soon as he said it, he wasn't sure why he'd bothered. *Just reflex, I guess.*

She didn't respond.

"Enid?"

"I—I'm fine.' She swallowed hard enough that he could hear it. "I just want to go home."

"Murray's on the ship," he told her. He couldn't keep the anger out of his tone. "He has it locked up tight."

"What about the others?" She sounded hopeful, stupid kid.

"What others?" This time he couldn't stop a sharp laugh. He'd yet to see anyone else from their party. "I'm pretty sure we're it."

Enid let out a long, high whine that ran at the top of his ability to hear it. He knew how she felt, but he wasn't about to own up to it. He might be stuck in a hole, but he was still Shrapnel. Still the baddest motherfucker of the mercs hired on for this fucking project.

He inhaled, steeling himself for the next thought that had to come. They couldn't stay in this hole forever. More than being marooned, his greatest fear was coming face-to-face with one of those hellish monsters, the ones the hunters were after. He had a far-fetched notion that he might be able to communicate with the hunters, but the other creatures out there were pure evil with too many sets of teeth.

Not to mention the winged ones. Fucking *wings*.

The only hope he could come up with was to make a run for it.

"How far back does this cave go?"

"I don't know," she answered after a moment. "I was too scared to look, but I think I'm at the end."

"Are you sure? Try going back farther."

"Okay." Shrapnel could hear the fear in her voice.

"No," he said quickly. "Wait." Crawling backward, he carefully headed toward where he'd heard her voice, until his hand brushed her foot. She sucked in air for a scream, but he made a *shushing* sound before she actually let it out.

"I have something," he told her. "A passcode card. You need to save me if you want to save yourself."

"Save myself?" She sounded confused.

"Like I said, the ship's locked up, if it's even still here," he said in a low voice, "but in case we get separated or something, if you can get back up top, the card's got the passcode for the number two cargo door at the rear. Depending on what Murray did after I left, it might or might not work."

"What about you?" Enid asked.

"I know the code—I have it memorized," he answered. "You'll need it and the card. Save me and we'll get the fuck out of here." He felt her hesitation, but after a moment he heard the displacement of dirt, and there was a shift in the ceiling as dust settled on his back. With the dust came the smell of damp earth and something else— something that made his eyes water.

"Careful," he grumbled. "You'll bring it down on us."

"My feet are dangling above something," she whispered. "It might be a step down. I think there's a cave back here."

Hope shot through Shrapnel. "Wait! A cave? Can you make it farther in?"

"Hold on," she said, and by the way she said it, he could tell her tongue was in the corner of her mouth. "I think I can—shit!"

Then nothing.

"Enid?"

Nothing.

"Enid, where are you?"

"I'm here," came a voice from further away than it should be. "The drop was a little more than I expected."

"Where's here?"

"I think it's another room in the cave. Do you have a light of some kind? I can't see a thing."

Shrapnel cautiously moved toward Enid's voice. As he went, he breathed in the sharp smell again, this time stronger. It was a chemical smell, and he knew instinctively that using fire would be a very bad idea. A memory tickled—he'd smelled something like this before, but he couldn't place it.

Yeah, no open flame.

"No, but..."

He scooted forward until his feet found the ledge. Carefully he slid his legs over the side, then balanced himself with both hands and lowered himself into something squishy. His boots sunk several inches into the ground and the reeking air floating around him made him gag.

"What the hell is this place?"

"I don't know," Enid answered from a foot or two away, still a disembodied voice. "Just a cave, I guess."

"What's all over the floor?"

When she didn't answer, Shrapnel reached down and drew his finger through what had to be some sort of stinking guano. Then he knew where the chemical odor had come from—a build-up of gasses in the small cave. This place was a bomb just waiting to be lit.

"For God's sake," he said. "It's a lair. Be careful and don't light anything. I think I've got something that'll work." He reached into one of his cargo pockets. At first he thought it was gone, then his fumbling fingers found it and he pulled it out and snapped it on. A small chemical light stick.

Sickly green light illuminated the den. Enid gasped and Shrapnel's mouth dropped open as he realized what they'd walked into. Dug into the walls surrounding them were dozens of haphazard smaller holes, each containing a pulsing white sac. The floor was mounted with speckled green droppings, and hanging from the ceiling was the largest riftwing he'd ever seen, far too fat and bloated with eggs to fit the narrow hole through which they'd entered.

"Oh, fuck," Shrapnel whispered. "Don't make a sound or we're dead meat."

As they stared, the riftwing's back end pulsed. The creature pushed, and a long rope of white mucus fell from it to the ground. Then the mucus coalesced into a long, worm-like mass that slithered toward them.

Shrapnel hopped out of the way, but Enid wasn't as quick. It snatched at her leg and held on.

Then she screamed.

3 9

Sta'kta struck the floor of the rift hard enough to knock all the air from his body. What saved him from death was the Xenowing's body. As they both hit the rift floor, it cushioned Sta'kta's fall in a sickening squelch of acidic liquid that flew in all directions.

Disoriented, he managed to roll over, the world a blur, like stars during a mad hyperdrive jaunt through systems. He tried twice to stand but fell back to his knees each time. Managing it on the third try, he felt as if he'd been too long on the receiving end of a crate of Gollanz ale.

He staggered to the wall of the rift, using its earthen sides for support. In doing so he disturbed a hive of native wasps, and slapped them aside as they buzzed angrily. Several landed on the dead creature, then sizzled and popped as the acid immediately obliterated them. Despite his circumstances, he grunted in humor.

Evolution sure was *gahn'tha-cte*—ruthless.

Several meters ahead, Ny'ytap was impaled on the sharp end of a tree branch several feet above the rift floor.

Beneath him lay a Xenomorph furiously struggling to get to its feet, despite its shattered legs. The creature looked up at Ny'ytap, dangling above, and it fought to reach the hunt leader's trailing foot. It was a hideously pathetic dance as the groaning Yautja jerked his leg out of reach.

He lives, Sta'kta thought, stunned and fighting with disbelief. The hunt leader's agony had to be indescribable, though—trapped, his flesh pierced, unable to defend himself against even the most pitiful attacker. His blood poured from the wound, ran down the branch, and pooled on the ground below. Even the slightest motion yielded another unintelligible sound.

The Xeno fought to pull itself inch by inch closer to where it could snag its prey's legs with its claws. Shaking off paralysis, Sta'kta lurched toward them. He was halfway there when another Xenowing emerged from the recesses of the shadows and swooped toward him.He let himself fall flat, and the creature soared over him and angled toward Ny'ytap.

To all appearances the hunt leader's fall had been broken by the side of the rift and, ultimately, the tree branch that had pierced his left side at an upward angle. His struggle to avoid the injured Xeno revealed that he was still alive but trapped, unable to gain purchase that would allow him to escape.

The Xenowing landed on Ny'ytap's chest.

Its position hid the body from view, the wings flapping as the groans became louder. Cursing as he searched for a weapon, Sta'kta found a thick length of dead wood. He used it as a cane to propel himself forward, and when he reached the broken Xenomorph, he plunged it into the creature's mouth over and over until the beast was dead. As the acid ate away at the branch, Sta'kta stumbled and fell, barely missing the pool of acid surrounding the dead form.

Before he could turn his attention back to helping Ny'ytap, he heard a sound like thunder and the ground beneath him began to shake. Sta'kta turned in time to see a herd of hexapod creatures bearing down on him, bright red figures in his night vision. He vaguely remembered a mention in the mission brief that such creatures lived in the rifts—large rodent-type fauna with six legs. They ran in packs for protection. The cacophony of the battle must have frightened them into a stampede.

Unable to hurl himself out of the way, all he could do was cover the back of his neck with his arms as they charged through the darkness toward him. He buried the front of his helmet in the dirt and the first dozen or so creatures went around him. Others ran through acid, sending the rest into a frenzy as the caustic liquid splashed over them.

Terror and pain made them go over him rather than around, and he felt trampled by hundreds of feet as the hexapods treated his back as if it were the ladder to freedom. Every time he tried to raise his head, the creatures would surge and press him once again to ground.

Claustrophobia started to creep into his senses. He couldn't stay here—he had to get up. He tried to roll left, then realized that doing so would take him into the deadly pool. Switching direction, he jerked himself to the right until he was again up against the side of the rift.

Without warning he was pulled to his feet, and Ca'toll slammed him against the earthy rift wall.

"What are you doing on the ground, Young Blood?"

"I—I—it was just that—"

"Enough," she growled. "We are still in the midst of battle." Sta'kta heard anger and derision in her voice. "You act like you are afraid of the jivenings."

Jivenings. That's what they were called. Omnivorous creatures that could eat their way from the inside of a whale, if necessary. Given enough time, they might have begun to chew on him. He'd instinctively tried to roll into a ball, but Ca'toll was right.

Better to stand and fight.

He pulled back his shoulders. "Where are the others?"

"Scattered, but still engaged in combat." This time there was a distinct note of accusation in her tone. He looked up at the thing still perched on Ny'ytap's now motionless body. Whatever life had been left had fled. What remained was a ruin.

"What are those beasts?"

"Some sort of polymorph," Ca'toll responded, "created by the merging of existing fauna and the Xenos. I've heard about it happening before, but never seen it. A flying Xenomorph changes the entire equation."

"Maybe we should abandon this rock and obliterate it."

"There are other mining colonies, a substantial distance away," she said. "No purpose would be served by killing those who live there."

"Why should we care?"

"Why?" She stood straighter and smacked him on the front of his helmet, hard enough to make his head rock back. "Because we only fight those creatures worthy of our attention. These oomans are no such thing."

Sta'kta glanced at his burned arm and shoulder. "It just seems that there's an easier way to conclude our business here."

"If our 'business,' as you call it, was easy, then it would not be fit for the Yautja," Ca'toll said. "We are the finest hunters in the universe, and there is nothing that can stop us once we start. That carries with it an unassailable code of conduct. You would do well to remember that."

Sta'kta pulled himself up. What she said fit with all that he had been taught. He needed to be above it all, and not descend to the level of their prey.

"What now?"

She clicked her mandibles. "Now we gather our dead, and get off the planet."

"What about the Xenowings?"

"They will remain for another blooding, if any wish to hunt them. Should they propagate, this will become a fertile hunting ground for future generations. About which others can tell tales to stir the song of combat in their hearts."

The sound of a plasmacaster cut through the darkness and caused both of them to turn. A short way down the rift, light flashed on and off, matching the sounds of the weapon. Sta'kta looked to Ca'toll.

"Stea'Pua has planted the plasmacaster," she said. "This is where we will all finish our battle." Without another word she sprinted in the direction of the lights, and Sta'kta's mandibles clicked in anticipation as he followed.

More action.

More hunt.

More tales of glory.

4 0

"Get it off me! Get it off me!" Enid bawled. She went down in the muck and thrashed in a panic, shaking her leg and splashing the disgusting slime that covered the floor of the hidden grotto.

Even as she fought, the mucus-creature wrapped itself around her legs as if it had a brain. But it didn't—this was some kind of prebirth, a weirdly animated organism whose only purpose was to find food. It gave off a smell like bleach that mixed heavily with the already nasty chemical solution of the guano.

Without warning, Enid stopped moving. Shrapnel pulled a knife free from a sheath on his thigh and, without thinking, grabbed at the slick white substance. As soon as his hand touched it, a shot of electricity jolted through him, paralyzing him where he stood. In the dim green light he saw the terror he felt reflected in Enid's eyes. He was unable to move, unable to release his grip.

His body wouldn't obey his mental commands, but his tongue was caught between his teeth, and he bit down hard. Pain razored through his face and released whatever strange hold the thing had over him. Shrapnel staggered backward until his lower back hit the edge below the entrance they'd used to get in here. His knees tried to buckle, but he caught himself before he dropped into the sludge under his feet.

Fighting to regulate his breathing and avoid hyperventilating, Shrapnel pulled himself together and headed back toward Enid. Instead of grabbing at the mucus, this time he sliced at it with his knife. It came apart like a length of rotting old cloth. The cut piece fluttered to the floor and landed lightly atop the guano, then turned gray and abruptly liquefied, melting into the riftwing shit.

The piece still attached to Enid writhed, but didn't let go. She jerked slightly, the creature's pain granting her the smallest amount of release.

"Get—get it off me," she managed to wheeze.

Shrapnel was reaching out to her a second time when the riftwing hanging above them began to undulate. He backpedaled just as a child-sized lump slipped from an opening in the creature's back end and squelched in front of his boots. Residue coated his legs and a piece of muck landed on his cheek.

Grimacing, fighting the urge to vomit, he wiped it away.

The thing that had just come from the riftwing was white, and he could see through the thin film of its surface to something dark and round on the inside. The object pulsed erratically at first, then began to find a rhythm as if it was becoming attuned to something other than the mother's womb. Shrapnel's lizard brain instantly wanted to kill it, stab it until it no longer moved and was just dead, dead, dead.

But he couldn't. Something else was happening, something inserting itself into his subconscious. The disgust he had felt was erased, replaced by an intense and almost painful need to *protect* this thing—to take care of it at all costs. The knife fell from his hand, forgotten, as his eyes fluttered, rolling up in his head. When his vision returned, gone was the urge to vomit, the sense that this thing was alien, replaced by the instinct a father might feel for a child.

It was unnatural.

It was horrifying.

It was wonderful.

He glanced toward Enid and growled. She needed to stay away. This was his!

She was a threat.

As if to confirm what he felt she growled back and, before he could react, approached the squirming form of the newly born riftwing. There was something hanging at her side, and he wondered if it was a weapon, something that might harm the infant. He barked at her to stop, but she lifted the small creature to her breast and held it with one hand.

Her eyes narrowed. As if thoughts could pass between

them, he knew what needed to be done. It was as if he'd become enmeshed in someone—*something* else's evolution. Become a part of it.

Shrapnel bent and searched the muck for the knife, moving his fingers stickily through the sludge until he came upon something hard. It wasn't his knife, but a piece of bone. He couldn't tell what kind it was, but one end of it was broken like a green fracture in a tree.

It would have to do.

He found a clear space on the wall and began to hack free large clumps of dirt. Somewhere in the back of his mind Shrapnel knew he was being controlled, but he felt the better for it. He was exhausted from making decisions about his life and everyone else's. Sometimes it was so much easier to be a follower, rather than a leader.

Just do what needed to be done.

In this case, the care and feeding of a beautiful new creature that would one day soar on the warm updrafts to the blue skies above. What more could he ask than to be part of such a process?

Once the impression had been dug deep enough, Shrapnel stepped aside, pointed at Enid and grunted. It was as if he had become incapable of human speech.

Enid took the newborn and laid it in the hollow Shrapnel had created. As if it had a life of its own, the remaining afterbirth slid up the wall and into place, forming a barrier that would protect the newly hatched creature from scavengers and hunters.

The two of them of them stood and stared, eyes dull, their tasks accomplished, waiting for their next command. Thoughts swirled in the back of Shrapnel's mind, ideas that he should be doing something else, but as soon as they surfaced they skittered away as paternal instincts took charge and squelched them.

A high-pitched whine pierced the chamber.

Shrapnel ducked his head and put both hands over his ears, trying to keep the sound at bay. It was coming from the mother riftwing, but he couldn't understand its meaning. Then he knew in his core that danger was present. Until now the only sound had been a subliminal hum from the huge creature, urging them to do what was needed.

This was different.

Something was coming.

Shrapnel scooped up the chemical light stick and shoved it between his teeth, despite where it had been. He knelt and again scrambled frantically for the knife he'd dropped. He found it, and an instant later the head of one of the monsters appeared in the chamber entrance.

He screamed.

Enid screamed.

Shrapnel went into a crouch, bone in one hand, knife in the other. He placed himself between the monster and the newborn. The creature extended its second jaw, teeth snapping, its deep black armored hide catching the green of Shrapnel's light as its mouth dripped what looked like venom. This was the closest he'd been to one, and he could see the claws on its forelegs. It gripped the sides of the small entrance as it peered inside, its teeth clacking as they opened and closed.

Against all sanity Shrapnel leapt at it, but it was too fast. As if he was insignificant, it launched into the air and latched onto the riftwing mother. The monster bit into her and the whine returned, this time so loud it drove Shrapnel to his knees, and he fell onto his side.

Suddenly the control was gone, the overwhelming compulsion vanishing in an instant. Yet somehow everything still seemed to be *wrong*. There was still something he needed to do.

Stop this mindless killer.

Shrapnel rolled to his left, covering himself in guano, and then stood, the light emanating from the chemical stick in his mouth. The motion got the monster's attention. It paused, then moved toward him. Shrapnel shoved the length of bone into its open mouth then brought the knife around and shoved it into the creature's skull.

Blood and acid spewed from the new wounds, coating his free arm. Shrapnel screamed as the skin bubbled away. Then the meat beneath sloughed off and fell into the offal beneath them, leaving behind exposed brown bones. As he watched his limb go up in smoke, a wave of intense pain filled his senses, so overwhelming he couldn't even scream.

Gone was the last hint of the riftwing's control. Barely hanging on, Shrapnel still managed to bring the knife back around, jamming it over and over and over into the skull of the beast.

"Enid," he ground out, "Save... yourself."

"I... I don't know how."

His back arched as his mouth opened impossibly wide.

"What can I do?" she cried.

He tried to laugh, but it came as a gurgling shriek.

"I'm done," he said around the stick in his teeth. His voice was little more than a cough. "Nothing left—too far gone to run. Get... the card."

Still alive, the monster clawed the air and tried again to grab Shrapnel. Enid reached for him as well, her eyes on the creature as she dug around in his pocket.

Then she was tripping back, the card in her hand.

Shrapnel mustered the last of his energy and tried to duck under the thing's belly, but one of its swipes sent him stumbling. The glowstick flew from his jaw. He landed face down in the guano and inhaled despite himself. Sputtering and gagging, he saw Enid frantically climb toward the exit. She pulled herself through, struggling with something that hung at her side, and was gone without a backward look.

The last nerves in his ruined arm were giving out, and although the limb was still functioning—barely— it wouldn't for much longer. Wherever he had been splattered with the creature's blood, blisters were building, then bursting, and Shrapnel knew he was as good as dead.

Beyond pain, he decided to do something he'd never considered before.

Go out like a hero.

After all, what the hell.

Yanking himself up, he almost fell against the monster's side. When it whipped its head toward him, Shrapnel shoved his ruined arm into its mouth, shoulder deep, pushing as far and hard as he could until he felt something on the inside. Whatever it was, he grabbed it and tugged. Prevented from biting down, the creature tried to shake him away, but he refused to let go, pulling as hard as he could—

—until in one great surge, he tore off a piece of the monster's insides and fell with it, kicking and screaming in the sludge as pain short-circuited the beast's brain. Shrapnel brought up the piece of mottled black flesh, no longer noticing as the acid blood smoked on his fingers. With a roar of triumph, he sunk his teeth into it.

An insane scream emerged from his lips, and the flesh inside his mouth burned away. As the monster shrieked and toppled next to him, the riftwing mother let out a keening sound that filled his senses. Its babies stayed silent in their protective grottos.

Shrapnel tried to stand, then fell again, this time on top of the writhing, dying monster. Acid from its wounds ate at him until there was nothing left but a vague sense of who he once had been. Then that was gone as well, his final sensations imploding into a black hole of non-existence.

4 1

When Ca'toll located Sta'kta, he was cowering on the ground beneath the jivenings, several meters away. Nearby burning bushes glowed brightly in her night vision, among the shadowy recesses of the rift floor.

The disgust that flooded through her at his cowardly behavior had almost—*almost*—been enough to make her leave him there, groveling under the weight of the repulsive creatures until he either found his *yeyin*—bravery—or died beneath the foreign rodents' small, sharp teeth.

Ultimately her own *yin'tekai* would not allow such an action, so as Ptah'Ra landed and began pounding a hole in the soil to plant the plasmacaster, she had kicked her way through the end of the stampede and hauled Sta'kta to his feet.

Now they crouched around the plasmacaster as it prepared to fire. Many times in the past Ca'toll had disparaged plasmacasters for not being able to fire continuously. In their present situation, however, recharge time was critical. Although each of them had a transponder that identified them as a non-target, the wait between firing afforded them the opportunity to engage the weapon's targeting system, and avoid falling victim to its lethal bolts.

The plasmacaster might be the only thing that kept them from being torn to pieces.

The three Yautja fought with wristblades and combisticks—the only weapons they could use in such close quarters. Above them, the other four young bloods struggled to keep Xenos of all sizes at bay, striking and slashing and never resting.

Between the plasmacaster rounds, Ca'toll weaved among their opponents, her extended combistick and longer wristblades a blur, anticipating the moves of both the attacking creatures and her two young bloods. Acid blood splattered everywhere, sizzling flora and fauna alike, but with the thrill of battle hammering through their bodies, the Yautja barely felt the stinging touch.

Ca'toll swung and sliced from right to left; the Xeno coming for her reeled backward as the bottom third of its face slid free and fell to the ground. She dodged sideways so the plasmacaster could fire—

Sta'kta fell right in front of its blast.

The center of the young blood's body exploded in a mist of green blood and flesh as the upper and lower halves flew in different directions. Then she saw movement at the far left of her display—Vai'ke, who had dropped from his cable.

Sta'kta was pushed!

She knew immediately what had happened.

"*Pauk-de s'yuit-de*," she gritted. "Fucking idiot!"

Vai'ke's head whipped toward her.

"It was unintentional!"

"And you are a liar," she spat. "I will deal with you later." A juvenile Xeno lunged at her, and she twisted away, slamming her combistick into the side of its face and pitching it, screeching, into the darkness. Her brain told her not to turn her back on Vai'ke, but the situation offered no other choice—there were too many creatures to focus on one of her own kind, even if she no longer trusted him. She would have to rely on the other four young bloods to watch her back.

They wouldn't be expecting a traitor in their ranks, though.

Rather than her back, Ca'toll should have been watching above her. She cursed herself for an unblooded as a Xenowing pulled her off her feet. It was the biggest one they'd encountered so far. With long front claws hooked under the armor on both shoulders, it lifted her as though she weighed no more than a jivening. Unexpected pain spiked through her shoulder muscles and Ca'toll hissed, but there was no time to dwell on it. If this creature took her up too far and she destroyed it, the fall might kill her— or worse, leave her to a fate like Ny'ytap's.

If she was destined to die today, she would not go quietly. By all that she held holy, she would see to it that this monster never attacked another living soul.

With her arms free, it took barely an instant to reach up with her wristblades and shear off the legs holding her captive. Her attacker screeched, and the fall was minimal, twenty *noks* at the most.

Ca'toll landed on her feet at the same time the Xenowing came after her again, apparently unfazed by the loss of its front appendages. So far she'd seen them only in the chaos of combat. One-on-one combat presented an entirely new set of challenges. She relished the prospect; the progeny of two savage creatures, the Xenowing was an *ui'stbi*—an abomination.

She threw herself backward as a mouth lunged out of its insectoid face. Pointed teeth splattered her facemask with the disgusting slime of a Xeno. Ca'toll arced one of wristblades at its head, but the Xenowing was quick and nimble. First it was on the ground, then it wasn't, teeth out and ready every time. She whirled and there it was, behind her back while on the ground again.

Despite its size, the monstrosity was skipping around her so fast that each time the plasmacaster targeting system locked onto it, her transponder canceled out the signal. It leaped and bit at her again, this time giving her helmet a groove along one side.

Ca'toll's back arched, and within the mask her mandibles spread.

She let out a deep snarl and turned again to face the Xenowing.

She was in for the fight of her life.

4 2

They'd come close to discovering him too many times for Fetch to count. He'd managed to stay beneath a thick bush with red and yellow flowers. It was lighter now, so the sun must have risen, but down here in the rift there were still dark shadows that might be hiding any sort of threat.

On two occasions a wind had shot through the bottom of the canyon and released a thick cloud of pollen from the brush surrounding him, but the mask he wore protected him from any possible effects. Who knew what it could cause? The Khatura gave him that special high, but perhaps these flowers did the opposite. This was the way his mind worked, he mused—especially when he wasn't high.

Always trying to find connections.

Always needing to know the reasons for things.

It was why Fetch had been so good at gambling—he intrinsically knew the relationship between chance and attainment, and the law of attraction that bonded everything together. It was both a curse and a gift. He was capable of understanding events and ideas in ways others found confusing and, frankly, emotionally debilitating.

Fetch waited, and watched, and figured out what everyone else couldn't. He had done it with the monsters. They came in all shapes and sizes, from the crazy long-tailed acid crabs to the human-sized clawed things that seemed capable of ripping him in half. Were they filled with acid, too?

Seemed that way.

Then there were the monster *hunters*.

He'd watched one hunter push another in front of their laser weapon, the kind that up top had cut in half the monster that was about to feed on him. The larger hunter, who appeared to be the leader, had *almost* seen it. While she thought she knew what was happening, she'd missed something in the guy who did the pushing. A tilt of the head that could only be cunning. From his hidey hole, ten meters away beneath the bush, Fetch had seen it. No mistake.

That guy looked familiar. It was the second time he'd done something that seemed out of place. The first time had been when he'd been harvesting. Shrapnel had been watching over them, but he wasn't the best protector. He hadn't paid attention to ninety percent of the things he should have. He probably would've been a better harvester than guard.

What Fetch had seen was that the hunters had the ability to appear and disappear. Not all of them. Not the small ones—at least so far—but the larger ones had some special technology that allowed them to be there and then—*poof!* Gone.

The murderer—the one who'd pushed the other in front of the laser—had been talking to a larger hunter who'd gone invisible, and then remained hidden from the others. It was weird. Fetch thought these guys were all on the same team.

Something was afoot.

Something the other hunters didn't know about.

But what had the smaller hunter done to get killed? Had he seen something? Had he somehow discovered the invisible one? Since they had technology that made it possible to become invisible, it seemed logical that one of them might be able to override another's equipment, if he became suspicious of something.

It occurred to Fetch that he might be able to curry favor with the large female, who definitely seemed to be the group's leader, if he was able to parlay his information. That was predicated, however, on his ability to communicate with them.

Although he kept perfectly still, Fetch's brow creased. Out of the corner of his eyes, he kept thinking he saw another hunter, but when he looked in that direction, there was nothing. Was he imagining things? Could that be the invisible one? Maybe it was because of his ability to see the connections between things. Things that, to someone else, wouldn't be there.

Then it came to him.

The invisible hunter was *hunting*.

It was hunting the leader, and she had no idea she was being targeted. She was fully engaged in fighting the flying monsters—not the riftwings, but the others. Every time they killed one, they acted like it was a victory, like everything they did was for sport. A nasty, senseless sport that just got people killed.

Fetch never thought he'd be in the game again. He'd assumed the Khatura, and being trapped in servitude, would destroy his skill, his insight. When he'd been forced to go back into the rift and hide like an animal, he'd thought it was hopeless—that he'd never escape. Now he knew otherwise.

Escape was possible, if he did it right.

All he had to do was not look, and he would see.

Suddenly an enormous creature, one of the hybrids of the riftwings and the black monsters, swept down and grabbed the leader. Its wings beat as it lifted her, but then she made it let go. *Cut off its fucking legs.* She dropped but it came after her, hopping so quickly and in so many directions that the laser weapon kept missing.

The smaller hunter ducked and flung itself out of the creature's range, making no effort to help his leader. She faced it alone as it hovered, placing herself between it and the laser weapon. Showing no fear, she pulled herself to her full height and gave a ferocious, ugly growl. The hair stood up on the back of Fetch's neck.

Without disturbing the soil, the huge, mutated creature set down and time seemed to stop. It appeared to wait, evaluating her. She went into a crouch, leaning first to one side, then the other; her adversary followed her movements with its head but stayed where it was, watching. The hunter repeated the same back and forth motion, then again, and again, until it looked like she was trying to hypnotize the creature. Fetch felt himself being lulled.

Abruptly she sprang straight at it.

With impossible speed, a sort of second mouth shot out of its face, with blunt teeth that Fetch knew were still somehow deadly, dripping fluids as they tried to fasten on her head or body. When he thought she would run right into its maw, she dropped and slid feet-first under its massive head, like the players in that old Earth game, baseball. The bite missed and for a moment the creature fumbled, unable to figure out where she was.

That instant of hesitation cost the winged mutation its life.

The hunter twisted beneath it, bringing up a short weapon that suddenly extended into a long rod with a sharp-edged, hooked spear on the end. She thrust it upward through the center of the beast's neck, then yanked sideways with both hands until the weapon came free.

The riftwing-creature's shriek was so loud and piercing that it took everything Fetch had to stay still and not slam his hands over his ears. Its head wobbled then fell to one side, too many of the muscles severed to hold it up. Blood sprayed in all directions as its appendages spasmed wildly. Wherever the blood landed, there was a burst of smoke.

The leader dodged out of the way as the monster fell, twitched, and finally died. Rivulets of air moving in the rift caught the smoke of the burning brush and leaves around the corpse.

Swiping absently at the splatters along her arms, the female glanced at the other of its kind, where he still stood out of the circle of battle. She stepped toward him, then they both glanced upward as two more of the hunters descended on steel cables and landed beside her. They were talking and gesturing, but Fetch couldn't understand anything.

They pointed, his gaze followed, and he understood.

They were preparing to gather their dead.

4 3

Enid was still shuddering from Shrapnel's fate. He'd saved her, but his death had been too grisly to even think about. Climbing out of the riftwing chamber, she'd felt around in the utter darkness and discovered a tunnel larger than the one they'd entered.

That was how the monster made its way in.

Spurred by the knowledge that Shrapnel's dead body was behind her, she made her way out of the cave, stumbling through the undergrowth until she came upon a grisly scene. A body—huge, more than twice her size. It had been wearing some sort of armor and a frightening helmet, but that hadn't done it any good.

It had been cut in two.

There were burns all over the corpse, especially the creepy-looking top half. They looked as if they were caused by some kind of acid.

Like Shrapnel...

Had he really given his life for hers? She'd always thought he hated her and her kind—addicts. It had been pounded into her mind, that they were the worst kind of people, unable to control their own appetites, willing to beg, steal, betray or worse to get what they needed. She'd hated Shrapnel for everything he had done and said to her, all the while knowing that she secretly agreed with him— about her own failure as a human being.

Then, in the end, he had inexplicably been there for her in a way no other person in her life would have even considered.

The lower half of the body was large enough that she could crouch behind it, beneath it, and not be detected. Green blood pooled around it, and she hoped that in the eyes of the monsters she would appear to be part of the corpse—dead and unworthy of any attention.

Now that the sun was up, Enid had more options. For the first time since she'd arrived on LV-363, she had free will. The Khatura was all hers—the vacuum bag was still hanging from her side—but she could also be free of the drug. She could walk away, maybe even escape. People had talked about other harvesting colonies, but she didn't know if they existed, or how far away they would be. Whether the monsters had destroyed them, as well.

Murray might still be there, although he could have taken off while she and Shrapnel had been holed up inside that cave. As long as there was a chance, that would be her best option. She just had to get out of the rift.

If she could walk away right now, if she could dig deep and go straight, pull the willpower from where it had retreated way down inside her brain, then she could finally be free of the parasite that was always on her back, whispering in her ears, lying to her about how everything was going to be okay.

Like it was right now.

Just a little.

She didn't have to overdo it.

Just enough to tide her over.

No, she answered.

Enid ground her teeth together until her jaw ached, hoping the pain would be a diversion. She wouldn't give in. Because of all the shit that had happened, it had been more than twelve hours since her last high. If she could just make it a while, it would be out of her system completely. Thirty hours, they said…

She almost laughed aloud.

Thirty hours.

So much time.

Thirty hours was eighteen hundred minutes. Eighteen hundred minutes was a hundred and eight *thousand* seconds. Each one would be a challenge, and it would get worse as each painful second crawled by. An eternity. It was impossible. One slip, one accidental inhalation, one teeny snort, and the clock would start all over.

Addict math.

Fucking addict math.

She hated the Khatura for it.

She hated herself for it.

Enid hated Murray and the cartel for bringing her to this godforsaken planet, a place where the only thing going for it was a plant that fed the greedy and enslaved the rest. She had had a family, back on the mining platform orbiting the Thuron Gate sun. A son and a daughter. Her husband had long ago disappeared into the bottoms, where he sold his body for Khatura. She'd been the solid one. She'd kept the family unit together, moving on without him.

Then he'd come home and tried to take her son—he'd actually wanted to *sell* the boy so he could get a bigger stash. Enid had said *"Fuck no!"* and a fight had ensued. He'd been bigger than she was and thought he could overwhelm her by sheer weight, but she'd be damned if she'd allow that druggie bastard to come between her love for her family and her responsibility to her children.

Enid had stabbed the sonofabitch as many times as she could before the police broke down the door and relieved her of her knife.

Dirty cops, always dirty cops.

She should've expected it.

They'd taken her into custody, and the captain decided he wanted a piece of her. All her protests and fight had evaporated in a cloud of Khatura, and then *she* was hooked. Used up, abandoned, kicked out and left to beg in the space ports.

Such was life lost.

But she could reclaim it.

Enid scrunched her eyes shut and ran her hands across her face as hard as she could, ignoring the greenish goo that was all over her, thanks to the half-body of the alien. It felt strange to feel the skin of her face against her palms, especially when there was so much Khatura pollen within reach. What, she wondered, did she look like now? She'd been pretty once, with shiny light brown hair and eyes that were a deeper, almost chocolate brown. With her mind clearer than it had been in too long to remember, she could almost recall what she looked like back in the day. And now?

She had to stop herself from braying laughter. Khatura was the greatest thief in the universe, and it sure as fuck hadn't skipped her. Yeah, she still had hair. She fingered one of the thin, filthy strands that poked unevenly out in tufts across her skull. If they had a color, it would be called dirt. Her fingernails were split and discolored, and she didn't want to think too much about the material caked under the edges.

There was movement, and guttural sounds.

Moving slowly, she inched upward until she could see over the ruined corpse. There, about ten meters away, more of the same. The largest—was it a female?—made the loudest sounds, and seemed like the leader. Different species or not, there was no mistaking the furious tones and sharp gestures as she faced off with a smaller one. When the leader pointed in a direction that included the half-body, Enid decided it was time to get out of there.

Taking a quick glance behind and overhead, she managed to ease backward a couple of meters. The rift floor was a mess—broken branches, smashed bushes, and shattered rocks were everywhere. To add to her misery there were splashes of acid blood from the black insect monsters. Each time she touched even the smallest amount, she had to bite her tongue to keep from whimpering.

Finally she slipped behind the wreckage of a spindly, twisted tree that had been uprooted, just a couple of meters from the bottom half of the corpse. The pain was hard to bear, and she fought to keep silent. She just had to hope that the aliens were too busy taking care of themselves to bother about her. After all, as far as she knew, she wasn't on their list of prey or whatever it is they were after.

Licking her cracked lips with a too-dry tongue, Enid kept going.

4 4

His attention fixed on the hunters, Fetch watched them assess their casualties, including the upper and lower pieces—*ugh*—of the one cut down by their laser weapon. But where was the invisible one?

He looked by not looking, took several deep breaths and trusted his peripheral vision, and there it was. Behind a tree by the rift wall, only a couple of meters away. It stood, watching everything.

Fetch didn't move a muscle, and neither did the watcher. There had to be a way to turn what he knew to his advantage. He'd love to sit back and let things take their course, but not here, not now. In this situation, it was better not to leave the vicissitudes of life—especially *his* life—to mere fate. He needed something better, something more realistic. Somehow he needed to introduce his uncanny luck into this game, and make it work for him.

Once before, he'd been in a similar position during a massive game of chance he'd come upon one evening in the bottoms of a station around New Ganymede. While everyone topside was down for the night, stomachs full, thirst quenched, and not even thinking about where their next meal might come from, those on the bottoms were always scrabbling over one another for the simple chance of survival.

Fetch had been on the edge of the ruckus when it broke out.

Thugs vied for the central position so that when the garbage filters rotated and emptied, the garbage would drop right on top of them. Everything spilled from above, from rotten food to half-eaten lunches discarded by the jet set. The largest bullies always claimed the best spots, and when they didn't get what they wanted, they fought for it.

Fetch had been watching the events for a week before he worked out a better way. Rather than wait beneath the scrubbers, it was wiser to wait *above* them. When he confided to one of his frequent cohorts, the man warned him against it.

"It's been tried a bunch of times, but no one ever survives."

He worked the problem out in his head. To survive meant to be able to walk around the grinding gears without being sucked into them. As starving as he was at the time, this seemed like a perfectly reasonable risk. After all, to do nothing was to die; if he died trying this, at least he'd been *doing* something.

Then he had an even *better* idea.

Coming at the problem from a different angle, he had

moved amongst the group waiting for the food to fall. One at a time, he planted the idea in their heads that if they were the first up top, then they'd be able to get the food before the others, before it was mixed and dirty. At first no one listened to him, but when some began to starve because the strongest always held the front ranks, they grew more despondent, and more desperate.

With that desperation came the need to try something new.

Fetch had realized that they'd never be able to effectively retrieve the food before it went into the ever-churning garbage filters. But others didn't, and they began to fall into the mechanism, adding their mass to the rest of the biologicals coming out the bottom, dropping onto the thugs who, at first, didn't realize what was happening.

Finally, the entire mechanism froze.

Because of him. He'd convinced them to jam the system.

The idea had always been to get someone else to do the work.

Once the scrubbers were jammed, he and a few others walked atop the pulped and mashed bodies, and were the first to collect the food—the *only* ones to collect the food. Below them came cries of those who were still hungry.

The filters had lurched. They'd soon be running again.

When they were, Fetch would repeat the process. Until then, his stomach was quite full.

* * *

He pressed the memory back into its slot and took a deep breath, steeling himself for what he was about to do, then pulled himself free from beneath the bush and stood. They spotted him immediately and he held up his hands in the universal symbol of *please don't fucking shoot me.*

Sometimes the way to win at something was not to play, but to get someone else to play in your stead. This was what he would do. If he survived.

Underbrush burned behind them, but they didn't appear to care. He felt his entire body pucker as they brought their weapons to bear on him. Three triangular points of light hovered on his chest; he did all he could not to spin and run. Instead, he opened his hands and held them out so that they could see they were empty, and he was no threat. Then he walked carefully toward them. Once his foot came down on a branch that snapped in the night, as loud as a gunshot.

Everyone jumped.

Fetch remained steady. Had he done otherwise, he was sure he would have been shot. He approached the largest of the hunters. Judging from the curve of the torso, it seemed to be female—though he didn't know the biology of this species any more than he understood the finer points of intergalactic space travel.

She allowed him to get within three meters, then shook her head. She hissed, her body silhouetted by the burning brush.

Fetch stopped and slowly squatted. He never took his eyes off the large hunter. He motioned for her to see what he was doing, then began to draw pictures in the soil. With each picture, he pointed at who he was drawing. First, he drew and pointed to himself. Then he drew and pointed to her. Then he drew the two smaller hunters. He pointed at each picture and their real-life counterpart, over and over until he thought they realized what he was doing.

Then he drew a picture of the one hiding behind the tree, thirty meters away. The female hunter glanced at the location and back at his drawing, then stared at him. Fetch nodded and jerked his head toward where the other hunter was hiding. Then he pointed to the drawing and nodded vigorously.

The female hunter seemed to understand.

She called one of the smaller hunters over and spoke quietly to him. He glanced at the mark on the ground, then toward the tree line where the shadow hid. Fetch thought he saw movement.

The smaller hunter activated the blades in his wrists, and for an instant Fetch thought his heart had stopped. But the leader thumped him on the chest and stopped him where he stood, growling out something in their strange language. Fetch pointed again, more insistently this time.

There were no more threats. He sat back on his heels, and grinned. At least now he was an agent of action, instead of an agent of reaction.

He liked it when he was able to get others to do things that benefitted him.

* * *

Ca'toll glared at the newcomer. From her xenobiological studies, she knew of the oomans, and while she'd known they were busy conducting their own business on the planet, she'd never felt interaction was necessary.

Now this one, a male so puny and looking diseased, had the temerity to come along and act as if they were battlemates. He wasn't armed and was trying to communicate with her.

She watched as he drew and knew immediately what he was trying to relate. She glanced at Vai'ke, who was also watching carefully. Let her eyes range to where the ooman inferred another Yautja stood, but saw only a tree. Was she to believe the ooman? Was there another Yautja, using a cloaking device to avoid being seen?

That was illogical.

Why wouldn't a fellow Yautja reveal him or herself?

Ca'toll's thoughts flashed to Vai'ke, and how he'd pushed Sta'kta in front of the plasmacaster. Her teeth wanted to click inside her helmet but she forced them to be still. Something was going on here that she hadn't yet figured out, and she had a gut feeling she would pay dearly if she didn't do so, and soon.

Why would this ooman want to be involved?

Vai'ke snapped out his wristblades.

"Leave him." Ca'toll stopped him using her combistick to thump his chest. The smaller young blood glared at her. "Let's see what he wants." The ooman cocked his head and gestured again, more emphatically, to the childish drawing and then over toward the trees. Again, Ca'toll glanced in that direction.

There.

Had she seen something? A flash or a movement, a displacement of air? She shook her head and looked back at the small ooman.

He stood, his full height barely coming to her chest. He was as thin as one of the older oomans she'd seen, but had probably yet to see half of his life. He wore a metal mask, one she'd seen others on this planet wearing. Ptah'Ra had said that they were slaves of the stronger oomans who farmed drug pollen that was then taken and sold. She shook her head. It mystified her, the very idea that someone would find their excitement at the end of a leafy plant rather than in battle.

Ca'toll scanned the area around them. She could easily kill the ooman, but he wore no armor and had no weapons. There would be no honor in it. He was not a threat. Such an action would be beneath her.

Without warning, a shriek split the air.

The ooman threw himself to the ground as the plasmacaster tracked something airborne and fired three times, until its power was depleted. The sound of the weapon echoed through the rift, and Ca'toll could feel the hum through her body. A Xenowing suddenly flopped in several pieces along the rift floor.

Vai'ke pointed at the human. "We should kill it."

Ca'toll watched him warily. "Like you killed Sta'kta?"

"That was an accident."

"Was it?"

"You saw it."

"It did not look like an accident."

"What are you trying to say?" Vai'ke asked. He pulled himself to his full height, even though he was still only to her shoulder.

She sneered at him. "I don't believe you are being truthful. I think that's obvious." Without responding, Vai'ke glanced down the rift to where Ny'ytap's body impaled on the tree, several meters away.

"He was a great hunter." Vai'ke made a sound of regret. "It should have been you."

"What do you mean by that?"

"The Xeno should have taken you, not Ny'ytap."

She narrowed her eyes as her tongue ran over the edges of her mandibles. Where was this going?

"Ny'ytap wasn't paying attention. He was too busy celebrating to remember that the battle isn't complete until the ships are back in orbit."

"I watched you," Vai'ke said. "Everyone but you celebrated."

"What was there to celebrate?" She glared at him. "We'd lost a large part of our party. Did you want to lose more?"

"Such is the way of things," he answered impudently. "If everyone could be a young blood, it would hold no honor."

"Still, there is a time for celebration, and a time for care and concern. That was not the time for festivity." Watching Vai'ke carefully, she waited for him to respond, but he went still. It was if he were staring at something behind her. Frowning, Ca'toll turned just in time to get a kick in the face.

Another Yautja!

As befit an experienced hunter, she caught the details even as the kick connected. Finally visible, he was wearing all black—no clan colors. This was what the ooman had been trying to tell her!

She rolled with the kick and let it propel her backward, where she collided with the plasmacaster. She felt the sharp ridges of its hardened shell as her body knocked it aside. Reaching around as she fell, Ca'toll grabbed it, brought it around, and fired. The burst missed, and then there was a dry click.

The weapon needed time to power up.

The razored end of a combistick was turned away by her armor. She yanked up the plasmacaster and let the next blow scrape nastily from the edge, sparks dancing like deadly fireflies in the night.

"Stop!" she bellowed, but if the other heard, he clearly wasn't going to obey. Who was this, and why wasn't Vai'ke coming to her aid? In the corner of her display she saw the young blood. He stood back, arms crossed, as if he'd been waiting for this moment. She wondered what his game was.

To one side, the ooman crawled away. He had tried to help her, and she'd been far too slow on the uptake.

Ca'toll rolled to her left and kicked out at the smug Vai'ke. He jumped out of the way as she regained her feet and threw the plasmacaster at her attacker. Something deflected it and the still-charging weapon flew off to the side.

Then Ca'toll could see her attacker. He was taller than Ptah'Ra had been, wearing all black with red bands down his legs. She'd never seen his colors before, so it was unlikely this was a blood feud. Then what? She flicked open her wristblades.

"Who are you and what do you want?" she demanded. He growled in response and lunged with the extended blade. She leapt to the side. "*Who are you?*" she cried again.

The Yautja attacker ignored her question and went into a full combistick kata that forced her to back away, ending when stopped by a tree. At the last moment she dodged, and the blade scored the tree where her heart had just been beating.

Diving to her right she somersaulted across the ground. He tried to follow, but she was too quick and caught him with a kick to the jaw that sent him reeling. Then Ca'toll jumped and spun again, this time wrapping both her legs around his neck as they both slammed to the earth. She twisted as they fell and landed on his chest, chopping the combistick from his hand. Before he could retaliate, her wristblades were pressed into the flesh just below his helmet.

"I'll ask you again. *Who the* pauk *are you?*"

The answer bubbled from deep in his throat.

"You should know."

"What does that mean?"

"Why don't you tell your young bloods how you left me to die!"

"What?" She had no idea what he was talking about. Then something clicked in her brain, a memory.

Oh, hell.

"Ar'Wen." He laughed and she recognized the sound from decades previous. Abruptly she stood and backed away, retracting her wristblades. *He couldn't be. Could he?* Both her hands went to her head. She removed her helmet.

"Ar'Wen? No—it can't be—"

He mirrored her movement, removing his own helmet.

"You left me," he rasped. "You left me to *die*."

"No! I did no such thing." Ca'toll's thoughts whirled. In her mind she could see the young blood he once was behind the now-adult features. His smiles. His frowns. His laughter. His tears. They'd once been friends. "I saw you go over the edge. You were dead!"

"Far from it, Ca'toll," he said, saying her name like it was a bad taste in his mouth. He pushed to a sitting position. "I was more alive—more in pain—than I ever thought possible. And when I finally recovered, you had already taken the ship back home. You *left* me there."

"That's impossible." She shook her head. "Your indicator lights went dark—the display registered you as dead."

"A malfunction," he hissed.

Part of her was thrilled to see the familiar Yautja in front of her, her battle companion and the one with whom she'd been blooded. The other part was mortified. What if she *had* left him alive? How could she have done such a thing? It was the opposite of honor—it was disgrace. She asked the only thing that came to mind.

"Why did you wait so long to show yourself?"

Ar'Wen had gotten all the way to his feet. "The oomans were terraforming the planet," he answered. "I had to smuggle myself out in one of their ships."

Ca'toll fought to keep her voice steady and strong.

"What have you been doing all this time?"

He appraised her, then hissed. "Working out how I was going to kill you."

"It was an accident!"

He stared at her, motionless, before he finally spoke in a low voice.

"Never leave a body behind."

And there it was, coming back to haunt her. The others didn't know her history—no one did. There'd always been a reason she was so relentless, and that reason was standing right in front of her...

Living proof of her failure.

4 5

The rays of the sun began to slip past the crest of the rift's edge, high above.

The darkness dwellers would seek the shelter of their holes until night fell again. An enormous scar across the surface of the planet, this rift—and others like it—was a deadly place for anything that could become prey. With no place to flee, they'd created ingenious ways to hide from predators.

Like the jivenings—when daylight struck them, they burrowed and pulled the ground over themselves. The only creatures unafraid of the light were the myriad insects that went about their pollination duties and sought to use the light to their best benefit.

* * *

Fetch raked at the side of his metal mask, desperate to be free of it. Not only was the weight becoming unbearable, his body was ringing with the need for

Khatura—triggered by the sudden rush of adrenaline. Hiding behind a tree, he slammed his face several times against it, but to no avail. He managed to dent the mask and make his cheekbones throb, but that was about it.

Meanwhile, the two hunters fought.

The larger of the pair, the one who'd tried to remain hidden, had finally decided to show himself, which meant Fetch had nothing more to offer. To prove the point, the other smaller hunters had descended on cables and appeared on either side of Fetch. Two of them grabbed him by his arms and shoulders and forced him to the ground, while another righted the laser gun.

"Whoa," Fetch protested. "Wait a second—there's no call for that!" For once he wished Shrapnel was around. The big asshole would have been more than happy to fire on the pair. Who knew what they intended to do to him now?

Meanwhile, the two large ones had stopped overt fighting, but judging from the sounds they were making—guttural grunts rising and falling—it seemed as if the violence could erupt again at any moment. They had removed their helmets, revealing deep-set staring eyes beneath thick brows, wide mouths with tusks and pointed teeth, and thick braided hair bordering a spotted bare skull.

If the masks had been fearsome, the faces were the stuff of nightmares.

Fetch willed his luck to return. He needed it to survive, and the way he was being held left it impossible for him to defend himself. He wouldn't stand a chance with these things.

Then something happened he didn't expect.

The smaller hunter, who he had seen collaborating with the invisible one, attacked the female leader from behind. Without warning, he swung a long stick with a meter-long razor spear that sliced through her suit and drew blood.

She leaped away from the assault, then twisted to face both opponents, but the smaller of her two attackers grabbed the newcomer by the arm and they both sprinted for the other side of the rift. A moment later Fetch could hear them climbing noisily upward.

He wished he understood what the hell was going on. Besides a few burning pieces of flora and some eviscerated fauna, there was nothing left here. As if to underscore his worthlessness, the pair who held him let him go and rushed to help their fallen leader. She groaned as she settled back onto the ground. One hunter pulled some kind of spray from a pouch and handed it to the other, who sprayed the wound. Fetch's eyes widened as he watched it close and the blood ceased flowing.

Damn, *that* would come in handy.

Wanting to see more, he started to inch forward then he felt something tug at him. Then another tug, followed by a flash of pain.

Was this how a fish felt?

Fetch turned to glare at whatever was holding him, then realized he was looking directly up at the underbelly of one of the flying monsters. He couldn't stop the scream that bubbled out of him. The laser gun pivoted around and affixed three dots of light on the chest of the creature, just inches above Fetch's head..

"Don't!" he cried, throwing up his hands, even though it would be useless. If they fired, he'd be drenched in an acid bath. He'd much rather a faster death than having his blood, bones, and organs boiled away. In his peripheral vision he saw the female poke her fingers at something on her shoulders. An instant later, the target dots blinked out.

The beast above him focused momentarily on the hunters, giving Fetch the chance to grab one of the claws that had sunk into his shoulder. He felt his way down to where the joint might be, then he twisted with all of his might and brought his metal-encased jaw around and hammered at it, over and over. The thing began to rise into the air and released him, but Fetch didn't let go—they already were six or seven meters above the rift floor. The fall might not kill him, but it would definitely hurt.

Where was his vaunted luck now?

A bolt of energy suddenly struck the rear of the monster's wing, and sheared away its back legs. Its resulting screams overpowered every other sound, and its body spasmed. Acid slid across the side of his facemask and began to burn. A single drop made it inside and landed on his cheek, and Fetch added his screams to those of the creature. Instinctively he jerked as hard as he could to get away and suddenly he was falling, his arms wind-milling, down, down, down—

—into the arms of the female hunter.

They both went down, but where Fetch rolled into a mewling ball, banging his head against the ground to try and stop the acid's pain, she rolled to her feet and lifted a spear weapon from the ground. She whirled it in the air, ready for another attack.

None came.

Fetch clawed at his face and suddenly, blessedly, the metal mask cracked. He pried it open and hurled the pieces as far away as he could. His fingers found where the acid had eaten away his flesh and left a throbbing, raw wound. He'd need to clean it and keep it sterile. He knew where there was a spring, but he couldn't be sure of what lived in the water.

And with the mask off, now—

Fetch's gaze followed the side of the rift upward to where he knew the Khatura flowers grew. A single thought filled his mind. There was no one to stop him from ingesting as much of the magnificent pollen as he wanted. He would be playing into the cartel's hands, he knew that, but the pull of the high was just too rich an opportunity to pass.

Climbing to his feet, Fetch took two steps toward the wall of the rift where a cable dangled, then felt a hand grasp his collar and jerk him back. Wondering who the *fuck* was trying to get between him and euphoria, he spun—

—and looked into the face of the largest hunter.

She hadn't put her mask back on, and her jaws were moving, causing the teeth to clack and look more like mandibles. Four vicious-looking fangs jutted from the gums, which spread wide, and two shorter ones pushed upward from a smaller mouth at the center, with pointy extra teeth adding to the effect.

He didn't want to take too close a look, lest he pass through them on the road to her digestive system. Instead he grinned with false bravado.

"I am Fetch," he said, then he pointed to his chest and repeated it. "I am Fetch."

With her free hand, she pointed to her own chest and responded in a voice that sounded like her mouth was filled with grit.

"I am Fetch."

He grimaced and shook his head "No, no. That's a chest." He made a circle around his smiling face. "Fetch."

She circled her face.

"Fetch."

He groaned and rolled his eyes.

She copied him.

"Stop copying me."

"Stop copying me," she said back in his own words as if it had been recorded—badly.

He pulled carefully out of her grasp, then ran his hand up and down his body.

"This is Fetch," he said, then he picked up a piece of a branch, pointed at it and said, "This is stick." He picked up a rock and said, "This is rock."

"Fetch. Stick. Rock." She nodded, then repeated. "Fetch. Stick. Rock." She nodded again and thumped him hard in the chest. "Fetch."

He staggered, but nodded. "Yes.

She thumped herself in the chest. "Ca'toll."

"Ca'toll," he said, letting his mouth work the letters. "Is that you? Are you Ca'toll?" He glanced at the two younger ones who were watching and pointed at them. "Ca'toll?"

She shook her head. "No. T'See'Ka—" she pointed, "— Ba'sta." She pointed again. Waving her arm to encompass them all, she added, "Yautja."

"You are Yautja," he said. It sounded to his ear like *yowt-jah*. "That must be your species. I am human."

Again she repeated the words. "I am ooman."

He shook his head, which seemed to be a universal non-verbal gesture for *that's wrong*. She gave him what he took for a frown, and he quickly changed his approach, pointing at her.

"Yowt-jah," he said, then he indicated himself. "Oom... er, *human*."

"Yautja," she agreed. "Hunter."

Theirs seemed to be a rudimentary language and Fetch smiled. She mimicked his expression, and the result was genuinely hideous, but he didn't show what he was thinking.

This meant they could communicate. It also meant these creatures must have encountered humans before. Perhaps they even coexisted somewhere in the universe. He started to say just that, then Ca'toll peeled back her mandibles and hissed at the other two, causing them to scamper up the cables.

Perhaps they didn't exactly coexist, but at least they could survive.

4 6

The chasm between who she had been then and who she'd become now, *where* she was now, wasn't lost on Enid. She was standing before a rift, but it was different from the one that was her life—that had been her life for a long time.

On one side was the mother she had been. On the other was the pathetic remnant she'd become, and in the middle? Oh, the middle was the Khatura, the great equalizer. It treated everyone with the same disdain, promising things that were beyond its ability to provide. The great *liar*.

As surely as the monsters below, Enid was at war with herself.

She could feel need prickling across her face, a physical craving for the blush the Khatura would stimulate in her cells. It promised to soothe her, to relieve her of the memories of everyone she had let down. To blot out the shame and the guilt—oh, the *guilt*. In the end her husband had taken not only her son, Daniel, but her daughter Hannah, as well. Between hits—during the few seconds of clear-headedness—Enid had imagined Hannah begging, just as she herself had, and Daniel being used and tossed away like her husband. Then addiction had overtaken her, and all she could do was surrender.

Some things were better left unremembered.

Better left unspoken.

Some things should be forgotten, but they always came back.

Like now.

Her head was clear but her veins were starving. She could almost feel them writhing beneath her skin, screaming for sustenance, as her brain reminded her of all the terrible things she'd done, how she'd abandoned her children for a fleeting chemical euphoria.

She was overwhelmed. By need. By guilt. By both. There was a way to forget, but only if she embraced the inevitable.

Enid had made it to the top, climbing to the harvester nets then using them to cover the remaining distance, and every muscle in her body burned with pain. A couple of meters away from the edge she turned back to the rift, its scar deep upon the planet. The sun still bathed a good portion of the fissure, and winding through the nets were Khatura flowers, all being pollinated by a thousand busy insects.

After everything she'd been through—riftwings and insect monsters, that horrible cave, everything that had tried to kill her—after all that, her vacuum bag full of

Khatura had been with her. A promise, like that last bottle of booze in the ship when you were trying to quit, the one that gave you comfort because you knew if your resolve failed, it was there for you.

Except now it wasn't.

Somewhere during her ascent, the strap had broken. Maybe a branch had snagged it, or one of the innumerable thorns on the ugly plants that grew on this wretched world. She'd tried to grab it, had very nearly jumped after it. In any case, it was gone.

Enid closed her eyes and imaged herself as one of those insects, flying from plant to plant, her legs thick with pollen, transferring, propagating, then returning to the hive to feed a queen.

If only she had been a queen.

But she *was*. She was all of it—queen, jack, and joker.

* * *

Enid was climbing back down the side of the rift before she registered what she was doing. Then she was face-to-face with a bloom, the large, creamy petals cradling a pirouetting insect inside. That forced her to wait, but not long enough to change her mind.

When the stinger-loaded bug flew to the next bloom, Enid buried her face in the flower and inhaled. When she pulled back an instant later, a ray of sun lit the pollen as it danced across the air in front of her face.

She'd once had children.

Daniel. Hannah. Those children—

—she couldn't remember.

All that existed was her, the center of a halo of golden light. All at once, her energies were at one with the planet as she inhaled more of the bounty it so gloriously provided. All was well in the world.

All was well.

From below came a shriek.

She inhaled and laughed.

She'd once been a—

What had she been?

Did it really matter?

She was living in the now.

Now. Now. Now. Now. Now.

Forever and ever in the now.

4 7

The ooman seemed harmless, but Ca'toll was a warrior and warriors were trained to trust no one but their *mei'hswei*—their brothers. Her young bloods still wore their helmets, and their displays would have indicated if their unwelcome visitor had a weapon, but he was unarmed and posed no immediate threat.

That meant it would be dishonorable to simply eliminate him and be done with it. She wanted to tell him to leave and not come back, but she didn't know the right words for it in his language. She'd tried gesturing that he should go—as in anywhere but here—but in response he just kept stretching his lips, showing his teeth, and moving his head up and down. As a result, she had no idea what to do with him, or about him.

So here he remained.

Hissing under her breath, Ca'toll decided to continue with the things they needed to do. Ar'Wen's appearance had shaken her to the core, but she could not allow that to cause her to shirk her duty. She was a hunt leader.

"It is time to retrieve the bodies of our dead," she told the remaining four young bloods. While she donned her helmet and reconnected the display to the links on her shoulder, Ptah'Ra, Ba'sta, Stea'Pua and T'See'Ka pulled in a little closer, waiting solemnly for her instructions. "That one," she glanced at Fetch, as the human had referred to himself, "is *hulij-pe*—unhinged. We must all be aware of him at all times. Never trust him."

"Can we not just kill him?" T'See'Ka asked. "Leave him as *amedha* for the beasts of this planet to feast upon? He is an annoyance."

Ca'toll lifted her head and stared hard at him. "You speak of a dishonorable act. Would you follow one affront with yet another? You took credit for a kill that should have been credited to Stea'Pua." Before he could jump out of the way, she was directly in front of him; an instant later she slammed her helmet against the bridge of his. T'See'Ka staggered backward. "How can you call yourself a *sain'ja* when you would kill a defenseless animal? That is not the action of a warrior."

T'See'Ka found his place again, although she could tell he was uncomfortable standing that close to her. And he could not let it go.

"But if we must watch him at all times, he will hinder us, don't you see?" he said, his voice whiny and testing her patience. "We might miss an attack, or—"

"Silence!" Ca'toll's frustration with him showed in her voice and she inhaled deeply, fighting against anger so that she could return to teaching mode. "You must learn to balance multiple tasks, and at all times. It does not matter if one of them is *inconvenient*. As a warrior you must be able to track everything in your surroundings, no matter how trivial." She stared at T'See'Ka until, finally, he lowered his head in submission.

Ca'toll stepped back, noting the wariness among the other young bloods and the way they tracked T'See'Ka—more watchful of him than the human about which he complained. Disappointment flared through her—this was not supposed to be the prevailing mood at the end of a hunt. Regret at those they had lost, yes, but at the same time jubilation, the pleasure of youth knowing that they had progressed along the long and difficult path toward their destinies as the galaxy's greatest and most feared hunters.

"Return to the task at hand," Ca'toll instructed. "Now is the time we gather our fallen Yautja and return them to the ship. We will leave no one's body behind." The irony in her words stung harshly, but she did not let it show.

"Hunt Captain?"

She turned her head to regard Ba'sta. "Speak."

"Our team's hunting captain—"

"Ny'ytap."

"Yes. He was—is—suspended in the foliage back there." Ba'sta gestured with one hand. "He may be—"

"It is a certainty that Ny'ytap is dead," T'See'Ka interrupted with a shrug, "and there is likely very little left of him. He was spiked on a tree and dying, when one of the half-riftwing, half-Xenomorph creatures began feeding on him. He has most certainly become *amedha*." He shot a glance at the human, who still hovered close to their group. "A salvage attempt would be useless, a waste of time." He shrugged again, this time with more emphasis. "We would be scraping his pulped remains into containers using the edges of our blades. No one wants to do this."

T'See'Ka's words made the other three young bloods hiss almost in unison, and for a moment Ca'toll was so angry she froze.

But only for a moment.

Then she was in front of him again, the talons at the end of her left hand digging into his throat.

"You are an *ui'stbi*," she hissed. "An abomination. How dare you say such a thing." T'See'Ka didn't move, but this time he stared back at her with his head held high.

"You talk about dishonor," he said. "Wasn't it you who left Ar'Wen behind?" He glanced at the others, who all nodded.

Ca'toll hissed and felt like squeezing the life out of the disrespectful young blood, but...

The truth was that he couldn't—and shouldn't—be punished for telling the truth, no matter the effect it had on her.

"Do you want to make my mistake, then?" she demanded. "How do you think I will feel going forward? I feel as if I dishonored Ar'Wen, and that is something I have to live with. Would you choose that for yourself?"

"You have the *yin'tekai* of a *zabin*," T'See'Ka declared. "The honor of an insect. Why should I listen to you? Why should *any* of us? T'U'Sa was my hunting captain—not you. A Yautja without honor is worthless."

She laughed, and the sound was unpleasant.

"Now you choose to speak of *yin'tekai*. You, who wanted to leave a hunt leader, whether he was dead or alive. You are the *zabin*. You are the creature that goes about his business without care for anyone but himself, thinking that competence is all you need. There is more to being a Yautja than being *competent*, Young Blood."

It was his turn to laugh. "Says the one who left her best friend behind."

"Enough of this," Ca'toll said. "You are insubordinate. Whatever my actions were then, I have reclaimed them now. I have shown honor and have lived honorably. You are seeking *u'sl-kwe*, and if it is your final rest you desire, I can make that happen."

"I am only being honest," he responded. "I am the only one brave enough to say that which we all believe."

"No." Stea'Pua stepped forward. "You are incorrect." All eyes turned toward him—even the ooman's. There was curiosity there.

"Perhaps I should not speak for the others who are gathered here," Stea'Pua continued, "but I will not be included in your disgraceful conduct. We heard and understood what she did before. It was done without intention. What you wish to do now is with intention. There is a difference."

Ptah'Ra nodded. "Nor shall I."

T'See'Ka said nothing, still standing rigidly beneath Ca'toll's nails.

Ba'sta, the smallest of them, surprised Ca'toll with his next, bold words.

"I believe you have another motivation, T'See'Ka," he said. "I believe you do not want to gather our deceased comrades because you are a coward, and are afraid to face the Xenomorphs and the riftwings again. Just as when you did not retrieve T'U'Sa's body after his death. You are *h'ko yeyindi*, and I do not associate with cowards."

T'See'Ka growled his rage and tried to push Ca'toll away.

"*Ell-osde' pauk!* Let me go, bitch."

"I will not." She stepped back, but pulled him with her. Her right hand slid around his waist and they stood, helmet to helmet, almost like mates in a farewell embrace. Then Ca'toll let go of T'See'Ka's throat and shoved him backward.

He faltered for a moment, then suddenly his legs buckled and he sat down hard. Bright green blood pumped from a deep wound that started just under his armor in the center of his waist, and didn't end until the spinal bone on his back halted it. T'See'Ka looked down and saw his internal organs slip into his lap in a slick puddle of flesh.

Without a word of warning, Ca'toll had gutted him.

Ca'toll re-sheathed her ceremonial dagger. It had been a very long time since she had used it. With her move into blooding, rather than hunting, she hadn't felt the need to take trophies. She would use it to take the head of a Xenowing on this trip, but only because it represented a new species. It would also ensure that the last blood on its blade was not from a Yautja.

Regrettably, T'See'Ka couldn't even die with honor. Instead he reached out, trying to grab at anything and showing his pain as he implored the other young bloods to help him. No one moved, and no one tried to assist him. If any of them disagreed with her actions, none said so.

With the others, she watched T'See'Ka die. She felt no sadness, and certainly no guilt. If there was anything in her heart, it was regret that he had been born without regard for the laws of the Yautja. Young bloods had much to learn, and in experiencing the hunt itself—especially during blooding—mistakes often happened.

Ny'ytap had granted T'See'Ka leeway, and though she disagreed, Ca'toll had done the same. But she had been unable to make him comprehend his own behavior, and preferring to leave his hunt captain to the creatures of this planet had been the most incontrovertible evidence that he was irredeemable.

She'd had enough.

When T'See'Ka's had breathed his last, Ca'toll finally looked up at the others.

"To speak of this will bring great shame upon his family," she told them. "This we will not do. We will bring his body to the ship with the others, and it will be written in the records that T'See'Ka's life was ended in combat." Her gaze stopped on each one. "Is this understood?" When they indicated they did, and only then, did Ca'toll turn away. "Then let us begin retrieving the bodies of our fellow Yautja."

The ooman called Fetch was still standing in place; his eyes were wide and fearful—as they should be. For a moment she considered ordering him to assist in the collection, then realized how inadequate he would be. He was thin to the point of emaciation, and looked as if he could barely haul himself up one of the oomans' nets, much less carry even part of the body weight of a Yautja.

He was one of their species who ingested chemicals on a regular basis, substances that were neither necessary nor beneficial. Although they had encountered the oomans many times over the centuries, this particular aspect of their behavior remained a mystery. While she wasn't considering killing him, she *was* beginning to feel some of the frustration T'See'Ka had espoused.

Why wouldn't the ooman just go away?

Ca'toll clicked her mandibles in annoyance and turned. For now the creatures of the rift had ceased their attack, or perhaps their numbers had thinned to the point where they no longer had the courage. Taking advantage of the lull, the young bloods gathered the grisly remains, strapped them to their backs, and began the upward climb. One hand was kept free, in case the attacks resumed.

Before joining them, she stood over the massive, dead Xenowing she had killed. Ca'toll had already claimed a trophy from a traditional Xenomorph, but its importance paled when compared to this new mutation. She pulled out her ceremonial dagger. Two strokes later, the creature's head was suspended from her fist.

The dagger had been used as it was intended, wiping the blade free of the corruption of T'See'Ka's dishonorable blood.

Good riddance.

INTERLUDE

Ar'Wen watched the entire confrontation, from the moment T'See'Ka rose on his heels to challenge Ca'toll, to his eventual demise. The young blood had fallen victim to her dagger. She had never been one for patience.

Ca'toll was old school. She believed in blood feuds, and in a concrete right and wrong. As with T'See'Ka, she would offer a warning, and if that went unheeded, she would remove any opponent from the Yautja lifecycle, his body brought back in dishonor so that it could be torn asunder and thrown into a volcano. That accomplished, it would disintegrate into its finer qualities before the cycle began again.

In truth Ar'Wen admired her. It would be a loss to the Yautja when he killed her, but just as she didn't allow disrespect to occur without retribution, neither would he. In fact, she had done far worse than disrespect him— she had *dishonored* him. She seemed to have forgotten him entirely, even though the arc of his life was carved into the universe by her own artifice.

He had no doubt that if their situations were reversed, she would respond in the same fashion he had devised. He wondered if he really had been planning for this meeting all of these intervening years. Putting together the pieces, becoming one of the coveted seeders for the hunts, all the while knowing that eventually he and Ca'toll would meet in some fashion or another.

The synchronicity was just too perfect.

Ar'Wen squatted on a wide tree branch, again invisible to the naked eye. He watched the young bloods retrieve the dead. First they went in pairs to retrieve the bodies, then laid them out at the top of the rift. Once all the dead—and pieces—had been accounted for, the corpses were hauled through the dense foliage to the ship, where they were taken into the hold and, he assumed, placed in cryogenic tubes to halt decomposition.

Although he couldn't see the faces behind their helmets, he was a good enough reader of Yautja character to understand when someone was recalcitrant. Ca'toll had shown them more in the last two rotations of the planet than they had learned their entire adult lives.

There were no takebacks.

Stupid got you killed.

Dying was forever.

Now that they had learned the basic secrets of the universe, it was time for Ar'Wen to present himself so that Ca'toll could be taught the same. For no matter what good she'd done in her life, it didn't remove the fact that everything she'd done as an adult had been predicated by leaving him behind, and by a lie that he couldn't in good conscience allow to remain unrevealed.

Ar'Wen toggled off his cloaking and leaped down from the tree. It was time to engage. This would be the culmination of more than fifteen years of rage, and Ca'toll would be the worse for it.

4 8

Following her directions, the young bloods completed the final, unpleasant trip back from the bottom of the rift to the ship, when Ca'toll turned and saw Vai'ke trying to slip quietly back among the group. When he realized she'd seen him, he straightened to his full height.

"Stop," she said sharply. "You are not welcome or wanted here."

He cocked his head to one side. "You are incorrect," he said. "I am Yautja."

"You are *ic'jit*—bad blood," she shot back. "Bow your head in shame and leave us."

In response, one of Vai'ke's big hands went to his neck and he disengaged his helmet. He lifted it from his head and while staring at her, flung it aside. Then he flexed his back and his mandibles flared at her as he dropped into an attack stance, combistick out and set.

"What do you think you are doing?" Ca'toll demanded. "Stand down, young blood." She had no time for a rogue Yautja. There were preparations to be made so that the bodies could be put into the cryonic chambers, functions to be activated, and a trajectory sequence plotted to guide their ship back to the mothership.

Although she would always cherish the hunt, she'd had enough of this despicable planet and its overage of death and humans and betrayal. It was past time to return to Yautja Prime, where the elders would be expecting a full accounting of the successes and failures of the mission—and there were many.

That Ny'ytap and Ta'U'Sa weren't there to recount them meant she would bear the brunt of whatever anger the elders would feel at the end. So be it. Right now she had to deal with the traitorous Vai'ke. Instead of responding in like, Ca'toll stayed where she was, waiting.

"I know what you did," Vai'ke spat when she didn't come at him. He eased out of full attack posture, but she could tell he was still ready to fight. "You are the worst of us. Do you really think you can make up for what you did?"

Her jaw flared in anger. Ar'Wen—this had to be his doing.

"What is it you *think* you know, Young Blood?"

"I know that when you went for your blooding you cheated." Vai'ke switched the grip on his combistick, keeping it light. "You were never blooded." He lifted his head triumphantly. "You returned unblooded, but claimed the blooding!"

Ca'toll's jaw tightened. Her greatest secret. Something for which she'd spent her entire life trying to make amends. When a rescue team had found her, wandering and covered in blood, with a head wound that made it nearly impossible for her to communicate, every indication had been that she had become blooded. There were no witnesses—but that meant nothing under the honor code of the Yautja. She herself had believed it for a long while, but the more time passed and the longer she pondered it, the less certain she became.

Until one day she became positive.

She had never finished her ceremony.

At first she did not know what to do. Go to the elders and tell them they had made a mistake? That they needed to allow her to return to the planet, and embark on a new blooding? She'd already been treated as a young blood. The entire hierarchy of her family would come down—they would be shamed. She would break that which should never be broken… their honorable way of life.

When she *did* try to reconcile it with her family, the result had been disastrous. Ca'toll had since been blooded a hundred times over, but her worst memory, her worst fear, was being thrown in her face by a rat-faced, soulless Yautja young blood. A youth who did not know. She would have to address this here and now.

"With whom have you discussed it?" she asked. She kept her voice calm when her insides felt as if they were shaking with fury.

The truth…

"So, you don't deny it?" Vai'ke responded, knowing that the other young Yautja were carefully following the conversation.

"I do not answer to you."

"Clearly you don't believe you answer to anyone." Vai'ke sounded triumphant.

Ca'toll lifted her head. "You've been listening to the wrong Yautja."

"Does he lie?"

"He doesn't know half of what he thinks he knows."

"But does he *lie*?" Vai'ke gaze was fierce. *"Did you fail your blooding?"*

This was the moment. She could find a way to deflect it, or she could face up to what she had done—and *hadn't* done. Ar'Wen's return certainly wasn't going to make her life easy. Then again, she *had* left him behind. Hadn't informed anyone that he might still alive. As such, she'd let down her clan, and she'd failed him.

"Did you complete your blooding?" Vai'ke demanded again.

"No," she said simply. "I did not." Vai'ke seemed displeased at her response, because for a few seconds he had nothing to say. He might have been hoping for more verbal sparring, but she was past that.

"Then I must place you under guard, to return to answer for your crime against the clan." He retracted his combistick and stepped closer to her.

"You will do no such thing." Ca'toll stared him down. "You do not have the authority. If I am going to return home and speak with the clan elders, then I shall answer for my past actions with my head held high."

Vai'ke shook his head. "You have no choice in the matter," he said flatly. He held out a hand. "Pass over your weapons."

Now she laughed. "You have a better chance at mating with a Xenomorph," she said. Her mandibles clicked rapidly.

"There is nothing amusing about this situation," he said.

She stopped laughing, but only with great effort.

"I will never give in to the likes of *you*."

Vai'ke glanced at the remaining young bloods. Ptah'Ra, Ba'sta, and Stea'Pua made a half circle behind Ca'toll's back.

Stea'Pua seemed ready to fight, but Ptah'Ra and Ba'sta clearly wanted to be somewhere else. And who blamed them? They'd just been informed their hunt leader—the only one remaining—had not fulfilled the initiation ceremony they had been required to complete. This rendered her a false example.

And yet, everything they'd endured together had still earned her their respect.

"Then I will be forced to take you in," Vai'ke said. He seemed to puff out his chest. For a second, Ca'toll was speechless.

"Don't be foolish. You can't take me."

"I am a young blood," he said proudly. "Unlike you."

"I was never a young blood, but I went straight to hunter. Think about that a moment, Vai'ke," she said, the last heavy with emotion. "The past is what it is. Do you think I'm proud of it?" she asked. "Do you think I would do it again? It was not my choice. I was badly injured and removed from the ceremonial field, never given the opportunity. If anything, my chance at blooding was stolen from me."

"That excuse would have been valid had you informed the elders the moment you realized the truth of it," Vai'ke said, nodding pointedly toward the other young bloods. Ca'toll sighed. Ar'Wen had stirred the pot so that the feasting insects would never be able to land. She saw where this was heading and she didn't like it—not at all.

"Do you really want to do battle with me?" she asked. She studied him, but saw only an inexperienced youth. "You are not thinking clearly. I have hundreds of bloodings to the few you have accumulated here, on this wretched planet."

"None of your bloodings count."

Surely he wouldn't be so foolish as to believe that. Would he?

She snapped her combistick out to full length.

"I urge you again not to do this. I have every intention of returning to Yautja Prime. If you feel it is your right, you may accompany us, to tell your story." That decision stung, but it was necessary. "Know, however, that when we do, you will be expected to confess to the murder of Sta'kta."

Vai'ke growled in his throat. "That was an accident."

"You lie."

In an instant Vai'ke's mandibles flared in rage. Then he extended his combistick, arched his back—and lunged.

Ca'toll easily swept the strike aside. Vai'ke reversed the combistick, tried again, and again she knocked it to the side.

"Do you not remember who taught you how to fight?" she asked. Her voice held more than a bit of sarcasm. "Ny'ytap and I trained and hunted together. I know all of your moves." In response, Vai'ke leaped to the left and swept the combistick along the ground, trying to trip and injure her at the same time. The attempt cost him dearly when Ca'toll easily skipped over it and came down with her own weapon, sliding it down his shoulder just outside of his armor.

Unused to such injury, Vai'ke cried out as it parted flesh.

A split second later he hooked one leg over her stick, trapping the weapon. Ca'toll's eyes went wide. This was a move favored by Ar'Wen, and something neither Ny'ytap nor she had taught him. She was forced to release her weapon and dive to her left as Vai'ke brought his own combistick down to his right.

She rolled and came to a standing position, facing Vai'ke as he held both combisticks.

Although his tactic had surprised her and gained him another weapon, Ca'toll knew Vai'ke did not have the advanced training to wield both at the same time. Feinting to her right, she saw him almost drop her stick as he tried to follow her movement. She feinted again and he swiped downward.

Ca'toll allowed the combistick to hit the ground and vaulted over it, using Ar'Wen's move against Vai'ke. Then she spun, twisting the stick out of the bad blood's hand. She bounded backward so quickly that Vai'ke's own momentum made him fall forward. Before he could regain his balance and stand, she thrust her combistick forward and down at an angle through Vai'ke's neck. The power of the blow pushed the combistick's blade all the way through his torso and out his lower back.

Vai'ke stumbled away from her.

"This... this..."

Ca'toll shook her head. "I know," she said, experiencing genuine sadness. "This is not how your blooding was supposed to end." She approached him and placed a hand on his head. "I am truly sorry, Vai'ke. You are as much a victim as I am in this. Ar'Wen used you to try and exact a revenge to which he really has no right."

Vai'ke sank to his knees. He coughed. Rich, green blood sprayed from his mouth and down his chest. Then, without a sound, he fell to the side and died.

Ca'toll and the remaining young bloods stared at the body in silence, then stepped away from the corpse and turned to face them. "Am I to face more battles? If so, let us commence now and be done with it."

They looked at her and without hesitation shook their heads.

"Then get behind me," she said and motioned to the area between her and the ship. "This situation remains unfinished." When they were in place, she faced the tree line. "Ar'Wen," she called out. "I see now what you have been trying to do. I think it's well past time we had… a discussion."

The only response was the sigh of the wind and a faraway *JAI-REEE!*

"Enough, Ar'Wen," Ca'toll said angrily. "Are you going to slink around until our departure, and then leave via your own ship? Or you have your own unblooded, or brand new young bloods do more of your dirty work?' She gave a caustic-sounding laugh. "Somehow I don't believe you are as resourceful as you want everyone to think you are."

A figure slipped out of the trees ten paces in front of her.
"Ca'toll."

She hadn't had enough time in the rift to really examine him. He was taller and more built out, but other than that, he hadn't changed much.

"*Mei'hswei*," she said. *Brother*.

He hissed at her. "I should leave you here and tell them you are dead."

Ca'toll looked at him, unfazed.

"That wouldn't be the truth."

"The truth?" He laughed roughly. "Where is the truth here? You cheated and you had a life. You left me and I had to run for mine. Run for fifteen years."

Ca'toll tilted her head. "There was no need. You could have chosen to return to Yautja Prime—there were ways. You chose not to. You chose to run. You *chose* to be a *bha'ja*—a ghost."

Ar'Wen just nodded. "That I did, and now it's time for a reckoning."

4 9

Enid came back to herself rolled into a tight ball. She was lying, literally, in the center of a large and very prickly bush on the outskirts of where they had all been camped. Her eyes were at ground level and she could see through the branches that there was nothing salvageable.

Within a pall of slowly dissipating smoke, the tents had been flattened and torn, and the cooking equipment overturned and strewn in all directions. At the same time, it sank into her brain that she was unlikely to find anything of use among the mutilated piles of bloody fabric and body parts, too many to count.

She shuddered and tried to move. Pain streamed along her limbs and the back of her neck, even along her scalp. She stopped, finally realizing that, although her position in this overgrown scrub provided a decent hiding place, it had also been an extremely poor choice as far as self-harm went. Of course, she didn't remember choosing it, so her Khatura-soaked brain probably hadn't been registering much of anything as the ragged branches and nasty thorns carved a new landscape into her ragged skin.

Well, she could grit her teeth against the sting and get the hell out of here, or lie here and die. The planet wouldn't care either way.

But did *she*?

Sucking in air, Enid decided she did. She wanted to live. Yeah, she had given in to the call of the Khatura yet again, and maybe she would always be an addict, but she didn't want to die on this rock and become riftwing food.

Checking her pockets, she found that she still had the card she'd taken from Shrapnel. Was the ship still here? There was only one way to find out.

Extracting herself wasn't easy. Her vision was rolling, making her dizzy, and her muscles desired nothing more than to just stay put. The branches wanted to pop and crack, and she was terrified the noise would be heard by monsters, riftwings, or that freaky, flying combination of the two.

As scared as she was, she finally extricated herself and squatted next to the bush for a few moments, trying to pant through the throbbing wounds that stippled her skin. There was plenty of blood, oh yeah. It ran down her arms and legs and made little pools around her grubby shoes. She had nothing to wrap herself with and the truth was she didn't care enough. Could the creatures of this place *smell* her blood?

It was a definite possibility, so it was time to get moving. If the ship was still here, she would find it.

* * *

Her memory was spotty, so it took Enid more than an hour to make her way to the ship. Fear twisted in her stomach the entire time. At any moment she expected to feel the ground vibrate as the ship's engines fired up, to hear—as well as feel—the painfully loud *boom* as Murray lifted the vessel off the damned planet and left her behind forever.

But there was the ship. Enid wanted to beat feet straight to the main hatch and hammer on it, but she hesitated. Making a lot of noise might be the worst thing she could do, short of standing in front of the cockpit window while screaming and waving her arms.

Hello monsters and riftwings; goodbye Enid.

Caught in her own indecision, she stayed still for quite some time, her head cocked, listening for any sound other than the wind. It was hard because of how high she still was. Everything was tinged with the full spectrum of colors. If she glanced too fast in one direction there was a kaleidoscope smear across her vision that caused her to both grin and groan, as if she was aboard a ship and it wouldn't stop rocking.

The clearing around the ship was empty of man or beast, although there was plenty of churned-up earth to evidence previous activity. The main door was closed and no doubt locked, and as far as she could tell—which admittedly wasn't much—there was no one in the cockpit. There were cameras all around the spacecraft and she knew there was no way to approach it without being seen—but that was a good thing, right?

Whoever was on board certainly had nothing to fear from her, a skinny addict who didn't have the strength to pick up and aim a weapon. Had she even possessed one. Which of course she didn't.

But it was so... *quiet.*

She touched her face and sighed. Oh, but her fingers felt so good. She squeezed her cheeks. Had they ever been so big—so soft and tender? She realized then that her nose was numb. She couldn't smell anything but the lingering scent of Khatura pollen.

Finally Enid shuffled forward, taking painfully small steps. She craned her neck and watched the sky until her muscles twinged, but there was nothing—no riftwings, no monstrous, mutated insect-things. She made it to within a meter of the ship, but nothing leaped from the tree line, nothing skittered toward her from the bushes.

Just empty, eerie silence.

She swallowed and crossed her arms, her ragged fingernails digging into her skin. She wanted to run to the back of the ship as fast as her almost-useless legs would take her, but she was afraid that too much active movement would draw unwanted attention from the things she most feared, as well as a thousand others she likely didn't even know about. Instead she moved slowly, carefully, crossing the intervening distance and making her way along the hull.

Tension made her ears ring, the whine so loud she wondered if she'd even hear one of this planet's nasties coming for her.

A few feet beyond the first cargo door Enid halted, her jaw dropping. Her objective was just ahead, but she wasn't going to need that passcode after all. There was something... some*one*... there, waiting for her. Was it a person?

After another fearful scan of the sky, she made herself move until she reached the body—or what was left of it—in front of the cargo door. There wasn't much to the remains, just small pieces in a wide, thick pool with jagged, uneven edges that made it look like something had... *played* in it. She tried to imagine one of the monsters doing that, flying or otherwise, and couldn't—they were all business. Bite, kill, eat. Was there something else, something *new*, on this hellish world?

Who had this been? Had they exploded? Spontaneous human combustion. The idea made her giggle and she covered her mouth with her right hand. She shouldn't laugh at people exploding. Such a messy business. After all, she might be next.

Sucking in a breath, Enid finally made herself move closer, where she discovered she hadn't yet been shocked to the maximum, after all.

Now that she'd closed the distance, saw that the cargo door *wasn't* shut—at least not completely—and she understood why. The dead puddle—*man*—the exploded human—was the big boss, Murray.

His boot was the identifying factor. Lightweight and expensive, way too high-end for any of the mercs to be able to afford. The light tan color of the synthetic leather was blotched with mud and scarlet, and a number of other mystery things she would never care to identify. His initials were branded in ornate letters around the back of the ankle.

There was only one boot...

With his foot still inside it, wedging the cargo door open.

That was it for Murray, all that was left. Enid had never known his last name and couldn't begin to guess at it, especially since only the "M" was still visible—the other two letters had been obliterated by muck and, well, teeth marks.

She stepped over the boot and into the cargo bay. She was *in*. Against all odds, she'd made it there even without Shrapnel's passcode—but she still had to close the door, to keep out any unwanted visitors.

A childhood song came to her about a little boy with just one shoe. She started to hum it, then covered her mouth again, this time with both hands as she looked toward the sky. She had to be super quiet. No telling when one of the flying monsters would return.

She glanced down at the key card.

The *useless* damned key card.

She let it slip through her fingers and watched as it hit Murray's leg and tumbled outside.

Moving the appendage was probably the most difficult thing she'd ever done, but the fact that there was nothing else to be seen that could identify Murray, especially his face, made it something she could accomplish... barely. Even so, she had to tug and twist it to make it come loose, an effort that almost landed her on her ass in the smelly muck that represented the rest of him.

With his foot finally out of the entrance, Enid felt some of her anxiety let go. The door slid shut of its own accord.

"Thank you, Murray. You were a complete and terrible asshole of a man, but you were all we had. You could have killed us or thrown us down the rift or spaced us. I know we were a pain in your ass, but we really didn't—"

She forgot what she was saying.

Enid turned and headed into the cargo bay...

Only to be confronted by the worst thing she could imagine. She didn't know if it was real or Khatura-induced, but it didn't matter.

It was there, and it was waiting for her.

5 0

"I'm afraid this isn't the surprise you'd hoped it would be," Ca'toll said.

"What does that mean?" Ar'Wen faced her, standing with his own modified combistick. It appeared as if both ends held blades that were electrified. Thin, jagged bolts of energy danced, then faded across the mean edges of the blades. He'd already removed his helmet. Ca'toll took off her own helmet and tossed it aside. She let her mandibles flare as she hissed her anger from deep inside.

"I knew you had been rescued. I knew you were alive."

He flared his mandibles, as well.

"How did you come by this knowledge?"

"When you were rescued, they held a special court for me where I had to answer for my actions. They wanted to know why I left you behind. I told them the truth and I was acquitted."

"And what was your *truth*?" he demanded. The word sounded like poison coming from his mouth.

"That I tried to get you to return with us, but you were too battle hungry to listen."

He laughed and nodded. "I certainly enjoyed the flavors of blood, when I was younger."

"Still, I regret leaving you behind. I never should have done it."

"No," Ar'Wen said. "You and the others should have found a way to bring me back. I was at the crossroads of my own sanity."

"You threatened to kill me if I attempted to force you. You were so enamored with killing." Ca'toll shook her head. "You were blood crazed."

"You could have figured something out." He scowled at her. "You gave up."

She sighed. "As you can see," she said to the three young bloods, "nothing is black and white. Everything is a shade of gray."

"Yet gray is still a color one should attend to," Ar'Wen told her.

"If you think I feel sorry for you, then you are significantly mistaken." She shook her head. "I understand that I should not have left you behind. I own that. I've never done such a thing again, nor shall I."

"Could it be that you left me behind because I knew your secret?" he asked. His gaze was sly as he twirled his combistick with false nonchalance.

"Not at all," Ca'toll replied. "For years I thought of little else. I considered that might be true. Wondered if it were, and imagined myself doing it subconsciously. But you see, I recovered my wits, and admitted my doubts about my blooding to my hunt captain before we reached the home planet. So there was no secret.

"What he chose to do with the information is not for me to know," she continued, "because I never saw him again. After I returned, I went back as a hunt lieutenant and immediately achieved my first kill. In fact, I completed my first eighteen kills within a very short time." She took a step forward. "Ar'Wen, your words have no power over me."

"All this is as you tell it," he said, but she could hear the confidence bleeding from his words. "That does not make it true."

"I've never lied." She stood straight and tall. "I've owned up to my actions. Tell us, do you remember what you told those who rescued you?"

He pulled himself up and puffed out his chest.

"I told them I was left behind."

"And was that true?"

"Yes, it was."

"Yet whose fault was it? Are you really going to say it was my fault, because I didn't sneak up on you, hit you over the head, truss you up, and lock you in the hold?"

He glanced at the ground. "No, not as you say it."

"Is there any other way?"

"Perhaps not," Ar'Wen replied. His voice was losing volume.

"Then I am innocent of your charges," Ca'toll said firmly, "and always have been."

"No." He shook his head. "No. You were my sister," he said, his voice filled with emotion. "We were to be responsible for each other. You *failed*."

"And because of that, our parents never spoke to me again." She pointed her combistick at her brother. "I have not had contact with them in years. That is *your* fault."

Ar'Wen was silent for a moment

"I went to them after I returned."

"You did?" Ca'toll's eyes widened. "What did they say?"

"They wouldn't speak to me." Again he looked down. "They said they had already had... my funeral. I was dead to them."

Her mandibles flared. "So much like Father," she growled. "Even if he was wrong, he always refused to reconsider, once he made a decision."

"Mother agreed." Ar'Wen's voice was gravelly.

She shook her head. "What are you going to do?"

His head raised and he met her eyes.

"For a very long time I have wanted to fight you."

Ca'toll felt a stab of regret, but she didn't back down. "Does that mean it's too late for us, brother?"

"It was too late the moment you left me."

"Then we should get on with it." She glanced at the sky. "None of us wish to be attacked like Ny'ytap was."

"He was a bully," Ar'Wen said. "He got what he deserved."

"He was a bully when he was young," Ca'toll agreed, "but he became a great hunting leader. We all change, brother."

"I haven't." He glared at her.

"It's because you left the best of yourself back on that planet," she told him. "Who you were then—as impetuous as you could be—you were my brother."

"And now?" His hand tightened around the combistick.

"I don't know who you are."

"Now who sounds like Father?"

"You." Ca'toll regarded him solemnly. "You refuse to even consider changing your mind."

Ar'Wen snarled at her, then lifted his combistick above his head and spun it. Both blades sizzled with electric energy. Regretfully she stepped back, holding her stick at the ready. She could not bring herself to make the first strike, so she would begin in defensive mode.

Lower mandibles flared, he came toward her. Ar'Wen was perfectly on balance, his combistick flowing through an offensive kata that forced her to back away, then at the last moment dive to her left. She brought her own stick down in an attempt to trap his, but she was a second too late, ending up backpedaling until she was against a tree.

Ar'Wen came in high and she swung low, but he caught her stick between his legs and twisted it from her grip. Instead of using it, he tossed it to the ground and stepped over it. If she wanted it, she'd have to take him down.

Ca'toll backed away and put her hands up, ready to parry. She could use her wristblades, but those were reserved for creatures, genuine prey, not her brother. Leaving the tree behind, she began moving left and right and making him turn back and forth, not giving him a moment where she would be an easy target.

He swung once where she was and then another time where he thought she'd be, missing entirely on both occasions. She danced to the side and went low, sweeping her leg just as he brought his combistick up to attack. That took him down, then she kicked him hard in the side. He made a sound as air escaped him, then laughed nastily.

"That's the Mei-Jadhi Kaail I remember. Sister Rage—she can't be stopped." He shifted on the ground and brought his stick down. She moved, but not fast enough: he caught her in the leg with the flat end of the blade. Electricity shot up the limb, deadening it as the pain and pleasure receptors were overloaded.

Ca'toll crab-walked back on one leg as fast as she could until she felt a tree on one side, then pulled herself back to her feet. She realized that Ar'Wen had mentally played the battle between them a thousand times, and was ready for anything, whereas she had never considered the concept.

"One to you, brother."

"It will be more than one," he hissed, the blood lust again rising to the top. He came at her, his combistick making small circles toward her chest. Ca'toll watched the motion and timed it, then stepped forward—

She collapsed because her right leg still refused to hold her. Still she found the advantage by using her arm and ribcage to do what Ar'Wen done with his legs: trap his combistick. She felt him jerk her upward and turned with the movement, backhanding him in the face. With their helmets off, it was fist on flesh and his head rocked back.

Without hesitation she wrapped her arm around Ar'Wen's neck, then used her good leg to kick his legs out from under him. She went down on top of his body, bringing her elbow down repeatedly into his chest, using the point of the bone as her solitary weapon. She hit him four times before he punched at her. He caught her on the side of the face and, for a moment, the two of them just kept hitting each other, over and over, until the pain in her face made her block his next blow.

She captured his wrist and bent it forward until it pinched the nerve, bringing a scream out of him. Then he cut it off, gritting his teeth as he brought his other hand around. Instead of blocking, Ca'toll concentrated on his captured wrist and pressed hard until she heard it snap.

Again Ar'Wen screamed and he stopped punching her, instinctively trying to pull free. She grabbed for his other arm, but he easily avoided her move. He punched and kicked, rocking her so that he was able to escape and roll away, minus his weapon.

Ca'toll stood, using his combistick as a crutch. She shook her leg to get the feeling back into it and tentatively put her weight on it. The limb held and she flared her mandibles at him. She threw his combistick off to the side.

"Are you ready for round two?"

Without replying, he held his broken wrist, defiant.

Suddenly Stea'Pua pointed to the sky.

"Watch out. Here they come!"

Three Xenowings came from the top of a tall tree, diving as though they were in attack formation. The young bloods scattered, each wielding a combistick, the blades pointed skyward. One of the creatures landed on Ca'toll's back. The other two dove for Ar'Wen, but he leapt away, scooped up his electrified combistick, and whirled back swinging. As it connected with each of the Xenos, they jittered and fell to the ground, electricity racing through their systems.

Before the Xenowing holding her could take off, Ca'toll reached over her head, grabbed the sides of its face and dragged it over her body. It hit the ground and she snapped out her wristblades, raking back and forth across the exposed stomach. Carapace and flesh parted until she could see internal organs.

Acid spurted from its wounds, drops hitting her face and arms, boiling through skin and making her bellow. She rolled away and tried to find one of the other Xenowings, but the pair had recovered and were already off the ground. Struggling between them was Ar'Wen, hauled more than a hundred feet in the air. He still held his combistick, and she could do nothing but watch as he brought it up.

It was the wrong thing to do—he was too high.

But what other option did he have?

Ar'Wen struck one, then the other. He and the Xenowings plummeted in a jumble of thrashing wings, snapping jaws, claws, arms, and legs. They hit high on the side of the ship, bounced off, then landed hard on the ground. One was trapped beneath Ar'Wen, but the other was on top.

Ptah'Ra, Stea'Pau and Ba'sta didn't hesitate.

They were instantly at Ar'Wen's side, stabbing at the two monsters. Acid blood shot everywhere—some on them, but most on Ar'Wen. The alternative was to allow the Xenowings the opportunity to recover and launch a new assault.

Acid blood was everywhere on Ar'Wen's body, pooled heavily across his midsection. He tried to scream, but could only make a breathy sound that seemed to come from the very back of his throat, more air than anything. Ca'toll ran and kicked at the dying Xenowing that lay atop her brother, then clutched his arm and pulled him free.

It was too late. Kneeling next to Ar'Wen, she realized his armor had been destroyed and she could see his spine, surrounded by the bloody and scorched lumps that were what remained of his organs. There was too much of the deadly liquid inside his body cavity. Even as she watched, the corrosive blood ate at everything it touched, leaving nothing but blackened meat and sickly smoke in its wake.

Ar'Wen looked up at Ca'toll and coughed.

"I guess there will be no—no round two."

The young bloods formed a defensive circle around them, combisticks aimed toward the sky. They tried not to look at the dying Yautja, but the acid had an almost hypnotic effect, like oil poured into water, swirling into different colors until it eventually mixed into nothing.

"Brother…" Ca'toll began, but the word was more of a sigh than anything else. Was this how she wanted Ar'Wen to die? No. He'd wanted to kill her because his anger had become so great that he'd let it encompass everything he was, but once he'd been her battlemate, her friend—her *blood*.

She reached for his hand, but there was nothing left to grasp.

In the end, the acid won: taking down a Yautja nothing and no one else had been able to kill. Ar'Wen—someone Ca'toll hadn't thought of for years—had come back into her life and been laid low by the creatures he himself had brought to the planet.

She would mourn him.

He deserved at least that.

But now was not the time.

5 1

There had been times in Enid's life she thought were nightmarish, but nothing compared to this. There was an old belief that a person's life played out in their mind the instant before they died. Enid had never believed that, and now, facing certain death, she didn't have time for her mind recall *anything*—before or after the Khatura.

Right now, there was only survival.

She faced the monster. It was a *baby* monster. She'd never considered there might be anything but the big ones she'd seen in the rift and attacking the camp, but of course there would be. Nothing was born a fully formed adult, right? Well, she didn't know that for sure, but right now it was pretty damned clear the monsters began small.

Small enough to fit through the opening made by Murray's leg. Enid didn't know if this was the creature that had killed the cartel boss, but it seemed unlikely.

For the longest second of her life, Enid and the little monster stared at each other, almost as though it was as surprised to see her as she was to see it. She didn't know why, but it wasn't black like the others. Maybe it was some kind of throwback, or a mutation like the flying things that looked like a cross between the monsters and riftwings. Instead of black, it was a dirty mustard color with darker brown coloring that melted into the crevices and indentations of its body. This was something different.

The lighter color made it easier for her brain to make out other things that she had never been able to see on the black ones. No eyes, claws that were long and pointed, four spikes coming out of its back, and spindly legs that were probably twice as long as the bony tail jutting out of its ass end. It didn't have the black carapace that the bigger ones had, but maybe that developed later. It did, however, have blood streaking its mouth and head, dribbling down its body. Horrifying.

Then a desire to live slammed adrenaline through her bloodstream and Enid whirled and bolted down the corridor as fast as she could. She didn't know the ship at all, and had no idea where she was going—there were crew quarters in here somewhere, where the mercs had been housed, but the workers like her—addicts—stayed in the shitty recesses of the lower levels, and she had no clue how to get to either place.

So she just ran.

For a moment there was no sound behind her. The baby monster must have hesitated, as though it didn't know what to do. Then the sound of scrabbling began, and she looked back over her shoulder. It was leaping so clumsily it didn't seem like it knew what to do with its own legs. Sometimes it tried to jump on the walls, like a grasshopper, but it always slid off and fell. There was more traction on the floor, but still it clambered and tripped over its own feet. Was it newborn? If so, from what?

As she fled, Enid had the insane urge to laugh, high and loud, because she felt like she was being chased by some kind of weird-looking puppy. She careened around a corner, out of its line of sight.

An open doorway on the left seemed inviting and Enid went for it, bouncing off the farthest jamb and ricocheting into what appeared to be a breakroom. Before the baby monster could follow her she upended several tables and chairs, then ducked behind one of the tables she'd overturned and waited, fighting to keep her panicked inhalations quiet.

Did it have good hearing? Eyes or not, it certainly didn't seem blind. Then it was inside the room with her, jumping up and balancing on the rails of a chair that had tipped over on its side. Its elongated head swung first one way, then the other, as it tried to locate her.

Keeping the juvenile creature in her peripheral vision, Enid scanned the breakroom. There had to be something in here she could use for a weapon, a knife, a fucking spoon, *anything*. There wasn't much around because— *duh*—anything of use had been hauled over to the camp.

A meter off to her left was a bank of cabinets, but she had no idea what was in them; not much if everything had been offloaded, but there wasn't much of anything else to consider. She slid over, trying her best not to make any noise. When the little beast's head jerked in her direction, she realized that, even if she couldn't see its ears, it definitely had some way to track noise.

Enid forced herself to pause, even though every nerve in her body wanted to jump up and dig into every nook of the room until she found some kind of a weapon. After a couple of seconds the creature dropped off the chair and onto the floor, its moves still ungainly. Enid's breath caught as she realized it was heading toward her. She put a hand on the floor to brace herself, but stopped when she felt something beneath her palm.

When she looked down, she saw a synthetic cheese puff. There were a number of them scattered around and she realized that if she pressed down, they would make a *crunch* sound and give away her position.

Her position…

Enid snatched up two puffs and flung them as hard as she could to the right of the baby monster. They landed behind it and to the left and, as she had hoped, the creature twisted around and flung itself toward the sound. The puffs made a miniscule amount of noise, but the creature took it for stealthy movement. It scrabbled awkwardly between the legs of the tables and chairs, upending several more as it proceeded. That was just what Enid needed, and the banging of the furniture enabled her to get to the first cabinet door and pull it open.

Empty.

Completely fucking *empty*.

Terrified, she tracked the baby monster's movements. Again she had to choke back an urge to bray hysterical laughter—the ugly little shit was *playing* with a cheese puff like a cat with a fucking dustball. She yanked her gaze away from the bizarre sight and stretched to the next cabinet door, easing it open and trying to process its contents: hard plastic containers of cleaning fluid, rags, a small, open tray of tools.

The cabinet under the sink.

Without thinking about it, Enid reached into the tools and pulled out whatever her fingers folded around—

A heavy screwdriver.

It was long, maybe half a meter from tip to the end of the handle. She wanted to reach for something else, but a scrabbling behind her meant she was out of time. She whirled and realized her attacker was almost on top of her. She flung one arm in front just as the baby monster dove. Its mouth, rimmed with tiny but deadly sharp teeth, locked firmly on the underside of her forearm.

Enid screamed and dropped the screwdriver. The sound seemed to surprise the thing and it let go, pulling back as if it had never heard such a noise. Before it could bite her again, Enid scooted away and kicked at it. The workers weren't given ass-kicker boots like the mercs, but her shoes were still fairly sturdy and she connected with its head.

It went flying backward and thumped hard against the leg of one of the tables. It popped back up like some kind of horror jack-in-the-box and launched itself at her again, this time with its own ear-throbbing screech. With no time to do anything else, she pulled the same arm up to protect her face. Predictably it bit her again, this time harder. Its legs came up to claw at her and it tried to shake its head like a vicious dog.

Enid grabbed the screwdriver and rammed it into the side of its head.

She was surprised at how easily the tool punctured the thing's skull. The baby monster's mouth opened, freeing her forearm, and Enid let the trajectory of her swing carry the creature to the floor. The screwdriver embedded itself into the textured flooring. The screech the monster gave this time was louder and more painful than the previous one, and it thrashed violently, its limbs twisting in every direction and leaving brutal, bloody welts on her face and arms, shredding the fabric of her uniform and tearing into the flesh beneath it.

The creature's blood pooled on the floor and the screwdriver began to bend in her grip. She didn't dare let go, the most primitive part of her subconscious telling her what she already knew: release the baby monster and she would die.

The deck began to smoke where the blood had fallen as the thing rattled its death dance. It took a painfully long time for the creature to stop. By the time it was still,

Enid's hand, wrist, and arm were spotted with pinpoints of acid that would have probably made her scream if she hadn't been so high. Red clouded her vision as her skin burned—it was as if she'd been whipped with a spiked leather belt. The one thing she was grateful for was that the puncture wound on the baby monster's head was clean and small; the battles in the rift had shown her what their blood could do. This one had bled onto the floor rather than spraying her in the face.

The minutes passed like mini-eternities. She spent most of the time holding her breath, but no matter how hard she listened, the ship seemed devoid of any other sound.

She was alone.

But was she really?

Enid had to get out of here—what if there were more of these things on board right now? She wasn't safe—she'd seen the way they could climb in the rift. This one hadn't been able to do the same, but she didn't doubt for a second that its skills would have improved the longer it lived. And the way those things could squeeze through small openings—like fucking rats that could get into *anything*.

Once the idea gained hold in her head, that there were more on the ship with her, she was lost. The paranoia was overwhelming. With a final angry jab to make sure the monster was truly dead, she let go of the screwdriver and crept back to the doorway, into the corridor.

She didn't dare move fast, and was afraid to make any noise. Head jerking this way and that, up and down, she worked her way down to cargo door number two. She'd rather take her chances outside, maybe sleeping in trees or whatever—anywhere but in the claustrophobic spaces of this vessel. Checking behind her for the tenth or maybe fiftieth time, Enid shoved her hand in her pocket—

The card with the passcode wasn't there.

"Nooooo." She moaned low in her throat, fingers digging as deep as they could. It just wasn't there.

Blinking furiously, Enid searched the area around her. Not on the floor, not in her pocket, not in the other one. Where the hell could it be?

Then she remembered.

There wasn't a window in the cargo door, but suddenly she slammed both hands against the cold metal. Enid knew where it was. Because it was the only place that made any sense.

It had fallen outside before the cargo door had closed.

She was trapped.

5 2

The ship's coordinates were set and all of the dead, including Ar'Wen, had been prepped and placed in cryogenic chambers. Ca'toll had cleaned and smoothed the edges of her Xenowing trophy, which would remain stored in her quarters for the duration of the flight back to the mothership. The three young bloods were strapped in and ready for takeoff.

Another hunt had been completed, but this one had unquestionably been different. The death toll had been substantial, with only three of the unblooded surviving and completing their test. An unforeseen mutation, unanticipated humans on the seeded planet, and bad bloods! Those Ca'toll had truly never expected. In her lifetime, she had only seen one—*one*—such twist before this mission. To have two during the same hunt was unheard of, and yet there it was.

Making the situation even worse had been the dishonorable competition between team members, reticence, even cowardliness. Vai'ke, a young Yautja making all the wrong decisions for all the wrong reasons.

And then, of course, Ar'Wen.

She stared out the viewing portal at the landscape of LV-363. She had been on many hunts, so many that if she wanted a count she would have to check the computer records. Hunts much more deadly on planets so far beyond hellish that this world was nothing in comparison. And yet this one, *this* one, was the worst. No other could compare to it in terms of cost: the loss of life, the treacherousness of team members, the disregard for that most sacred thing.

Honor.

Shaking her head, Ca'toll reached for the control board and keyed in the take-off sequence. The engines responded instantly, their sound smooth and low. She hit the final set of switches and the spacecraft slowly began to lift. There was no hurry, nothing to gain but a higher usage of fuel should they accelerate any faster.

When her gaze cut back to the portal she saw the human, Fetch, standing among the trees at the edge of the clearing, staring up at the ship. The fool had tried to come with them, and she had done him a mercy by forcibly refusing. What did he think would happen to him on Yautja Prime, surrounded by younglings who'd never seen a human before?

Ca'toll lowered a dark filter over the portal so he could no longer see her. She input the setting for the ship to pilot itself up and out of LV-363's atmosphere, and secured herself in the pilot's chair.

One day, likely sooner rather than later, more Yautja would come to hunt the new and worthy prey, the Xenowings, that would proliferate on this planet.

It was true that she would have many things to answer for when she faced the elders and gave her report. If her hunt captain had not reported her confession, then the record would need to be set straight. Even so, she believed that the hundreds of Xenomorphs she had single-handedly dispatched between that long-ago time and the present, as well as her reasons for not disclosing it, would more than balance her actions.

Ca'toll was certain that the honor of the blood would go to her and the young Yautja who had survived this hunt.

5 3

Enid made her way back to the breakroom, and crouched behind one of the tables she had turned on its side. Even though she had built a kind of fort between herself and the door, using more of the tables and chairs, she didn't feel anywhere close to safe.

It was a joke of a shield, she knew, but last time she'd been able to hold off a monster. She'd made double-damn sure the thing was dead, and tried to pull the screwdriver out of its lifeless skull. All that came up was the handle—the rest had been melted by the acid.

She'd searched frantically for another weapon and found a knife that was used for cutting up meat and vegetables. Not much of a weapon, but it was better than nothing, and would have to do.

As she crouched again in her makeshift fortress, her breathing slowed but was nowhere near normal. It increased every time her mind turned over a new *what if*, right along with her heartbeat. That pounded in her temples.

What if there was another monster on the ship?

What if there was *more* than just one?

What if there were *adult* monsters on the ship?

What if...

What if—

What if.

She was going to go crazy if she stayed in this room.

Most likely there was enough fuel in the reserves to provide light and keep the essentials running. There might even be enough to fire up the engines, not that she had a clue how to do so. She'd never even seen a control panel, or whatever they called it.

There was water from the faucets. Somewhere on the ship was food, but that entailed getting off her cowardly ass and looking for it, finding the storage bays. Enid wanted to, although if she was truthful with herself she really didn't care about the food. Addicts like her didn't eat to satisfy hunger, they just did so to keep their body from collapsing. Her food hunger had peaked a long time ago, and all she felt in her belly was numbness.

No. She wanted—*needed*—to find the Khatura.

That was the thing that made her want to live, that tried to overthrow the mind-numbing fear running through her body. She'd woken from her last high on the planet's surface, and had gone to the ship instead of back down into the rift. Her body wanted the rift's bountiful pollen, but her brain—or what was left of it—knew that the Khatura alone wouldn't keep her alive.

The last of her high had been bled out of her bloodstream by adrenaline, and that had been… well, she didn't know how long ago. She was past the point of thinking she would ever give it up. So why bother? Everyone on this miserable rock was dead—the humans, anyway. She didn't want anything to do with the hunters, and they looked pretty fucking evil. If she was stupid enough to get in their line of sight, they'd probably kill her.

Enid was trapped on the ship so she might as well find the food. Then she could venture out to find the Khatura and enjoy however many she had left of the rest of her days.

Okay, then.

Time to grow some balls and get out of this room. She'd go the opposite way from the exit hatch, and see what there was to find.

* * *

So much for inter-species alliances.

Despite his best efforts, Fetch's attempt at befriending the aliens had bombed. He'd hauled himself up the rift wall as they dragged up the bodies of their dead, then followed them to their ship. Hanging out with a bunch of non-humans was exciting to begin with, but then—*wow*!

The two that had run off in the rift showed up again, and the shit hit the wind. It didn't seem to him like the female leader was very popular, because they'd both ended up attacking her. She'd killed the first one, then the secretive one Fetch had discovered down in the rift showed up. It wasn't easy, but he could tell them apart from the markings on what they wore.

And then, man, that was the fucking battle royale!

She'd killed that one, too, then her underlings—that's what they had to be—had loaded those bodies onto the ship. It was obvious they were done and heading off LV-363, so Fetch had taken a chance and tried to follow them up the ramp.

They'd knocked him on his ass for the trouble.

It was all past tense, so Fetch had to cast around for other options. The camp had been obliterated by the monsters; there wasn't enough of anything left to even warrant going back there. Besides, the monsters would probably check from time to time for any idiots who tried to scavenge among the ruins.

He wasn't stupid enough to be dessert.

There was the rift, of course. He could climb back down, try to camouflage himself behind a net or in the underbrush, and let himself drown in Khatura oblivion. As pleasurable as that idea was, it wouldn't last. Even if he managed to avoid the riftwings and the monsters, his high would eventually dissipate and thirst and hunger would kick in. He sure hadn't seen much he'd want to eat down there—or for that matter, on the surface.

That left one choice.

The ship. The one the cartel had used.

So he made his way through the trees and spotted it. He jogged across the clearing, ducking and weaving in case something tried to fly at him from the sky. Then he circled the ship, only to find every door sealed tight.

It wasn't like there was a fucking doorbell, and if there was no one onboard to let him in, he was shit out of luck. there was no way he could gain entry.

Except...

He stopped dead at a door toward the rear—it probably led into a cargo bay. The area around it looked like an abattoir. There was a large, nasty puddle of blood and what he assumed were chewed up pieces of flesh. The blood was still a deep crimson in the middle, but it was dried to black at the edges and where it had splashed onto the door.

Flung a few feet away was a boot with a foot in it. The foot was still wearing a ragged sock, but there was nothing else, so Fetch had to assume the guy had been eaten. The boot was too nice to have belonged to one of the mercs—they favored thick artificial hide with metal inserts at the toe and heels—*the better to kick with*.

That meant it was a supervisor, or maybe even the boss.

Whatever. Fetch didn't give a shit.

He did, however, care a lot about a little light-colored rectangle buried in the muck that had once been inside a body.

Fetch bent over and poked gingerly through the blood and chunks of meat. He fished out the object, held it up, and just as he'd hoped, it looked like a passcode card. If his ever-trusty luck had finally come back, this was the way he would gain entrance. His fingers dripped with gore and he couldn't read the numbers, so he wiped his hand and the card on his pants.

Then Fetch stuck the card in his shirt pocket, keyed in the numbers, and the door in front of him slid open.

Bingo!

He stepped onto ship and made sure the hatch sealed behind him.

Wouldn't want any of those monsters to follow him inside.

* * *

Enid had never been in a ship's cockpit before. It was crammed full of buttons and switches and levers and screens, not a single one of which she could turn on, much less understand. Even so…

Jackpot.

She'd found a weapon.

It was some kind of pistol, but that was about as much as she could tell. Her knowledge of guns came from entertainment, vids and games played with her kids, way back in her life before Khatura. Looking at the thing and turning it over carefully, she tried to remember.

"Don't point the barrel of it at yourself."

"Don't aim it at someone if you don't intend to fire."

"Keep your finger off the trigger until you're ready to shoot."

Those were the rules in all of the vids. Did the weapons she'd seen onscreen even exist in the real world, or were they all made up by drunk movie directors and hopped-up game designers?

The pistol had been sitting on the console in front of one of the pilot chairs. Not the big one. That was positioned in the middle of a semicircle, in front of the most complicated-looking panel. No, the one to the left of it.

It had been shoved off to the side, as if it was the most unimportant thing in the world, and yet for Enid the pistol could mean life or death. It seemed pretty straightforward, too, the kind of point-and-shoot handgun the hero in action movies always gave to the victim, usually a woman—some things never changed.

She could do that, right?

Enid stood up straight and squared her shoulders. She felt like a different person now. Armed and ready, that's what she was. Bring on a fucking monster, baby or otherwise. She'd blow its damned head right off.

Grinning like a fool, she headed back up the corridor. It didn't take a brainiac to conclude that if she'd been in the cockpit, and where she'd come in was cargo door number two, the main cargo hold itself had to be farther back. She didn't know how many cargo doors there were, but it wasn't a huge ship.

Besides, she was armed now. "*Packing heat,*" as they always said in the vids. The idea made her giggle a little as she strode confidently down the corridor, and she tried to remember what her favorite one had been. Not a romance, that was for sure. Her asshole husband had made sure of that. Maybe one of those spy—

Shiiiiiiiish.

Enid jerked to a stop, holding the pistol out in front of her with both hands. She'd been feeling fine, oh yeah, all that and more, and then that noise, that *noise.* Now her teeth were clenched and her hands were jittering like popcorn over an open fire. Cold sweat pushed out of her pores and ran down the sides of her face and the center of her chest. She didn't know how many synapses had to fire before her brain identified the sound.

One of the doors had opened.

Enid didn't know how it happened, but dropped to her knees. Her pulse made her temples throb so hard that the sound blotted out everything else. Then she heard movement, something coming onto the ship, and the noise had sent her heartbeat through the ceiling—

Thump.

Thump.

Thump.

—and her vision shimmied along to the same rhythm, making it impossible to focus.

The monsters had gotten inside. It didn't matter how—

No, maybe it *wasn't* one of the monsters.

Maybe it was a *hunter.*

That had to be it. None of her fellow humans were alive. Like Murray, they'd all been killed or eaten or carried off.

The monsters were nothing more than primitive eating machines, but the hunters had smarts. They had weapons, and technology, and had come on their own ship.

She'd dropped Shrapnel's card outside and one of them had found it. With the humans out of the way, they'd decided to claim the ship and its contents as salvage, taking what they wanted and leaving the rest to rust.

They sure as hell wouldn't want *her*.

More noise, and this time she recognized footsteps. Her terror wanted her to turn and run, find a place to hide and then wait it out. But that was stupid—they would find her, and they would kill her, either to claim salvage or, face it, just for the fun of it.

Enid bit the insides of her cheeks hard enough to bring blood, trying desperately to override her flight instinct. She sucked in as much air as she could, then for no reason she could think of, held her breath and aimed the gun at the space where the corridor turned and she couldn't see any farther.

A figure stepped around the bend with a shit-eating grin plastered across its dirt covered face, and her mind screamed *hunter!*

She pulled the trigger mechanism

Then did it twice more just to make sure.

* * *

Enid kneeled in front of Fetch's corpse. He looked pretty fucking sad, with his chest and stomach opened up and more or less vaporized. His eyes were open and staring at her, making her feel like she should say something over him, a prayer or whatever, now that her ears had stopped ringing and she could think again.

Maybe *I'm sorry I killed you*.

Or *rest in peace*.

Not that she believed in that stuff, and the truth was, she wasn't sorry. Being an addict had a way of wiping out a person's conscience. The main thing that had occurred to her after she realized what she'd done was he must've found the card with the passcode on it. That's how he'd gotten in, and there it was. Or rather, there were the *remnants* of it, because the holes she had put in Fetch had blasted him into about a thousand pieces.

Nope, she thought. *Not going anywhere*.

Enid felt sure the racket the weapon had made would have drawn any other monsters out of hiding, but nothing showed up. Unless the ghost of Fetch decided to join her, she was alone.

Just her.

And the Khatura.

EPILOGUE

A thumping sound came from deep in the hull of the Yautja dropship. A knocking that no one could possibly hear. A muffled sound that was confined to a small area in the hold.

The young bloods and the hunt leader were in the command suite, waiting to dock with the mothership. Not that far behind where they sat, something made small sounds that were undetectable over the noise of the ship.

Several bodies lay dead in the confines of their technological coffins. More than one had been torn in half. One corpse, mangled mercilessly, was hunt leader Ny'ytap, who had been impaled on a tree. The fierce Yautja had managed to survive for a time, until a hungry Xenowing had found him, eaten its fill and moved on.

Left behind was a still-warm compartment, ready for the most basic of Xenomorphic building blocks. Left with remnants of something called *Plagiarus Praepotens*. A liquid pathogen.

The thumping continued, less due to a desire for freedom than a need for change, the instinctive requirement to move on, to go to the next stage. The cryogenic hold echoed with this dull noise for a long while as the ship auto-piloted into the docking bay, and those in the command suite progressed through an after-action report, reviewing their successes and failures as they remembered those who had been lost.

Finally the noise ceased and everything was once again quiet.

Ny'ytap's corpse remained as it had been. His face has been chewed beyond recognition, the soft outer meat below his body armor consumed, making emergence a simple task. The newly born creature tucked its wings around itself for protection and pushed itself into the space between the heavily muscled arm and torso. It would wait out this cold by slipping into a deep sleep, slowing its body function down until only enough sentience remained to monitor itself. It could not free itself from its surroundings.

Yet.

Eventually freedom would come. Different surroundings, a new environment in which it could mature.

Then it would fly.

And its offspring would flourish.

A SHORT GLOSSARY

OF YAUTJA TERMS

amedha: meat

ell-osde' pauk: fuck you

gahn'tha-cte: ruthless

h'dlak: fear

h'ka-se: now

h'ko yeyindi: no brave one, coward

hulij-pe: crazy or unhinged

ic'jit: bad blood

ka'rik'na: let's go/ summoning of other Yautja

mei'hswei: brothers

n'dhi-ja: farewell/goodbye

nok: a Yautja unit of distance, about a third of a meter

pauk: fuck

pauk-de: fucker

pauk-de s'yuit-de: fucking idiot

sain'ja: warrior

ui'stbi: abomination

u'si-kwe: final rest (death)

yin'tekai: honor

yeyin: bravery

zabin: insect

ACKNOWLEDGEMENTS

Being part of the *Predator* Universe has always been a dream of ours. Each of us has written short stories in the universe, and finally we were offered the opportunity to play in an even larger sandbox—an *Aliens vs. Predators* novel.

As most of you know, we are best known as horror authors. Even when we write science fiction, it's "dark as hell" science fiction. But that's okay, because both *Aliens* and *Predators* have never just been science fiction. They've always been horror, or even terror—the terror of a hunter from outer space come to hunt a beast or two, perhaps even an Alien. The last thing you want to be is caught in the middle of a hunt.

Which is where us authors come in: enter stage left. So, thank you to agent Cherry Weiner and editor Steve Saffel. Thanks to those in the Wiley Writers group for constant encouragement. Thanks also to the Titan crew, including Nick Landau, Vivian Cheung, Fenton Coulthurst, Paul Simpson, and Kevin Eddy. A big shout-out as well to Nicole Spiegel from 20th Century Studios. Most importantly, thanks to the readers. Without you, we'd be nothing but monkeys scribbling on a wall in a cave in the dark.

ABOUT THE AUTHORS

The American Library Association calls **WESTON OCHSE** "one of the major horror authors of the 21st Century." His work has won the Bram Stoker Award, been nominated for the Pushcart Prize, and won four New Mexico-Arizona Book Awards. A writer of more than thirty-five books in multiple genres, his Burning Sky Duology has been hailed as the best military horror of the generation. His military supernatural series SEAL Team 666 has been optioned to be a movie, and his military sci-fi trilogy, which starts with *Grunt Life*, has been praised for its PTSD-positive depiction of soldiers at peace and at war. His shorter work has appeared in DC Comics (*Shazam*), IDW comics, *Soldier of Fortune Magazine*, *Weird Tales*, *Cemetery Dance*, and peered literary journals. His franchise work includes *The X-Files*, *Predator*, *Aliens*, *Hellboy*, *Clive Barker's Midian*, Joe Ledger, and *V-Wars*. Weston holds a Master of Fine Arts in Creative Writing and teaches at Southern New Hampshire University.

He lives in Arizona with his wife and fellow author, Yvonne Navarro, and their Great Dane.

* * *

YVONNE NAVARRO is an award-winning author of twenty-three published novels and a lot of short stories, articles, and a reference dictionary. She writes in a wide variety of genres, but favors horror or dark fantasy. Her work has won the Bram Stoker Award, the Chicago Women in Press Award, the Illinois Women in Press Award, the Unreal Worlds Award, and the IATW Award, among others. Her shorter work has appeared in hundreds of anthologies and magazines. Her franchise work includes *The X-Files*, *Predator*, *Aliens*, *Hellboy*, *Clive Barker's Hellraiser*, *Ultraviolet*, *Elektra*, *Buffy the Vampire Slayer*, *Angel*, *Supernatural*, and *V-Wars*. To make sure she stays busy, she's also an award-winning artist. She lives way down in the southeastern corner of Arizona, is married to author Weston Ochse, and dotes on their rescued Great Dane and talking parakeet, BirdZilla.